VIOLET TENDENCIES

An uneasy sensation swelled through my body as I walked with trepidation toward our float. Something about the huge, cavernous space felt foreboding.

"Hello!" I called again.

The only answer was the sound of my own voice bouncing off the walls.

Shouldn't the other decorators and volunteers be here by now? We were supposed to report by seven thirty for the morning meeting. Had I missed a message? Was the parade canceled?

I thought about turning around but I willed myself forward.

Bad choice.

When I made it to our float I looked up in horror. Our float had been destroyed. The arbor and grapevines that we had meticulously secured had been torn apart and were scattered in broken pieces throughout the floor.

I stepped forward and let out a scream.

Sham's body was sprawled out among the ruins. A noose of purple violets twisted around his lifeless neck . . .

D0483616

Books by Kate Dyer-Seeley

Published by Kensington Publishing Corporation

Violet Tendencies

Kate Dyer-Seeley

KENSINGTON BOOKS
www.kensingtonbooks.com

KENSINGTON BOOKS are published by

Kensington Publishing Corp.
119 West 40th Street
New York, NY 10018

All Kensington titles, imprints, and distributed lines are available at special quantity discounts for bulk purchases for sales promotion, premiums, fund-raising, educational, or institutional use.

Special book excerpts or customized printings can also be created to fit specific needs. For details, write or phone the office of the Kensington Sales Manager: Attn.: Sales Department. Kensington Publishing Corp., 119 West 40th Street, New York, NY 10018. Phone: 1-800-221-2647.

Kensington and the K logo Reg. U.S. Pat. & TM Off.

First Printing: December 2018
ISBN-13: 978-1-4967-0515-0
ISBN-10: 1-4967-0515-7

ISBN-13: 978-1-4967-0516-7 (ebook)
eISBN-10: 1-4967-0516-5 (ebook)

10 9 8 7 6 5 4 3 2 1

Printed in the United States of America

Chapter One

Portland was flush with spring color: blooming roses, bright flags flapping from the bows of navy ships docked along the waterfront, and neon carnival signs dotting the banks of the Willamette River. The end of the unrelenting rainy season brought a celebration like no other to the city—Rose Festival. The festival spanned three weeks from the end of May through mid-June, attracting visitors from all over the world who joined in Portland's annual street party at the queen's coronation, milk-carton boat races, starlight run, rose show, fleet tours, fireworks, and the *pièce de résistance,* the Grand Floral Parade. This year, Blomma, my aunt Elin's boutique European-inspired flower shop, where I had been working for the past few months, had been chosen as the showcase florist for the Rose Festival. It was a huge honor. And a huge undertaking. In addition to managing our regular clientele at the shop, we had been spending every waking moment at the

float barn, preparing our float and planning for
the dignitaries' dinner, which would take place the
evening of the Grand Floral Parade.

I'd never been so nervous about my floral designs. Blomma would be responsible for crafting
one-of-a-kind bouquets and centerpieces for world
leaders and visiting diplomats. Throughout history
flowers have marked monumental occasions, from
the coronation of queens to the burial of presidents.
We had to ensure that every flower and stem we
used for the dignitaries' dinner had been researched
and handpicked for its symbolism. It was my responsibility to track every bloom's meaning and history.
We wouldn't want to cause the next war to break
out after accidentally giving the Japanese ambassador
a bundle of begonias—known in many cultures as
inviting dark thoughts and a warning for the recipient to beware. Or to deliver a spray of foxgloves—
welcoming harm—to the visiting head of state from
Canada.

This year's theme for Rose Festival was Shine,
and we intended to make our float do just that. Elin
had sketched out a design plan that mirrored her
artistic, Swedish style. Many float designers opted to
adorn their moving masterpieces with Portland's
signature flower, the rose. Not Elin. Blomma's float
would consist of giant violet garlands that stretched
across a ten-foot bridge constructed from grape
vines. The float would be lush with purple violets,
dark greenery, and earthy vines, with touches of
brilliant white violets to signal the return of spring.
Elin had opted for the dainty flower because they
were often one of the first to push through the
ground in April. Violets connotate a delicate love.

In my research I had discovered many references in folklore to the violet. Dreaming of violets was a sign of good fortune, and purple violets were an ancient symbol of royalty and power. Elin and I agreed that the lovely, wispy flowers would convey the perfect meaning for the Blomma float.

Her vision for the float was to create an Oregon forestscape that was just beginning to bud to life. Assuming we could pull it off, her ethereal float could have a good shot at winning the judge's award for most outstanding. There were also awards for craftsmanship, best depiction of whimsy, life in Oregon, and community spirit. Winning a coveted award would be a boost for our growing flower shop and wine bar.

When it came to materials, the rules for the Grand Floral Parade were simple—everything had to be organic in nature. Seeds, bark, leaves, berries, flowers, and moss were all acceptable. Gluing thousands of tiny seeds by hand was a painstaking process, but I hoped that our efforts would be worth it. As of late, our biggest challenge (other than black, sticky fingers) was procuring enough product. Nicki Parks, the float-barn director, had told me in passing that each float used enough flowers to send someone a dozen roses every day for thirty years. That didn't even begin to account for the industrial-sized buckets of tapioca pearls, onion seeds, and cranberries lining every square inch of floor space in the float barn, along with stacks of twenty-foot evergreen boughs, corn stalks, and pumpkin vines. Trying to add up how many thousands of seeds and berries were being used in float production made my head spin.

For the moment I needed to concentrate. Elin had sent me to the Portland wholesale flower market in search of Shasta daisies. "Focus, Britta," I told myself as I surveyed Oregon's largest flower trading floor. Over fifty vendors offered fresh cut flowers, potted plants, baskets, vases, and floral accessories. From family farms to large distributors and importers, the wholesale market was floral Disneyland. Many mornings I would wander through the booths, stopping to admire freshly harvested bear grass or Italian ruscus, but this morning I was on a singular mission—Shasta daisies.

We received a last-minute call yesterday from a frantic bride whose florist bailed on her with her deposit. She needed six bridesmaid's bouquets, a bridal bouquet, boutonnieres, and headpieces for the flower girls by tomorrow, and her budget was minimal, given that her original florist had taken off with the cash she had put down for her wedding-day flowers. Elin and I both had a soft spot for brides in need, so we agreed to do our best. I had explained that the likelihood of finding enough Shasta daisies wasn't high, given that the Grand Floral Parade was in less than a week. Nearly every flower in the state had been purchased and accounted for. However, she had sounded so dejected on the phone that I couldn't turn her down. I assured her that I would give it a shot and that we could create something just as lovely with equally inexpensive white carnations and hints of greenery if necessary.

The trading floor was a mob scene, as always, despite the fact that the sun had yet to rise. Working early hours was part of life as a professional florist.

The market opened at five and stayed active until midafternoon, but any self-respecting florist knew that the freshest and rarest stems would be gone within the first hour.

I loved hearing the shouts of florists and vendors battling for the best stems and rarest finds. I loved the sweet, earthy smell of the cold market, and the dazzling color. Usually I enjoyed strolling through row after row of clementines, dahlias, and California figs. The fragrant scent of jasmine and the constant sound of vendors bartering were like home to me, but today there was no time. I squeezed past a florist I recognized who worked for one of the big national chains and made a beeline for the back of the humming warehouse. When I spotted the sign for Abundant Gardens, I nearly broke into a sprint.

"Morning, Britta," Chuck, the owner, greeted me with a smile, tucking a pair of shears into his overalls. "You look like you're in a hurry."

I felt a blush creep up my neck. My skin is naturally pale, which means that the slightest hint of color makes my cheeks look like two ripe cherry tomatoes. Elin has always told me that my porcelain skin is a gift. Fortunately, she also has been a fierce proponent of using sunscreen. "Britta, our Scandinavian skin is like an orchid. We must treat it gently and shield it from too much sun," she cautioned. It was wise advice, especially in our line of work, where visiting local farms and outdoor growers' markets came with the territory.

"Sorry," I said to Chuck. "I'm on the hunt for Shasta daisies. Desperate bride."

He gave me a knowing nod. "That's why I prefer

working in the field and on this side of the business. Don't have to deal with any crazy brides. Or worse, their mothers." He winked.

"Oh, I could tell you some stories."

"I bet you could."

My eyes drifted to large buckets that contained hundreds of black dahlias. Technically dahlias aren't black. They're actually a deep burgundy, but their overlapping petals make the flower look as dark as a starless sky. The elegant flower had earned a negative reputation thanks to a 1940s murder case—deemed the disappearance of the Black Dahlia. Dahlias represented strength, creativity, and dignity.

"Those are gorgeous," I said.

"Beauties, aren't they?" Chuck nodded. "Can't sell them to you, Britta. They're already spoken for. Special order for Rose Festival. Secret order. I'm under the threat of death not to sell a single stem or divulge who ordered these beauties. You florists sure get crazy around Rose Festival time." He gave me a lopsided grin.

"It's cutthroat," I bantered back.

"Don't I know it. You won't believe how many people have offered to pay double—even triple—the price. I have half a mind to take the money and run."

I wondered who was using the unique dahlias. None of the floats that I had seen thus far had incorporated the deep, dark stems. But then again, there were dozens of floats in various stages of construction in the float barn.

Chuck pointed behind him to a black plastic tub with bunches of white daisies. "However, you're in luck with the Shastas. How many do you need?"

I returned my attention to the task at hand. "Can I have all of them?"

"Consider it done. Let me to wrap them up."

While he bundled the Shasta daisies, I mentally reviewed my day. First, I would head to Blomma and assemble the bridal bouquets and our recurring corporate orders before we opened for walk-in customers. Typically, Elin hosts custom workshops in the cottage attached to Blomma, but we had put those on hold for a week until we were finished with our float and the designs for the dignitaries' dinner. She would oversee volunteers at the float barn this morning, and then we would swap places in the afternoon. With only four days to go before the big event, the organizers were allowing designers and volunteers to work late every night. We would grab a quick bite of dinner and spend the rest of the evening twisting grapevines and stringing evergreen branches into tight bundles. The float prep-work had to be completed by Friday. That's when the real fun would begin. The actual flowers would be the very last thing to go on each float. No floral designer wanted a droopy tulip or wilting rose on their float. The Friday before the parade would be a mad dash to the finish as everyone raced against the clock and the elements to cover their structure with fresh flowers. Elin and I had decided we wanted to create a test garland of violets tonight so that we could put together step-by-step directions for the volunteers who would help with the finishing touches.

I thanked Chuck for the daisies and headed for Riverplace Village. It was a short drive from the flower market. The village was located on the west side of the Willamette River and had cobblestone streets, charming shops, and an elegant yet laidback vibe. The small community of business owners in Riverplace Village were a tight-knit group. Most of the shops and the world-class Riverplace Inn had been operated by the same owners for decades.

Blomma sat at the corner of the village with welcoming brick-red, windowed garage doors that could be rolled up in the spring and summer months. In honor of Rose Festival, we had draped the front windows and door with strings of pink lights and filled the front display cases with pastel bouquets of roses in soft peach, creamy whites, yellows, and pale pink. A sandwich board propped near the front door greeted customers with a special Rose Festival quote:

TRUTH AND ROSES HAVE THORNS ABOUT THEM.— HENRY DAVID THOREAU.

As I pulled Elin's Jeep into a parking space in front of the shop, I wanted to pinch myself. I couldn't believe I was so lucky.

Of course, when I first made the decision to return home to Portland, I hadn't considered it luck. Quite the opposite. I had discovered that my deadbeat husband, Chad, had been having an affair instead of working on the next great American novel, as he promised. It turned out that his late-night trips to the library didn't involve writing. That is, unless you counted terribly cheesy poetry, "writing." At first, I'd been hurt and embarrassed, but after the shock wore off I recognized that his infidelity was actually a blessing in disguise. I'd been miserable for years. And as much as I hated to admit it, part of that blame was on me.

After graduating from the floral institute, I had imagined myself opening a shop much like Blomma, where I could leave my flower mark on the world, but instead I'd ended up in Minnesota working for a lifeless wholesaler. Chad couldn't take a traditional job because he claimed it would interfere with his creative process. That left me as our sole provider. Every time I suggested that Chad find a part-time job to help ease our financial burdens, he would have a burst of energy and swear that he was days away from finishing the book. Shocker. That never happened. Leaving Chad and the Midwest had been the best decision I had made in a long time. To be honest I didn't miss much about Minnesota, not the bitter cold winters or my unfulfilling job that had crushed my creative spirit. Portland in its spring-time glory had reawakened long-forgotten dreams and reignited my passion.

I shook myself from my thoughts and turned off the ignition. Then I removed the bunches of daisies from the back and went to open Blomma's front door. Immediately I was greeted by the scent of honeysuckle and sweet roses. I flipped on the lights, but kept the sign on the door turned to CLOSED. The chandeliers overhead cast a warm glow on Blomma's shiny hard-wood floors. Cozy furniture had been arranged in the front of the shop. Perfect for customers to take a break and breathe in the scent of flowers after a busy afternoon shopping in the village, and for casual meetings with potential clients. There were tins of fresh-cut stems and succulents displayed on tables. The back of the space housed a concrete workstation and sink, a display case with prearranged bouquets, and a distressed-wood wine bar with a black iron candelabra, complete with a wall of Northwest wine available to purchase by the glass or bottle. Elin had learned early on that flowers and wine were an excellent pairing. Our customers often came in looking for a gift and wound up lingering over a glass of Oregon pinot noir at the bar while waiting for us to create a gorgeous arrangement.

The cottage was attached to the main building through two sliding barn doors next to the wine bar. Walking into the homey, warm space with its exposed timber beams and stone walls reminded me of a childhood fairy tale. A large workstation in the center of the cottage had been crafted from salvaged barn doors and was stocked with every floral tool imaginable, from pruners to knives to clay, wire, and thorn-strippers. Whenever we hosted classes and workshops in the cottage, clients gushed about the space, saying it felt as if they were stepping into a rustic European castle. This morning, I left the barn doors shut and focused on our rush bridal order.

Before I began gathering supplies to create the bouquets, I quickly filled a bucket with warm water and a mixture of "love juice" to process the daisies I had bought at the market. It's critical when working with fresh flowers to trim their stems and douse them in a healthy bath of water, sugar, bleach, and vinegar. This preserves the life of the flower and ensures a long-lasting bloom. Once I had the vibrant, white daisies soaking, I removed a pair of shears, wire, scissors, and a silky forest-green ribbon from the workstation. For the bridal party, I wanted every bouquet to be symmetrical, with a tight weave and exposed stems. Next, I wound the bouquets with wire and wrapped them with the silky ribbon. I would finish them with a small bow and drape the ribbon on both sides to give the inexpensive flowers an elegant, romantic look.

Soon I was immersed in the creative process. Any worry about the Grand Floral Parade and our float faded away as I trimmed stems and plucked off any imperfections in the daisies' petals. Flowers are art and an expression of the soul. It was my job as a floral artist to infuse love and joy into every arrangement. I had found my true purpose, my calling. This was exactly where I wanted to be, and nothing could change that.

Chapter Two

Later in the afternoon, after I had handed off an overflowing box of flowers to a very happy bride, I sketched out an initial design plan for the dignitaries' dinner. Keeping with tradition we intended to take an innovative and European approach to the rose theme by blending Portland's signature roses with a variety of succulents. I roughed out a few options that included both high and low centerpieces bursting with peach, pink, creamy white, and yellow roses, dotted with purple-gray hens-and-chicks, flat rosettes with round edges, and dripping with gray-blue burro's-tail leaves. Additionally, we would create potted succulents in sand-colored clay pots that each guest could take home with them at the end of the evening. Succulents are ideal coffee-table arrangements that require little water and care and are almost impossible to kill.

I felt confident that Elin would approve of my ideas and that we could pull them off in time for the dinner. With that complete, I closed the shop and made my way to the float barn. To call the space a barn wasn't exactly accurate. It was actually a large warehouse owned by a carnival company. The carnival stored their rides and equipment during the off-season. It was an ideal location given its proximity to the parade route and the fact that the warehouse had been designed to store massive Ferris wheels and fifty-foot slides

The barn was located under the Hawthorne Bridge on the east side of the Willamette River. It was a quick ten-minute walk over the bridge from Blomma. I locked the front door and tugged on my windbreaker. The sun attempted to break free from a bank of clouds hovering on the horizon. I cinched up my jacket and headed toward the Hawthorne, with its green trusses and red trim. Hundreds of cyclists zoomed past in the dedicated bike lane. Buses rumbled over the metal grates. The Hawthorne was the busiest pedestrian transport bridge in the entire state, boasting close to ten thousand cyclists and twenty thousand bus riders a day, in addition to hundreds of runners, walkers, tourists, and families who used the bridge as a link from the east to the west side of the city.

I passed a group of joggers wearing RACE FOR THE ROSES T-shirts, a popular run that benefited a local charity. A choppy river stretched below me. I paused for a moment and watched colorful dragon boats cutting through the waves. On the banks adjacent to Riverplace Village white tents lined the waterfront. This was the heart of the action during the festival. There were outdoor entertainment stages that attracted performers from all over the country, a food fair, a live animal exhibit, craft beer, carnival rides, and the Big Thrill—a twenty-five-story-high catapult that shoots adventure riders into the sky. I shuddered at the thought of being slung through the air by choice, and continued onward.

On the east side of the river, I followed the pathway paralleling the river. The only drawback to the warehouse's location was that it was slightly creepy. A population of homeless people had set up camp beneath the bridge, and I hated having to walk past their miniature tent city on my way to and from the float barn. It was always a strange juxtaposition to pass people living in cardboard boxes and makeshift tarp-tents, on my way to work on a whimsical floral float.

A brisk, late spring breeze kicked up as I took the path from the bridge, down and around toward the float barn. A group of anarchists dressed in black from head to toe blocked the pathway. They had been protesting every day, and their numbers seemed to be multiplying. I guessed there must be at least thirty, with their faces masked by black and red bandanas. They held signs spray-painted on sheets and cardboard that read: SONS OF ANARCHY, GUERILLA WARFARE, CAPITALISM IS A CRIME, and THE SYSTEM HAS FAILED US. There was a massive banner made from a black sheet and spray-painted in red that said: A REVOLUTION IS NOT A BED OF ROSES—FIDEL CASTRO.

I recognized the group's leader, Sham, who wore a black bandana printed with the words *Dark Fusion* over half of his face. One of his fellow anti-fascist members, Zigs, was shouting into a megaphone.

"We are not going to let any of Portland's delicate little snowflake hippies distort our message. They can hold hands and sing 'Peace Train' in Pioneer Courthouse Square. We are here to riot! It's time to cause chaos. We need to rise up and fight the power! Who's with me?"

The crowd cheered and pumped their fists in the air. Some waved black and red flags, others held sticks and baseball bats.

I'd become accustomed to their presence, but it felt like things were beginning to escalate. Dark Fusion had been protesting the parade and every activity associated with the Rose Festival for the past two weeks. They believed that the Rose Festival was nothing more than a show of corporate power. A heated battle had been brewing between Sham and Zigs and Ted Graham, this year's grand marshal. Ted was the former mayor of Portland. He had been involved in Rose Festival for over forty years. He loved telling volunteers and the media about his memories from his first ever Junior Rose Parade, where he had marched with his junior high school band, the Fighting Lumberjacks. Ted was furious with Dark Fusion, especially because for the first time in the history of the Rose Festival he had to cancel the kickoff event—the Avenue of the Roses Business Parade.

Two weeks ago, Ted was supposed to have led the family-friendly annual event through some of Portland's oldest neighborhoods, but Dark Fusion had had other plans. They threatened to protest and disrupt the parade by any means necessary, even violence. Dark Fusion insisted that the Avenue of the Roses Business Parade was giving voice to Portland's conservative business community. Ted had met with organizers and business leaders before ultimately determining to cancel the parade for the first time in the festival's history. Dark Fusion had a well-documented record of violent clashes with police and destruction of property. It wasn't worth the risk.

Ted had demanded that every member of the anarchist group be thrown in jail. Without tangible proof (just verbal threats) the city's hands were tied. Dark Fusion took the city's lack of response as a win and had been escalating their threats. Ever since, tensions had been running high. Not a day went by that Dark Fusion wasn't camped out on the riverfront path near the float barn, screaming at poor, unsuspecting volunteers arriving for their shift, or engaging in a war of obscenities with Ted. Nicki, the float barn organizer, had sent dozens of emails to our incredible volunteers, informing them of the situation and offering alternative routes in and out of the barn so as not to have to come face-to-face with any members of Dark Fusion.

I felt terrible for Ted, Nicki, and the other organizers. It had to be a logistical nightmare. Hundreds of volunteers rotated in and out of the float barn every day. Some coming to work for a few hours, others for the entire day. Many corporations and nonprofits sent teams of volunteers. It was a great way to bond and meet people from all walks of life. Yet another reason it was hard to understand Dark Fusion's motivation. In challenging political times, events like the Rose Festival brought people together. I had worked side by side with an organic bee farmer, an army ranger, a vegan chef, and a BMX racer. If it wasn't for our float, I couldn't imagine any of our paths crossing in our normal daily lives. Why Dark Fusion wanted to tear down the community building, which occurred naturally while decorating fun and festive floats, was a mystery to me.

I pulled my hood over my head and was about to scoot past the group, when I spotted my friend Tomo interviewing one of the members of Dark Fusion. Tomo is a police officer who had helped solve a recent murder at Blomma. He and I had hit it off immediately. He was my first official friend in Portland, and like the brother I had always wanted. His family owned a drool-worthy authentic Japanese ramen shop, the Happy Spoon, near the village, which had quickly become one of my favorite eateries. Tomo had followed in his father's footsteps and joined the police force. They had only worked together for a short time when his father responded to a call at the ramen shop—a hate group had tagged the restaurant. Tomo's dad was the first person on the scene and had been shot. He was still recovering from his injuries. Portland had seen a string of targeted hate crimes in the city's mosques, temples, and churches, as well as vandalization of restaurants and businesses owned by perceived immigrants. The police had been tracking a suspected hate group, but thus far no arrests had been made. Tomo had made it his mission to find whoever had vandalized their restaurant and sidelined his father, while working double shifts on the force and at the ramen shop to help support his family during this difficult time.

He finished questioning the Dark Fusion member and turned in my direction. A look of surprise spread across his boyish face. He walked over to me with one hand on his police baton. "Britta, what are you doing here?"

"Nice to see you too, Tomo." I punched him in the arm.

His bright brown eyes softened. "Sorry. I didn't mean it like that." He pulled me away from the shouts and chants of the crowd. "Listen, there was an incident here earlier. A volunteer had a run-in with one of the DF members."

"DF?"

"Slang for Dark Fusion."

I noticed that he had positioned his body so that he could keep one eye on the protesters as we spoke.

"Right." I caught the eye of Sham, the huge, bulky leader who had a shaved head, a spiky metallic choker, and neck tattoos. He gave me a strange look. Was he trying to warn me not to talk to the police?

Tomo stared at me, then back to Sham. "Don't make eye contact. It's better to just ignore them. They want a response. They thrive on a response."

Tomo moved us to the gravel parking lot in front of the float barn. "Seriously, Britta, be super careful. I don't think that Detective Fletcher believes me, but I'm sure that DF is responsible for my dad's shooting. I don't know if I ever told you, but this is the same group that had been rioting in the village the week before the incident. I've been working under the assumption that whoever targeted our shop was motivated by hate and race."

I nodded. Tomo had shared some of the prejudices that his parents had faced as Japanese Americans when they first moved to Portland. It was hard to believe that anyone could target Tomo or his family. Anyone who walked into the Happy Spoon was immediately welcomed by Mrs. Iwamoto. Her noodles had become a thing of legend in Portland, attracting locals and tourists to the small restaurant for steaming bowls of her signature dish with bone broth, pork, bamboo shoots, eggs, leeks, mushrooms, spices, and fresh herbs. She ruled the ramen shop's open-concept kitchen with an iron spatula and a friendly smile. Since our first meeting, she had been trying to fatten me up with her handcrafted black sesame ice-cream and doughy pork buns. I hated the thought that the Iwamoto family could have felt unwelcome in Portland, even for a moment.

"Now I'm not so sure. Now I'm wondering if it was because of this," Tomo continued, tapping the badge on his chest. "What if DF came after my dad because he's a cop? He's been working the village beat and has had a few run-ins with DF. Nothing major. The usual. He cited them for rioting, setting off firecrackers, that kind of thing. What if I've been wrong this entire time? I think the guys responsible for shooting my dad have been right in front of me. I don't like this at all. I have a bad vibe, Britta. A really bad vibe."

"But Pete doesn't believe you?" Detective Pete Fletcher was Tomo's boss. He was new to Portland and tended to approach police work with a detached if not level head. I was surprised to hear that he doubted his young partner. Tomo looked up to Pete, and in the interactions that I had seen between them, Pete had seemed impressed by Tomo's natural intuition and follow-through.

Tomo kicked a piece of gravel. "I don't know. He doesn't want me jumping to any conclusions. But,

Britta, I'm telling you I have a bad feeling about this, and I'm worried. Look at them. These aren't peaceful protesters. Who brings a bat to a peaceful protest? DF are self-described anarchists who want to overthrow the city government. They're not going to stop with trying to intimidate volunteers here at the warehouse. This is going to escalate. I know it, and I don't want you around. I think they're planning something huge. Something that Portland has never seen. If they want to make a statement and take down the city, what better time than Rose Festival."

He was making me worried with his repetition of having a bad feeling. I felt my jaw go loose. "Are you serious?"

Tomo's face was rigid as he nodded. His round, almost cherub-like face looked as if it had aged a decade. "I don't think you should stick around here. Things could get out of control—fast."

"But I can't just leave. Elin and I are responsible for our float. I have to be here every day until the parade."

Tomo sighed. "I know. I'm going to talk to Detective Fletcher again, but in the meantime, don't go anywhere near them, and if you hear anything or see anything you call me. Don't call Pete, okay?"

"Okay." I nodded and headed for the entrance. Tomo's warning was unsettling. I'd never seen him so rattled. Was he on to something, or was he being paranoid? I wanted to hear Pete's take on the situation. Maybe I could stop by the precinct later. Any excuse to see Pete Fletcher was good with me, but I was worried about my friend and potentially my personal safety.

With a final parting glance at Tomo, who was heading straight for the protesters, I opened the heavy door leading into the float barn. The warehouse had been divided into twelve sections, each housing an individual float. At the front there was a small area with a microwave and a few folding tables and plastic chairs for volunteers or crew members. Rickety wooden scaffolding stretched around every float. The Blomma float was at the far end. I waved hello to familiar faces, carefully watching my footing because nearly every inch of open floor space contained buckets of seeds or floral tools.

Every float had been assigned a crew chief who was responsible for overseeing volunteers and ensuring that the float's design was carried out to the letter. No two floats were alike. There was a massive camel decorated in golden sepia tones with grasses, wheat, and dried hops; a rainbow-colored hot air balloon made from berries and pomegranates, echinacea pods, artichokes, and oranges; a float sponsored by the zoo with life-size tigers and bears; a strawberry teapot; and a rocket ship, just to name a few. The royal court's float where the princesses and Rose Festival Queen would wave to happy parade-goers would be completely covered with red and pink roses and was stair-stepped to offer everyone a view of each member of the court.

There were stations throughout the barn with chainsaws, sawhorses, drills, and an assortment of power tools. I weaved through buckets of peppermint, smoke bush, oak leaves, and branches.

"You're here, Britta. I had a feeling I might see you earlier than expected." A woman in her midsixties, wearing a vintage Rose Festival Volunteer T-shirt from 1970, greeted me with a smile. She was plump, with wavy silver hair, and reading glasses that hung from a chain around her neck. Gloria was our crew chief and knew more about the Grand Floral Parade than anyone I had met.

"Gloria, you know me, I can't keep my fingers away from that sticky glue." I pointed to a twenty-gallon bucket of glue resting on a metal cart. Gloria was using a soup ladle to scoop smaller portions of glue into half-gallon buckets. The volunteers would take the buckets and an assortment of paintbrushes, along with amaranth seeds, up onto the scaffolding to reach high points on the float. Gloria had ground white rice to make a fine powder that we used to cover the wheel wells. Not even the tiniest inch of the float could be bare.

I shrugged off my jacket and hung it on the edge of a wooden bookcase that was packed with knifes, paintbrushes, pruners, paddle wire, wire frames, twine, tape, and every floral tool imaginable. Gloria referred to the area as the pigpen, since it was a makeshift corral for storage and supplies.

"How did the morning shift go?" I ran my fingers through shredded coconut that had been tinted pink.

Gloria wiped her hands on a rag. "Pretty well. We had a team in from the high school debate club and a group of knitters from a local church. I sent the high-schoolers up on the scaffolding and had the knitting ladies focus on the wheel wells."

"Smart." Volunteers were required to sign waivers in order to participate in the decorating. The Rose

Festival took their safety very seriously. We never sent anyone who was uncomfortable with heights or unsteady on their feet onto the scaffolding. Many people were surprised at how physically demanding the tasks could be. I had learned to warn volunteers to expect to be sore by the end of their four-hour shift. And to take as many breaks as they needed. Float decorating was supposed to be fun. We didn't want to torture anyone.

"Don't you worry," she said as she finished unboxing dozens of empty water bottles. "I made sure that those kids took their tasks seriously. I explained that they can't just go and slap on a bunch of glue and slather on seeds. Some crew chiefs might not care about design and presentation, but the judges will dock us points for sloppy work. We aren't going to have any clumps on the Blomma float. I showed them how to press on the seeds so that the glue dries clear."

"Thanks." I appreciated her eye for detail.

"You missed some excitement earlier." Gloria removed her reading glasses from the bridge of her nose and let them hang loose on a silver chain around her neck. She motioned to the float next to us. It was in the shape of a dragon with a twenty-foot tail and fire shooting from its mouth. I had seen the preliminary sketches and knew that the flames would be made of orange begonias, marigolds, zinnias, and lion's-tails. I couldn't wait to see the finished product. The shot of orange against the green and purple body should be quite stunning.

"Trouble with the float?" I asked. A group of volunteers wearing matching name badges were gluing

poppy seeds on the dragon's body. They were joking
and laughing as they worked. There didn't appear
to be anything amiss with the float's structure.

Gloria motioned for me to come closer. She lowered her voice. "No, with Ted Graham."

I glanced back to the float. Sure enough, Ted was
talking to Nicki, the float barn director, near the
dragon's tail. He wasn't hard to miss in his Royal
Rosarian's white suit and straw hat. The Royal Rosarians were Portland's official greeters and ambassadors. They marched together in every parade as a
symbol of the city's outstanding character and kind-
ness. Nearly every Portlander could identify Royal
Rosarians by their classic suits, red ties, and hats.
They also served as hosts for VIPs and dignitaries
and represented Portland in parades throughout
the world. Ted's purple cape denoted that he was a
member of the executive council. "What happened?"
I asked. Neither Ted nor Nicki looked happy.

"One of the volunteers on the Mt. Hood float
claimed that she got hit in the head with a pinecone
on her way into the barn." Gloria flicked a seed
from her finger. Her hands were marked with age
spots and wrinkles.

"By Dark Fusion?"

Gloria nodded. "Ted called the police, but apparently there's no way to prove it. It's the volunteer's
word against that entire delinquent gang. Ted and
Sham got in a shouting match. Sham swore they
didn't do it. He said that if Dark Fusion takes things
to the next level, they won't be using pinecones."

"Yikes." I swallowed hard. This was getting serious. Tomo's warning repeated in my head. I figured

the volunteer incident must have been why Tomo had arrived on the scene.

"Mmm-hmm." Gloria furrowed her winkled brow. She had a kind face with deep-set brown eyes. "Ted told Sham that if Sham didn't leave the area within the next twenty-four hours, he's calling in the National Guard."

"Can he do that?"

"No. I don't think so." Gloria stared at Ted and Nicki. She let out a soft sigh. "Poor Nicki. This is her first year on the job and she's already been running around in a panic. I think this might push her over the edge."

Gloria was right. Nicki looked frazzled. She wore a rose-red short-sleeve polo with khaki pants and white tennis shoes. Her auburn hair spilled from a loose ponytail. She had a walkie-talkie in one hand and a clipboard in the other. A set of keys dangled from her back pocket. A black leather purse with a gaudy gold handle hung over one arm. I wasn't sure if she was agitated by whatever Ted was saying, but she kept bouncing on her feet like she had to go to the bathroom. Then she would dart her eyes toward the front of the warehouse and back to Ted. "She does look kind of jumpy."

"We can't exactly blame her, can we?" Gloria reached for a fine-tip paintbrush. "I've been a volunteer for my entire adult life and I can't remember anything like this in the past. Even during the Rajneesh attack back in '84, the parade and festival still went on as planned."

I remembered reading about the Rajneesh bioterrorist attack in high school. The extremist group had poisoned salad bars in The Dalles, Oregon, with salmonella, sickening over seven hundred residents, in an attempt to stop people from voting and ensure a win for their candidate. At the time it was the biggest and most successful bioterrorist attack in the United States.

"You think this is like the Rajneeshees?"

"No. Much worse. That crisis took place in the summer and fall, it didn't interfere with Rose Festival. However, people were still upset and nervous about further retaliation or acts of violence, but nothing happened. The thought of anyone trying to ruin Portland's most loved festival of the year makes me sick to my stomach." She flicked the tip of her paintbrush. "I've learned there's not much use in worrying about things we can't control though. So shall we get to gluing?"

I took the brush and followed Gloria to the front section of our float, stealing one more glance at Nicki and Ted. Were things about to explode between them and Dark Fusion? I never would have imagined that agreeing to design a Grand Floral float could be dangerous, but I was starting to wonder what Aunt Elin and I had gotten ourselves into.

Chapter Three

Gloria and I didn't have a chance to dive into our work because Ted grabbed a bullhorn and called the volunteers together. "Ladies and gentlemen, I'm sorry to be the bearer of bad news, but we have a growing situation with the punks who I'm sure you've all seen outside." He paused as volunteers murmured to each other. "As some of you know, the police were here earlier and they will be returning later tonight. They've offered to escort you to your cars. I don't want to scare or alarm anyone, but our parade is under assault, and I've just learned from the police that one of our volunteers was physically assaulted trying to leave the premises."

Ted's words made everyone gasp.

"It's okay." He swept his hand in a regal motion. "As your grand marshal, I refuse to allow these deviants to deter our mission. There is no need to panic. We're taking every extra precaution for the moment. Fortunately, the volunteer wasn't injured, but we don't want to take any chances."

Nicki stepped forward with a handful of bright yellow flyers. "I want to second what Ted said. We're working directly with the police. They are monitoring the situation and have offered extra patrols as well as helping anyone in and out of the barn. I've printed some flyers with more details about our response. Dark Fusion members are not allowed in any of the warehouses or even on the gravel parking lot. The waterfront path is city property, but the police will be patrolling the area to ensure that all of us as well as anyone walking on the pathway can access it without being harassed. Dark Fusion can't mount a protest here without a formal permit. Ted's working to try to rush through a restraining order. In the short term, should anyone approach you or attempt to block your path on the way in and out of the barn, my personal cell number is on here. If you need anything or witness anything suspicious or violent, call me anytime."

She passed the stack of flyers to a volunteer. Ted removed his straw hat and placed it over his chest. "What Dark Fusion is doing is incomprehensible. Let me repeat this again, as grand marshal of your parade, I assure you that their tyrannical acts will not go unpunished. Even if I have to hunt each member down, justice will be served and our beloved Grand Floral Parade will go on. They can scream and pound their fists, we will not be swayed from our mission. What's our theme this year?" He paused.

Someone near the back shouted, "Shine!"

"That's right." Ted waved his hat in the air. "Portland will shine come Saturday. We will march in the streets and not be deterred by a bunch of guerilla renegades determined to bring unrest and darkness to our peaceful city."

Gloria squeezed my forearm. "I hope he's right. I have a bad feeling about this." Her fingers were clammy.

"He sounds like he's taking it personally," I replied as we returned to the Blomma float. Although we had made considerable progress, every section of the float still had hours and hours of work left to complete. I felt a mild anxiety build in my chest.

"That's because he is." Gloria struggled to open a step stool. Her shoulders arched painfully, but the stool wouldn't budge.

"Let me get that for you," I said, taking the stool and locking it into the open position.

"Thank you. Creaky bones." She placed the stool over the black tarp positioned around the float. I kneeled next to her on a foam garden pad. Our task for the rest of the evening was to finish covering the base of the float with a combination of amaranthus seeds and ground rice. The float itself was actually a Suburban that was buried underneath our structure and camouflaged with thousands of seeds, flowers, and greenery. Come parade day, the driver would never even see the street.

Gloria's hands quivered as she painted a one-inch strip of glue onto the base. "I've never seen Ted like this." She turned to stare at him. He was talking to the float crew working on a float designed in honor of Portland's sister city, Guadalajara, Mexico. Their float depicted two flamenco dancers wearing bright, colorful, traditional folk-dancing costumes. Ted's cape billowed behind him as he motioned with his arms. I knew that he was speaking with passion but it almost looked as if he was trying to mimic the fluid motion of the dancer on the float.

"I can't say that I blame him," Gloria continued. "He's going to pop a vein in his head if he keeps letting Sham get to him like this."

"But what can he do? It's not like he has any control over Dark Fusion." I dipped my paintbrush into the glue and began coating it onto the float in one long strip. Next, I stuck a sponge into another bucket filled with the amaranthus seeds and pressed them onto the glue. It was a slow process, and a bit tricky because while pressing the seeds I had to place a bucket directly under the line of glue so that I could catch any overflow. As it was, seeds were scattered everywhere. I had a feeling that I would be hearing the tiny seeds hitting the plastic tarp in my sleep for weeks to come.

Before work began on any of the floats, tarps were tucked around the base of each vehicle. At the end of every shift the crew chief would direct the volunteers to carefully lift the plastic section by section and scoop the overage back into buckets. We wanted—no, needed—to salvage as much product as possible. Nicki's mantra this year was *No seed or stem shall go wasted.* It was a tall order. Seeds went flying everywhere. I'd found them in my hair and even inside my shoes at the end of a long day.

Gloria dabbed the fine rice powder onto the float. It looked like a first snow. "That's my point. He needs to let it go and let the police take care of it. I've told him again and again, but he won't listen. Stubborn man. He's making things worse. You can't argue with anarchists. Ted is giving them exactly what they want—a reaction."

"You're right." I tried to concentrate on decorating, but couldn't stop watching Ted. His face was scrunched in a tight ball and he looked as red as Portland's signature rose. He weaved his way through every float, stopping to promise volunteers that he would personally assure their safety.

When he made it to our float, he greeted Gloria with a pat on her shoulder and then appraised our work. "Very unique design, ladies. Excellent. Most excellent." There was something about his posture that felt condescending, despite his effusive praise. Perhaps it was the fact that he picked at a pile of moss I had set on the bottom step and tossed it to the side with distain.

"I knew that inviting Blomma would add a new layer of class to the parade." He tapped a twisted grapevine. "Lovely use of interesting and contrasting textures. I would say you have a good shot at winning an award." There was something off-putting about his tone.

Gloria tried to stand but her knees gave out. Ted hurried over to help her, as did I. We lifted her together. "Don't make a fuss. Creaky bones. Creaky knees." She brushed us off, but I caught a wince of pain flash across her face.

"Float design is a young person's game, Gloria. It's probably time for us two old fogies to throw in the towel, don't you think?" He shook a seed from his pristine white loafers.

"Never!" Gloria flinched as if Ted's words had struck her.

He didn't notice. "I haven't officially announced this, but this is going to be my last year as grand marshal. I'm passing on the torch to someone new next year, to focus on curating my international rose garden."

Gloria smoothed her vintage Rose Festival T-shirt. She appeared to have recovered from her shock at Ted's suggestion that they give up volunteering. She changed the subject. "Have you met Elin's niece, Britta? She's quite the flower expert. I'm sure she'd love to tour your garden."

"Ah, this is Britta. The famous, Britta. Your aunt has been talking about you for years." Ted reached to shake my hand.

I held up my hands, which were smudged with sticky black residue. "I'll just say hi."

He pretended like it was no big deal, but I noticed him smooth his white suit jacket as if my dirty fingers were contagious. "Where is Elin?"

"She's at the shop. We've been trading places—dividing up our time here and working on the designs for the dignitaries' dinner. She should be here in the next hour or two. Did you need something?"

"No. You heard my speech earlier and got a flyer?"

"We did," Gloria said. She had walked to the supply cart in the pigpen, and was cutting six-inch strips of twine. The woman never stopped. Her stamina was impressive, especially given her age and "creaky" bones. "Ted, you should head home and take a break. Nicki seems to have things under control, and I think that you being here is making things worse with Dark Fusion."

Wow. I was also impressed that Gloria was so direct. She didn't beat around the bush.

"No. I'm not leaving. That's exactly what they want. They want me out of here. I'm not about to give them that satisfaction. The moment we show any sign of weakness, they win. I dealt with much worse during my tenure as mayor, and I'm not about to give Dark Fusion an inch." His voice was laced with anger.

Gloria tried to calm him down. "Ted, how long have we known each other? And how long have we been doing this together? Thirty years? Longer? I know how much you care about the parade, but this is killing you. I'm worried about your health. You've been here around the clock. From the looks of the bags under your eyes, you probably aren't sleeping or eating well. I love the parade too, but I don't want to see you go down for the count." Her hands quivered slightly as she spoke.

Ted's face relaxed slightly. "Thanks, Gloria. You sound like my wife. I appreciate your concern, but I'm not going anywhere. We only have a few days left. I'll sleep once we've pulled off another successful Grand Floral Parade."

Gloria looked like she wanted to say more, but instead she nodded and kept snipping twine.

He turned to me. "Once this is over, please accept this as my official invite to my hand-curated rose garden. I have over two hundred varietals, heirlooms, and test vines. It's the largest personal collection of roses in the state. As a matter of fact, soon it might be the largest in the world. You and Elin are more than welcome to come take a tour. I'm sure you'll find a number of rare stems that you've never seen before. People tell me that my collection is the most incredible rose experience."

"Thanks." The man obviously loved roses, and certainly wasn't bashful about bragging.

"How are you enjoying float design and decorating?" Ted asked. He had shifted back into his role as ambassador of the festival.

"It's been really fun and I've learned so much," I said. I was about to ask him a question about the judging process, but suddenly a hush came over the barn. The sound of the power saw and shop vac stopped. Volunteer chatter ceased as all eyes focused behind me.

My stomach dropped. Had Dark Fusion infiltrated? I froze in place. They wouldn't do something drastic, like blow up the barn, would they? The sound of their chants echoed in the quiet, cavernous warehouse. Was the sound getting closer?

I watched Ted turn around slowly, and followed his lead, expecting to see a wall of anarchists waiting to take over the barn.

Instead, a tall, gorgeous woman, wearing strappy heels and a skintight black dress, stood in the doorway. She was clearly not here to work on a float. Decorators were given strict instructions to wear jeans or shorts, T-shirts or sweatshirts, and tennis shoes. Not only were sturdy shoes a necessity when climbing scaffolding or kneeling for hours, but volunteers would leave with glue and flower particles stuck to their clothing and coating their skin.

"She's here. She's finally here!" Ted sucked in his breath, and ignored my question. He flipped his cape behind him and raced toward the front.

"Who is *she*?" I asked Gloria.

Gloria pointed to the tiara resting on top of the woman's silky blond curls. "Queen Priscilla."

"Queen? I thought the Rose Festival court was high school students. Isn't this year's queen from Jefferson High School?"

"Yes." Gloria nodded. "Priscilla is this year's honorary queen. She's a former queen who reigned twenty-five years ago. She has been invited to crown this year's queen at the coronation and will be watching over the princesses. The media is going to do a series of short vignettes about a former queen imparting her wisdom to a new generation of girls. That sort of thing. Of course, she'll be on the float with Ted for the parade as well."

Was it my imagination or did Gloria sound almost envious?

Without pause Gloria continued. "Rose princesses aren't just pretty faces, you know. It's a once-in-a-lifetime opportunity. Did you know that members of the court spend weeks traveling? It's a full-time job—five days a week. The princess and Rose Festival Queen visit hospitals, youth groups, senior care centers, and civic groups. They meet with business leaders and politicians."

As Gloria spoke, a faraway look crossed her face. Now I had no doubt that Gloria longed to have been part of the court.

"It's more than that, too. The mission of the court program is to encourage community involvement and volunteering. The young women receive scholarships and countless networking opportunities. These connections will last them a lifetime and open many, many doors for them for years to come."

I watched as a number of volunteers ran over to ask Queen Priscilla for autographs. "She's quite popular."

Gloria placed the cut pieces of twine in a basket and reached for another spool. "Yes. She's a celebrity around here. She started a cosmetics company in LA—Juvenescence—about fifteen years ago and hit it big. You've probably seen her products in high-end shops, and those infomercials that run late at night? You know the ones where the fifty-year-old woman transforms into a blushing twentysomething after one application of Priscilla's proprietary night cream?"

"That's her company?" I was familiar with Juvenescence. Their infomercials ran nearly every night. It was impossible to miss the commercial that touted unbelievable results—like a complete reversal of the aging process—for the low, low price of five hundred dollars for a complete set of Priscilla's Juvenescence skin-care line.

"That's her." Gloria scoffed. "Everyone in Portland loves a local success story."

Ted ushered Priscilla away from her adoring fans.

"Rumor has it that her company is worth millions. She's the spokesmodel, and is constantly talking about the fact that her flawless face and skin are not only due to her wonderful products but also because of her attitude. It's rumored that she refuses to smile and keeps her face in a constant state of tightness in order to avoid laugh lines. I watched an interview she did with a local affiliate from Juvenescence's headquarters in LA. She sent out a warning for this year's court. Talking about the fact that back in her day, a princess was supposed to behave like a lady and carry herself as such. She told the reporter that she intends to be on the girls for slouching or chewing gum. She's a stickler for etiquette."

By the looks of Priscilla's perfect posture, I wasn't surprised. There weren't many people—if any—who could pull off wearing a tiara for no reason, but somehow Priscilla did. I felt self-conscious about my ripped jeans. I hadn't looked in a mirror for a while, but I was fairly confident that my pale skin likely didn't have the same dewy, natural glow as Priscilla's.

"If you ask me, the success has gone to her head. I don't even remember her coronation. Some queens stick out in your memory, but not Priscilla. She must have been an average queen during her reign." Gloria sounded disinterested, but she certainly knew a lot about the former queen. "Did you know that I've never missed a coronation or parade? I should bring in my scrapbooks for you. You might enjoy seeing how the floats and princesses' dresses have changed over the years."

"That would be great. I'd love to see them."

"I'll bring them in for you." Gloria returned to snipping twine. I returned to my station on the float, and spent the next hour chatting with our volunteer groups. Priscilla and Ted didn't stay long. I saw him sweep her out the back door not long after she arrived. I wondered if Gloria was right about him. He seemed high-strung. Part of me was glad that the parade was only a few days away, so that we could be done with Dark Fusion and the surrounding drama. Then looking at how much work was left to be done on the float, I wished we had another two weeks. If we didn't pick up the pace, the Blomma float would be a patchy, unfinished disaster.

Chapter Four

By the time Elin arrived, I had completed a third of the bottom section, and Gloria had cut most of the twine we would need to wrap the grapevines together.

"*Hej!*" Elin greeted us in Swedish. She removed her gray London Fog raincoat. Her pale hair fell to her shoulders and had been cut in a narrow, angular bob that accentuated her strong Swedish features. She wore her standard attire—a cable-knit sweater, jeans, and ankle-high rain boots. "You've made good progress. It's starting to look like a float."

"I want to show you a section over here," I said, finishing a row of seeds and then standing. The motion sent spots flashing before my eyes.

"Easy, darling." Elin caught my arm.

"I'm fine. I just stood up too fast."

Nonetheless, Elin held my arm as we walked around the float. Our vision for the top portion of the float involved stringing violets and grapevines through the tops of miniature evergreen trees. I was worried about the structure and how much weight it could hold. Violets weren't the issue, but once we bound hundreds of grapevines together it could bow out, giving the archway a saggy appearance. "Do you think these stakes will hold the weight of the grapevines?" I asked Elin, pointing out the section.

She deftly climbed onto the wooden scaffolding and tugged at the intricate pattern of stakes and four-foot cypress trees that we had secured to the second level of the float. "It should be fine, but there's only one way to know. Let's start assembling the grapevines and layering them into the canopy. If we can complete one section tonight, it should give us a good sense of how much weight will be compressed at the top."

"Good idea," I agreed. "I was planning to wrap a couple of the grapevines together anyway to use as a template for tomorrow's volunteers. The violets obviously won't last until Saturday, but if we create one or two as a guide, we can discard any wilting flowers and freshen them up Friday night." Fresh flowers would be the last addition to every float. Thousands of individual plastic water bottles had been salvaged for use in the parade. They would be filled with water and floral preservative on Friday evening. In a flurry of last-minute activity, volunteers would fill the makeshift vases with fresh-cut roses, daisies, violets, and dozens upon dozens of bright, cheery stems.

Elin came down from the scaffolding. "Sounds like we have our work cut out for us. Good thing I came prepared." She walked over to the storage cart in the pigpen and held up a soft cooler. "Dinner. First, we need to eat. Then we can put our fast fingers to the test. *Ja?*"

"You don't have to ask me twice." I grinned.

Elin cleared off a section of the cart and set out a spread of salmon pâté, rye crackers, sharp Väster-botten cheese, grapes, and one of my favorite child-hood snacks—spiced balsamic nuts. The traditional Swedish treat was a mixture of almonds, cashews, pumpkin seeds, and sunflower seeds that Elin toasted on low heat and then tossed in a spicy balsamic re-duction. "Gloria, will you join us?" Elin asked, open-ing a bottle of sparkling cider.

Gloria pulled on a thin Rose Festival sweatshirt dating back to 1983 over her T-shirt. I wondered how many Rose Festival shirts, hats, and scarves she had amassed over the years. "I begged Nicki to as-sign me to your float because I'd heard rumors about your Swedish feasts at Blomma and hoped that I might get a chance to taste for myself. Lucky me."

In addition to having an incredible eye for design and flowers, Elin was a wonderful cook. She and my mother grew up in Portland, but were raised in Swedish tradition. My grandparents immigrated from Sweden. They were attracted to Portland due to its European vibe. I remember many large family dinners where everyone spoke in rapid Swedish over a leisurely meal on my grandparents' patio. My early childhood had been blissful until tragedy struck when my parents were killed in a car accident. I was only seven, and in the years since their passing my memories of them had become fuzzy and distant. I remembered snippets, like running my fingers through my father's dark hair when he carried me on his shoulders, or my mother singing me Swedish folk songs to help me sleep at night. Part of me wondered if I could trust my memories. Were they real, or simply my imagination trying to offer comfort in the wake of devastating loss?

After the accident, Elin had swept in and adopted me. At the time I didn't know it, but she had given up love and plans for an adventure, for me. I had recently learned that Elin and her fiancé, Eric, had called off their wedding plans when she agreed to become my guardian. She never said a word to me, and I never knew that she had sacrificed her happiness for mine. Our years together had been filled with laughter, flowers, heartwarming food, and plenty of tears. Elin sat beside me in the early days after my parents' death and allowed me to grieve. She had lost her only sister. We grew inseparable in our pain, and came out stronger because of it. I owed everything to her.

"Britta," she said, interrupting my thoughts. "Come eat."

The three of us noshed on the decadent picnic. Gloria filled Elin in on what had transpired between Ted and Dark Fusion. I spread a thin layer of pâté on a rye cracker. The creamy salmon with hints of dill and lemon practically melted in my mouth.

"I saw them when I came in." Elin nibbled on a handful of the spicy nuts. "They didn't bother me."

"That's good," Gloria replied. "I was telling Britta earlier that I think Ted is making things worse. I know his intentions are good, but he keeps inflaming the situation. If we just ignore them, maybe they'll go away."

"Maybe." Elin looked thoughtful for a moment. "Dessert, anyone?" She unboxed a tin of homemade Swedish butter cookies.

I helped myself to a flaky cookie dusted with powdered sugar. The mouthwatering cookies are like a shortbread with a golden-brown crunchy exterior and tender center. The addition of maple syrup gives them a sweet, rich, buttery flavor. I devoured two cookies before raising my hands in protest. "We have to work tonight. I have to stop eating."

Gloria rubbed her midsection. "Tell me about it. You two might have to roll me out of here in Ted's golf cart."

"Golf cart?" I asked, trying to resist grabbing a third cookie.

"You haven't seen it? Ted zooms around everywhere on that ridiculous thing. He says it gives him access and speed to oversee float preparations. I wouldn't be surprised if he hopped on that thing and tried to mow down Dark Fusion."

Elin laughed and packed up the leftovers. "Let's hope not."

Gloria laid out twine and bundles of grapevines. "I'm serious."

Elin shot me a look. I shrugged. Then I went to consult our original sketches. Putting together a step-by-step guide wasn't simple. Many volunteers had never decorated floats before. Some had never even put together a floral arrangement. I needed to write instructions that would be easy for any novice to follow.

As I was working on my manual for tomorrow's volunteers, I spotted Nicki transporting supplies into the attached warehouse. We had been told that the neighboring warehouse was completely off-limits. Apparently, it housed carnival equipment and the owners were adamant that no one should enter the storage space. So much so that the door connecting the two spaces, which was right behind our float, had been locked and plastered with not one but three signs that read: OFF LIMITS, DO NOT ENTER, and NO ROSE FESTIVAL ACCESS.

In order to access the adjoining warehouse, Nicki had to pass our pigpen. She didn't make eye contact the first time she brushed by carrying a box of tools. I heard her fumbling to unlock the door. She muttered under her breath and jiggled the handle.

I put down my pencil and walked to the door. "Do you need a hand?"

She had set the box of supplies on the cement floor and was tugging the handle. "What?" Her hand flew off the handle as if it was hot to the touch.

"I just wondered if you needed some help." Why was she so jumpy?

She propped her foot against the door. "I'm fine, thanks. No one can come in here anyway. It's off-limits."

"I see that." I pointed to the signs taped on the door. "I thought you might need help getting the door unlocked."

"Nope." She blocked the door frame with her thin body. "I'm good. Just dropping off some extra supplies to make space. Sorry if I seem uptight. The owners of the carnival company are super strict about making sure that no one touches their equipment."

"I get it." I left her and returned to my design map.

However, it was impossible to ignore her as she came by two more times with heavy boxes. Between each trip she forced the door shut and locked it. Did she think we were going to sneak into the carnival warehouse and try to climb on the Ferris wheel or something?

My curiosity was piqued when she wheeled a wagon past the pigpen that was filled with buckets of the black dahlias that I had seen at the wholesale market earlier. "The dahlias!" I said aloud as Nicki rolled them by me.

She snapped her head and glared. "What?"

"Those black dahlias." I pointed to the mysterious dark stems. "I'm in love with them. I saw those this morning at my friend's booth. They're so gorgeous. What float are they going on?"

Nicki's lips formed a hard, thin line. "I don't know. Like I said, all this stuff is extra that we don't have space for at the moment." She tapped a red smartwatch on her wrist. "I'm sorry. I don't have time to stop and talk. There are a million things going on today and I'm about to lose it." With that she yanked the handle of the wagon and hurried to unlock the door.

Odd. I guess I couldn't blame her for being frazzled, given the state of things with Dark Fusion, but she seemed overly uptight about making sure that I didn't go anywhere near the other warehouse. It might be different if I were a high school student or new volunteer. I chalked it up to the fact that she was stressed, and concentrated on my directions for assembling the grapevines. To create a uniform design throughout our forestscape, I needed each bundle of grapevines to be symmetrical. Volunteers would clump the twisty, braided vines together at the base and wrap them tightly with wire. Then we would secure them to our arbor with fishing line. I couldn't decide if it made more sense to weave evergreen boughs and the violets into the vines before attaching them to the structure, or once they were already in place. I had a feeling that it was going to take longer than one might expect to arrange and cinch the vines onto the float. If that was the case then it would probably be better to add the final touches as a last step. However, that also meant our volunteers would have to precariously perch on the two-story scaffolding to do the intricate finish work.

Music played from a float nearby while I meticulously wrapped massive bundles of vines and twisted on delicate hanging violets. I documented each step in the process. By the time I had finished creating a ten-foot section of woody garlands, my fingers were achy and tiny blisters had started to form on my index fingers.

"Well, what do you think?" I asked Elin, who had completed covering one of the wheel wells with rice powder.

"I can't decide if it's going to be easier to assemble everything on the ground and then attach them to the arbor, or if we should get them up there and then layer in the flowers and branches."

We stood back to survey my work. "It is big, isn't it?" Elin studied the ten-foot section I had completed. "There's only one way to find out. Should we hoist it onto the arbor and see how it goes?" Elin asked.

I bit my bottom lip. "Yes, but I'm nervous. What if it crashes?"

"You wouldn't be the first float to have that happen," Gloria replied with a chuckle. "Like the year when the Bank of Portland tried to erect their big pink tower. It was nearly thirty feet in height, but they didn't account for the weight of the flowers—pink mums. About an hour before it was supposed to roll out for the parade, the tower toppled over and nearly took out two other floats. They never lived it down."

"That doesn't give me much confidence," I said to Gloria.

She pushed her glasses to the tip of her nose and stared at me. "You'll be fine. One of the high school volunteers was standing on the arbor earlier. It's solid."

"Let's hope so." I bent down to pick up one end of the garland. Elin grabbed the other side.

The garland wasn't as heavy as I had anticipated. I breathed a sigh of relief. As long as we could lift it over the second level of the float and secure it to the base we had built, I thought it would be okay. We made it onto the bottom of the float and then Gloria came to hold my end while I scrambled up the scaffolding. I could feel it bow as I stepped onto the two-foot-wide wooden structure.

The rickety ladder wiggled under me as I tied off the edge of the garland with green flower wire. "This side is good for a minute," I called to Elin and Gloria. I didn't want to break out the fishing line and really tie it onto the arbor until we were sure that this was the direction we wanted to take.

As I went around to the other side, I kept my body as close to the float as I could. I'm not afraid of heights, but the flimsy scaffolding looked as if it had been in use since the inception of the Rose Festival. I kept my line of sight straight in front of me. From this height it looked as if I could almost touch the arched metal roof. The view was quite amazing. I could see every float in the barn.

My shoe slipped on a pile of spilled seeds. I caught myself on the iron piping that served as a railing on the old scaffolding.

Watch your step, Britta, I cautioned myself, letting out a long breath before shuffling forward.

I had almost made it to the other side of the scaffolding when something exploded with a huge bang.

On instinct, I ducked and nearly toppled off the scaffolding. I caught the edge of a cypress tree at the base of the arbor just in time. My fingers dug into its pine-scented needles.

"Britta! Are you okay?" Elin shouted.

"Yeah." I inhaled through my nose, trying to calm my breathing. "What was that?"

There weren't many people left in the float barn this late at night. From my vantage point, I watched as Nicki sprinted to the front and out the door. A couple dozen volunteers and float designers emerged from behind their workstations to see what had happened.

Had the sound come from inside? Was it a gunshot?

I released my grasp on the cypress tree and turned behind me. We were the last float on this end of the barn. The door to the other warehouse was shut, but an emergency exit door on the opposite end of the far wall was flung open.

I could hear Nicki outside, shouting for someone to call the police. I left my supplies on the arbor and carefully climbed down the scaffolding. "Is that door supposed to be open?" I asked Gloria, pointing to the emergency exit.

She shook her head. "No. I don't think so."

Without thinking I ran to the emergency exit and checked outside. Cool air hit my face as I stepped into the darkness. The building's floodlights offered only the smallest sliver of light. I glanced to my left, then right. In the distance, I saw someone running toward the waterfront path. They must have been dressed entirely in black because they faded into the night. All I could make out was the motion of someone running.

I was about to return inside when my foot slid over something. I bent over and found at least a dozen rolls of firecrackers on the gravel. Were these the source of the bang? Had one of the members of Dark Fusion set them off and run away? Tomo had mentioned that Dark Fusion had used firecrackers in the past.

I left them on the ground and headed back into the float barn. "Where's Nicki?" I asked Elin and Gloria.

"She went out the front. I never saw her come back in," Elin said.

Sirens wailed nearby. *The police must be on their way.* I left Elin and Gloria and went to find Nicki. She was standing outside the front entrance with her hands on her hips, shouting at Sham.

Sham blended into the night sky. I was surprised that he had stepped onto the property. Ted had made it clear earlier that if any members of Dark Fusion so much as put a toe onto the gravel parking lot, he would call the police. Sham's bulky frame and the way the roof lights reflected off his bald head sent a shiver up my spine.

I scanned the waterfront. There were no other members of the anarchist group around. I wondered if they had taken off because of the fireworks or if they had just decided they'd had enough protesting for one night.

"The police are almost here," Nicki continued. She barely came to Sham's shoulders, but she was holding her own. She didn't appear to be afraid to confront the burly resistance leader. "This stops tonight. Understood? This is on *you*. You need to tell your guys to back off."

They shared a brief look that I couldn't decipher. "Sham, you know what you need to do, and the time to do it is long past." Nicki's voice was laced with anger.

Sham started to answer, but a police car sped into the parking lot. Its red and blue lights cut through the darkness. Tires spewed gravel in a long trail behind it. The car came screeching to a halt two feet away from Sham and Nicki.

The door to the squad car opened and a familiar figure stepped out. It was Officer Iwamoto. An immediate sense of relief flooded my body. Tomo was here. He would know what to do.

He didn't notice me as he exited the squad car. Instead, he yanked his baton from his belt and made a beeline to Sham. "I hear there was an explosion?" His voice sounded authoritative, but Sham towered over him in height and bulk. If he wanted to, it looked like Sham could take Tomo out with one swing.

Nicki pushed past Sham. I was surprised that he didn't react. "Yes. Just a few minutes ago. I don't know what they set off, but it sounded big. I think it might have been a bomb. Is the bomb squad coming? There could be more bombs."

A bomb? Why did she think that a bomb had gone off? The explosion hadn't been that loud. The equivalent of a gunshot maybe. But a bomb?

Tomo held the baton in one hand and took out a flashlight with the other. He clicked it on and started scanning the parking lot. "Is there any damage? Injuries?"

More sirens wailed nearby.

"Is that the bomb squad?" Nicki asked.

"That's my backup." Iwamoto continued to sweep the area. "Do I need to call an ambulance? Is anyone injured?"

"No." Nicki shook her head. "I don't think so. We were all inside when the bomb went off."

Sham spoke for the first time. "It wasn't a bomb."

"Of course, it was a bomb. It sounded like the roof was going to collapse." She turned to Iwamoto. "You should have heard it. It was so loud that my ears are still ringing." For effect she dug her fingers into her ears. "This is what Dark Fusion does. They destroy property. They're trying to destroy every float in the barn. They're going to destroy everything we've worked for. They're going to blow up the city, if you can't control them." Her voice was shrill. I couldn't decide if she was talking to Tomo or Sham.

Sham kicked the gravel with a combat boot. "It wasn't a bomb."

"How confident are you that you heard a bomb?" Iwamoto asked Nicki.

"One hundred percent. I'm positive it was a bomb. You have to call in more help. This entire place might be set to blow."

As if on cue, a fire truck and another police car pulled into the parking lot. I decided I had to tell Tomo what I had seen before he called in a bomb threat.

"Tomo," I said, walking over to them.

He flipped the flashlight in my direction. It hit my eyes, causing bright yellow halos to cloud my vision. "Britta?"

I reached my hand up to shield my face.

"What are you doing here?" Tomo lowered the flashlight. "I thought you were going to stay away from all of this."

"Working on the Blomma float." I motioned behind me to the barn. "I spotted something that I think you should come see."

Tomo frowned and looked to Nicki and Sham. "I'm in the middle of an investigation."

"I know. That's why you have to come see what I found on the other side of the barn."

"It's a bomb, isn't it?" Nicki asked, giving Sham a condescending glare. "Tell them, Sham. Admit it. You have to tell them." Sham hung his head and stared at his combat boots.

The firefighters and police officers ran over to us. "Is this a serious threat?"

Tomo held them off with his baton. "Hold up one second. Britta, what did you see?"

"Fireworks. Well, firecrackers. I think the sound we heard was firecrackers. There are a bunch of them by the emergency exit doors, and I saw someone running toward the waterfront path."

"No way!" Nicki shot me a furious glare. "It was a bomb. I don't know why you guys are standing around. Someone do something!"

Tomo motioned to the two other police officers. "You guys go sweep the path." He motioned for the fire crew to follow him. "Lead the way, Britta."

Chapter Five

I took them to the back entrance where firecracker remains were scattered on the cement. Tomo bent down and picked up a firecracker with a gloved hand. He showed it to one of the firefighters. "I think we may have the source of our explosion. No need to call the bomb squad."

Nicki fumed. "Firecrackers. What? No. That's impossible." She smashed one with the tip of her white tennis shoe. "It sounded like a bomb went off."

"Miss, I need you to back away. Please don't touch the evidence," Tomo said, giving Nicki a firm nod and motioning her away from the fireworks. Tomo was in his midtwenties, but was wise beyond his years. It showed in his calm yet firm manner. This was the Tomo I knew. He appeared to be in control of his emotions, unlike earlier in the day. I wondered if he had shared his theory with Pete.

"Wait! You said evidence. Does that mean you're going to make an arrest?" Nicki asked.

Tomo nudged her back. "That means we'll be surveying the scene. Please, return inside and someone will be in touch if we need anything further."

"Ted is right," Nicki huffed. "You guys are worthless. The Rose Festival is under attack and nothing gets done. Dark Fusion continues to walk free." She turned on her white tennis shoes that glowed in the dark and stomped toward the front entrance.

"I think she's under a lot of stress," I said to Tomo. He looked miserable.

The firefighters had begun searching the perimeter and marking the firecrackers with white chalk. "It's understandable," Tomo replied. "She's upset. Trust me, I get it. I'm upset. I want nothing more than to toss that entire crew of rioters in jail, but I can't. It won't do any good. I talked to Pete this afternoon, and I think he's starting to come around, but he made me promise to follow protocol. He's right. If we don't, then nothing we slap on them is going to stick. First, we need proof, and secondly—and she's not going to like this any better—the most we can do is cite the perpetrator with an illegal use of fireworks. It's a five-hundred-dollar fine. Setting off a bunch of firecrackers isn't going to land a single DF member in jail."

"Right." I watched the fire chief signal to one of his guys that the scene was safe. "I did see someone running down the waterfront path."

"Hopefully our guys will catch him." Tomo ran his fingers through his dark hair, giving it a tousled look. "Britta, I wish there was more I could do, and honestly I think Nicki is right. Things are going to escalate. I can feel it. I just don't have any idea how to stop it."

"What a mess." I reached for his arm.

Tomo's walkie-talkie crackled. "Look, I better check in. Stay safe and text me if you need anything, okay?"

"Thanks, Tomo." I left him as he answered his walkie-talkie. I didn't know the meaning of the police codes I overhead Tomo rattle off, but it sounded like they caught the guy not far down the path. Part of me wanted to wait and see what unfolded, but there was so much to finish on the float and I didn't want to intrude on Tomo's work.

Nicki was addressing the volunteers when I returned inside. "We're shutting down for the night, everyone. It's not safe for you to be here. The police think there could be more explosives planted inside."

The volunteers let out a collective gasp. What was she talking about? Tomo hadn't said a word about other explosives.

"Plan to report here at six a.m. Assuming it's safe to allow you back in, I'll be here with the keys first thing in the morning. We have a long day ahead of us, so get some sleep."

I had no idea why she was embellishing the situation. She made it sound as if the police had actually found a bomb on-site. Elin and Gloria ran over to me with handfuls of supplies, our coats, and the remains of dinner, which had been hastily stuffed into a large plastic bag.

"Britta, we better get out of here." Gloria's face was flushed from the exertion. Her glasses dangled on the chain around her neck. She kept rubbing the chain with such force that I thought she might snap it.

"It's okay." I took my coat from her arms.

"But the bomb." Her eyes were wide and frantic.

I placed my hand on her shoulder. "There is no bomb. It was only a bunch of firecrackers. I was there. I talked to the police."

Elin's eyes narrowed. "Are you sure?"

"Positive. Tomo's here." Elin was a fan of Tomo's, not only because of his dedication to his parents, but also because of his thoughtful community approach to police work.

"I don't understand. Why would Nicki say that we're in danger?" Gloria glanced around the barn.

We headed for the door. "No idea. It's a mystery for sure. I was stunned when I heard her announce that, because that is not what the police said."

Elin frowned. "I don't know what's going on, but I know I don't like it. It's very odd."

Gloria concurred. "Something doesn't feel right. You two go on ahead. I want to talk to Nicki for a minute. I think that Ted has gotten into her head. Maybe I can talk some sense into her."

We parted ways and agreed to meet back in the morning. On the drive home, Elin and I tried to rationalize why Nicki would have lied. The only possibility we came up with was that she was skittish from the ongoing Dark Fusion threats and felt responsible. "Likely she didn't want to risk anyone's safety," Elin said as she pulled into the driveway of her Swedish-cottage-style house. It was a two-story house on the hillside above Riverplace Village. The back deck offered a wonderful view of the Willamette River through the tree line. It had been a magical place to grow up. I remembered building fairy houses out of pebbles and bark and arranging them in the potted shrubs and trees around the deck.

The fairies—aka Elin—would leave me tiny sprigs of lavender and shiny copper pennies. Elin would spend lazy summer Sunday afternoons with a glass of iced sun-ripened tea, leafing through stacks of Swedish magazines. She let me run free through the wild forests below the deck. I would spend hours collecting Japanese maple leaves, thistles, ferns, and bleeding hearts. It was here that I first fell in love with nature's bounty and realized that I could leave my mark on the world by creating beautiful, simple things like a bundle of birch wood tied with rough string, or a dried bouquet of feathers, larkspur, and wild mushrooms. My creations took on a life of their own, and Elin always encouraged with praise and subtle suggestions.

We dropped the subject of Dark Fusion once inside the cozy cottage and went straight to bed, knowing that we would have a full day ahead. In anticipation of the final push to the finish, we had informed our customers that we would be closed through Sunday. Everyone we knew would be at the Grand Floral Parade anyway.

The next morning dawned early. I woke to the scent of Elin's strong coffee. Having been a tea drinker my entire adult life, I had made the switch to Portland's signature morning drink with little resistance. The rich smell wafting upstairs was all the motivation I needed to tug on a pair of jeans and a charcoal-gray hooded sweatshirt. I tied my hair into two braids and pulled on a pair of comfortable tennis shoes.

"Morning," I said to Elin, who was boiling eggs on the stove.

"*God morgon*," she replied with the slightest hint of a Swedish accent. "Coffee is ready. Would you like toast with your egg?"

Elin knew me well. I couldn't refuse my favorite childhood breakfast of a soft-boiled egg with toast and a side of her homemade lingonberry jam. I poured myself a cup of coffee and added a splash of cream. Elin's coffee was irresistible. She concocted her own blend by adding peppercorns, cinnamon, nutmeg, and cloves to dark Arabica beans. Then she ground the spices and beans together. The result was a decadent cup of sweet and spice. There was nothing else like it.

"I'll make the toast," I offered, breathing in the rich scent of the coffee.

"*Tack.*" She thanked me in Swedish. I'd forgotten how much I enjoyed hearing Scandinavian spoken. I didn't realize, in my lonely years with Chad, the dozens of little things I had missed about my life in Portland. Simple things like my aunt's accent and her Swedish phrases that had been such a part of my foundation.

"How did you sleep?" She tucked her silvery hair behind her ears, and wiped her hands on her lilac apron.

I popped two pieces of thin-sliced bread into the toaster. "Surprisingly well. What about you?"

Elin scooped the eggs out of the boiling water and placed each of them in a silver egg cup. She set them on the table. Topping off her coffee, she reached for two miniature egg spoons and sat at the table. "Not

well. Too much on my mind." Her brown eyes crin-
kled.

"The parade? Or could it be your visitor?" I sat
across from her and warmed my hands on the coffee mug.

"Britta." Elin tsk-tsked. "Eric's visit is nothing."

"Nothing?" I raised my eyebrows.

"*Lilla gumman.*" She paused and met my eyes.
"You know what I mean."

I smiled at the term of endearment. *Lilla gumman*
means little darling in Swedish. It was her affection-
ate way of reminding me that she was still the adult
in our relationship.

"I know." I reached for her hand. "But it's normal
to be nervous." Eric and Elin had been engaged
when my parents were killed. Shortly after, he left
Portland to pursue a publishing career in Europe
and they lost touch. Well, sort of. Eric had secretly
been sending Elin love notes and flowers every year
on the anniversary of what would have been their
wedding day. Neither of them had married. Apparently, they still held a torch for one another, and recently Eric had made it clear that he had wasted too
many years. He wanted to rekindle their romance.

The toaster dinged. I jumped up and plated our
toast. I handed Elin a plate. Then I got the butter
and jam dishes from the counter and placed them in
the center of the table. "He comes tonight? Right?"

She spread butter on her toast. "*Ja,* tonight at ten.
I feel terrible that I might have to leave you with so
much to do, and miss the celebratory dinner."

"Don't give it a thought." I patted her hand.
"I'm happy to help and so excited to finally get to

meet Eric." The dinner Elin referred to was an annual tradition. As a thanks to the volunteers, the
Rose Festival organizers hosted an outdoor dinner
at the float barn, complete with live music and visits
by the royal court and Rosarians. I had never attended, but Gloria had been chatting up the dinner
for the past few days, claiming that it was always a
highlight for the decorators.

"He's excited to meet you too. I wish there wasn't
quite as much going on." She stood and went over
to the sink where she snipped some parsley from
the pots of herbs on the windowsill.

"But that will be more fun," I replied, reaching for
the jam. "He'll get to see the float and all of your
hard work. I have a pretty good feeling that he might
even get to see Blomma take home the top award."

She returned to the table with a ramekin of fresh
herbs. Then she tapped the top of her egg with her
spoon to crack the shell. Once she had peeled her
egg, she sprinkled on fresh herbs and offered the
ramekin to me. "That would be wonderful, but at
this point I will be happy with the parade going on
as planned and without the threat of protest or violence."

"True." I ate my toast. The bright berries burst in
my mouth. Paired with the spicy coffee, it was a
swoon-worthy combination. My thoughts returned to
last night as I noshed my breakfast. Nicki's response
to the "explosion" had been odd. I wondered if Tomo
had caught whoever had set off the fireworks. Could
it have been someone from Dark Fusion? I didn't
think it could have been Sham, unless he was much
faster than he looked. He had been in the front the

entire time. It could have been Zigs, his second-in-command. But then again, firecrackers seemed like a lame joke compared to the level of violence Dark Fusion had used in the past.

If I had a chance to break away at some point during the day, I would walk over to the police station and see if I could learn anything more from Tomo. The police station was located on the west side of the Willamette River not far from Riverplace Village. A walk would give me a chance to stretch my legs, and a visit to the station might give me a chance to bump into Detective Pete Fletcher.

The handsome detective and I had met on a case when I first returned home to Portland. The chemistry between us had been hard to ignore. But I was coming off a bad marriage and didn't want to jump into any relationship before I had some time to reflect on what had gone wrong with Chad and me. I got the sense that Pete reciprocated my feelings, yet he played everything pretty close to his chest. He hadn't said much about his own past, leaving me to wonder if he was in a period of soul-searching as well.

"At this time in a few days, we'll be lining the floats up for the parade," Elin commented, taking her dishes to the sink.

I polished off the rest of my egg and downed my coffee. "True. It's hard to believe, isn't it?"

She took my dishes too. "I think we're in good shape. Gloria has the volunteers under control, and as long as we can finish the grapevines, we will be ready for the judges."

I hope so, I thought as we cleaned the kitchen and headed for the car. This was the chance of a lifetime.

Many florists would only get to dream about working on a float for one of the grandest parades in the country—if not the world. I was doing it. Regardless of what happened outside of the barn with Dark Fusion, I intended to soak up every moment and savor the experience.

Chapter Six

Elin and I were the first to arrive at the float barn. She steered the Jeep with the Blomma logo—a pale-mint-green scroll of the word *Blomma* with whimsical ivy vines—on the sides into an open parking space. The morning sky threatened rain. I was glad that I had brought my jacket at the last minute. There was no sign of Dark Fusion or the sound of protests along the waterfront. However, when we walked inside, Nicki was pacing back and forth by the dragon float. She didn't look like she had slept. Her clothes, which looked suspiciously like what she'd worn last night, were wrinkled and her hair unkempt.

"Nicki, is everything okay?" Elin asked with concern.

"Huh?" Nicki answered in a faraway tone. "What?"

Elin stepped closer. "Is everything okay? You look distraught."

Nicki shuddered involuntarily and stopped pacing. She seemed to realize that someone was speaking to her. "Oh, sorry. I'm in a daze. I haven't slept all night."

"You've been here all night?" Elin caught my eye.

"Yeah." Nicki brushed her off with a half wave. "It's fine. I thrive on no sleep. It had to get done. We have to turn this ship around, if you know what I mean?"

What was she talking about?

"Can we get you a cup of coffee or tea? You should come sit down for a minute." Elin tried to place her hand on Nicki's arm, but Nicki started to pace again.

I noticed that her hands were coated in dark glue residue. Had she been working on the floats? I was under the impression that Nicki's responsibilities as director of the float barn included overseeing every float, not working for or supporting any individual designers.

"There's no time to sit. Do you realize everything that needs to be done? The parade is in two days, and we have hours and hours of work to do. I don't know how I'm going to make it happen." She ran her sticky fingers through her hair. They got stuck.

Elin physically blocked Nicki's path and helped her untangle her fingers. "Come with us, my dear. We'll make you a nice cup of chamomile tea and go over what's left to be done. I'm sure that there are plenty of tasks that we, along with the other float designers, can help you with."

"But you can't. You can't help with what I have to finish," Nicki wailed.

"Trust me, we can," Elin assured her as she steered her toward our float. "Just the other day we received a call from a bride who'd been left at the altar by her florist. Britta put together bridal bouquets, boutonnieres, and flowers for the ceremony in a few hours. I've been in this business long enough to know that magical things can happen when people come together over a mutual love of flowers. Today will be no different. As soon as the designers arrive, we can assemble everyone together and cross things off your to-do list."

"But you don't understand," Nicki protested. "You can't help with this."

Elin forced Nicki to sit in one of the folding chairs next to our portable cart. She motioned to me. I took her cue and went to fill the electric teakettle. Had Nicki snapped? Maybe organizing something as elaborate and involved as the Grand Floral Parade was too much for her. Or maybe it was because of Dark Fusion. I waited for the water to boil, wondering why she was so insistent that we couldn't help. If she was overloaded and stressed, wouldn't she want extra hands?

The teakettle began to screech. I poured steaming water into a mug and found the box of assorted teas, hot chocolate, and coffee that Elin stocked for our volunteers. I brought the mug to Nicki, who appeared slightly calmer.

"Thank you, Britta," Elin said with a raised brow. She gave Nicki a stern yet kind look. "Drink this. It will help."

Nicki sipped the tea. Her white tennis shoes, which were now dirty and splotched with seeds and sticks, bounced on the concrete floor. "Thanks." She tried to smile. "I know I sound like I'm crazy, but if you only knew what was really going on."

Elin and I shared a look. I started to ask Nicki what she meant, but was interrupted by the sound of shouting. Nicki spilled her tea. She let out a yelp and began rubbing her thigh. Then she bolted toward the front entrance.

I picked up the cracked mug while Elin reached for a rag to wipe up the floor. Once we had the spill mopped up, we followed Nicki to see what the commotion was.

Outside the sky had clouded even more. Dull yellow street lamps cast halos on the gravel parking lot. The air felt damp and drizzly. Ted and Sham stood with their faces less than an inch apart. "How many times do I have to tell you that this is private property?" Ted shouted.

"The waterfront is public property," Sham retorted. Technically he was right. The tip of his steel-toed combat boot was at the edge of the path.

"I got a call about illegal use of firearms last night." Ted tilted his straw hat to shield his face from the rain. "The police said they'll be on-site today, so I would take my advice once and for all and get the hell out of here."

"Firearms?" Elin whispered to me.

I shook my head. "I think he means fireworks."

Sham threw his head back and laughed. "Are you talking about firecrackers? There's no proof those were set off by Dark Fusion, and again *firecrackers*, not firearms. You never listen. If you would just shut up for a minute."

Ted puffed out his chest and flung his cape. It made him look like a peacock, hardly intimidating. "Get off this property now or I call the cops."

Nicki ran over and pushed them apart. "Ted, you need to listen."

Ted ignored her and lunged closer to Sham. Sham tossed Nicki aside like she weighed nothing. She nearly lost her balance but recovered her footing before landing on the gravel.

"You should listen to her." Sham's nostrils flared. "Your holy attitude is why Dark Fusion has it out for this parade. You have to be the big man, prancing around in a cape. You look ridiculous, and *you* are the reason that things are going to turn violent." Sham hit Ted's shoulder with his index finger. "You! This one is totally on you. Don't say I didn't warn you."

He glared at Nicki and stomped away.

Ted sputtered. I couldn't tell if he was trying to come up with a response or if Sham had injured his shoulder. He massaged his arm and turned to Nicki. "Call the police. I want him in jail now!"

"But . . ." She couldn't get another word out before Ted flicked his cape. "Call the police—right now! I'm not putting up with another minute of this. Not today." He gave Elin a half bow and walked inside.

Nicki stared after him for a moment. "I don't know what to do. No one will listen to me."

"We'll listen," Elin said in a soft tone.

"Thanks." Nicki didn't sound comforted. "Look, I need to go try and talk to Ted. He's the only one who can fix this."

There was so much more I wanted to ask, but Nicki was already halfway to the door.

Elin linked her arm through mine. "I think this is our cue, isn't it?"

"Is this getting weirder and weirder or is it just me?" I asked.

Elin frowned. "It's not you, Britta. However, I don't think it's worth our energy to try to insert ourselves in the middle of this battle. Let's focus as much positivity as we can on our float."

"Deal." I leaned into her shoulder. She was shorter than me by a couple of inches. At first glance, we probably didn't look related. Elin looks classically Scandinavian, while I inherited my dark hair from my father and my pale skin from my mother. Many people over the years had drawn comparisons with Snow White. It wasn't my favorite reference, but it fit.

We tried to forget about Nicki, Sham, and Ted as we began securing ten-foot sections of grapevines to the arbor. By the time our first group of volunteers arrived, we had almost completed one entire side of the structure. I was beginning to feel more confident about our progress. If we could finish the grapevines by the end of the day, tomorrow we could focus on weaving in the evergreens, which retain their color for longer. Last would come the violets. Twenty-gallon buckets of African violets pre-soaked in Elin's signature love juice awaited us for the final push.

My fingertips were numb and raw by lunchtime. "Break time, Britta," Aunt Elin said, tapping my arm.

"I still have four dozen more of these to weave." I held out a section of the spirally grapevine.

"And they can wait until after lunch. Go get outside and take a walk or sit by the river. If we don't take small breaks throughout the day we'll be worthless later."

She had a point. I finished the strand I was working on and took her advice. The muscles in my legs had cramped. I stretched in an attempt to loosen them. "Do you want to come with me?"

Elin had a violet tucked in the corner of her mouth. She removed it and twisted it onto a grapevine. "No. Since I need to leave early to pick up Eric, I want to finish as much as I can."

"Let me at least bring you something. Ramen? A sandwich?"

"I'll be fine." Elin concentrated on the tedious task of weaving the violets together. We had decided to try a few different techniques with the delicate flowers and leave them out overnight to see which one held up the best. For one strand, Elin was hand-tying tiny knots of fishing line to link the violets together. For another she was using floral wire and wrapping the violets with floral tape, and for the last test she planned to use individual vials of water, and hot-glue the violets directly to the evergreen branches.

"I guess I'll just have to surprise you then," I said with a wink. On the way out, I grabbed my jacket, but I didn't need it. A welcoming amber sun greeted me as I walked along the waterfront path. Crows squawked overhead. I tucked my jacket over my arm and smiled. There was no place on the planet as gorgeous as Portland in the spring. Leafy cherry trees lined the pathway. Bright, colorful dragon boats cut through the river below me. Purple lilacs burst open with fragrant, heavenly blooms. The sounds of children's laughter filled the air as they zoomed along the walkway on bikes and scooters.

I had just started to say to myself how nice it was not to have the sound of Dark Fusion's raucous jeers assaulting an otherwise perfect afternoon, when I rounded the pathway toward the Hawthorne Bridge and ran straight into Zigs.

He was dressed in black ripped jeans with a Dark Fusion T-shirt, a black leather jacket, and combat boots. A gas mask hung from his neck. His mohawk stood like a spiky crown on top of his head. His beady eyes darted from side to side.

"Watch where you're going." He brushed past me, digging his elbow into my hip. Unlike Sham he was thin and wiry, with two gold teeth and tattoos covering every inch of bare skin.

I stopped and massaged my hip. I had a feeling that Zigs's stiff elbow was going to leave a mark. Good thing we were headed in opposite directions.

I started onward, but quickly realized Zigs wasn't alone. Dozens of the protestors, carrying baseball bats and sticks, crowded onto the pathway. They poured in, chanting "Death to corporate America." Zigs leapt onto a rock formation at the base of the bridge.

I scanned the area around me. Dark Fusion members were funneling in from both directions. Within what felt like seconds I was surrounded by them. My heart thudded in my chest. There was no way out.

"Have you had enough of this corporate crap?" Zigs spat on the ground. "Are you tired of being told what to do by the cops? Pushed around? Treated like second-class citizens?"

"Yeah!" a guy wearing a spiked collar around his neck shouted. "Time to bring them down!"

"That's right," Zigs replied. "We're not waiting for anyone's approval. Tonight we take up arms and take down the corporate machine."

Someone tossed Zigs what appeared to be a police

baton, which he proceeded to pound in his fist, riling up the crowd even more. I tried to make myself as small as possible. What did that mean? Did Dark Fusion intend to take violent action tonight?

Zigs wasn't done. "March with me, brothers and sisters! Portland belongs to the people and we are about to set this city on fire."

Cheers erupted from the crowd.

I thought I might throw up. A cold sweat dripped down the back of my neck. I had to get out of here. Were they planning to turn violent now?

Zigs pulled a lighter from his back pocket along with a string of firecrackers. He lit them and tossed them above our heads. I ducked.

The firecrackers exploded in the air and landed a few feet away.

He laughed. "That's just a taste of what's to come. You know what to do! Let's go!"

The group funneled onto the path and began chanting, "Fight the rich! Take them down! Fight the rich! Take them down!"

I waited until they were about a quarter mile away and then sprinted up the bridge. I needed to find Tomo—stat.

Chapter Seven

Normally I enjoyed a leisurely walk over one of Portland's many bridges. There was a reason that Portland was affectionately known as Bridgetown. Bridges stretched the length of the Willamette as far as the eye could see. The Steel Bridge, with its industrial black trusses, to the bright white tiered arches of the Fremont Bridge, which always reminded me of a roller coaster. However, there was no time to stop and admire the scenery. Zigs's ominous threat and maniacal laugh rang in my head as I hurried over the Hawthorne Bridge.

By the time I made it to the police station I was short of breath and damp with sweat. *Please let Tomo be here*, I said to myself as I entered the precinct's lobby. A huge American flag hung from one wall. Smaller flags of Portland and its sister cities stretched along the ceiling. Posters reminding citizens to stay alert and stay vigilant lined the lobby.

That's what I'm doing, my duty as a citizen, I thought,

squaring my shoulders and stepping toward the counter to speak to the receptionist. To my equal delight and horror, Pete Fletcher came inside at the same moment.

"Well, well, well, if it isn't Portland's petal pusher." Pete's golden-flecked eyes landed on me. I felt acutely aware of my messy jeans and grubby sweatshirt, as he stared at me for a moment before stepping closer. "What a coincidence. I was just thinking about you."

He was thinking about me? I willed my cheeks not to flame. "Really?"

He held a coffee cup from Demitasse in one hand. "I was down in the village this morning and noticed that Blomma is closed for the weekend. I was going to pop in and say hi, but it looks like I didn't need to. Fate stepped in." He winked.

"Right." Why couldn't I think of a witty reply? Probably because I couldn't stop staring at Pete. He wore a pair of black slacks with a white dress shirt. The sleeves were rolled up, revealing a small tattoo on his left forearm. It was too small to make out what it was. Maybe a heart? Was there a name written on it?

"It's good to see you, Britta." The way Pete said my name and ran his hand along his short auburn beard made my knees want to buckle. "To what do I owe the pleasure?"

I tried to regain my breath control. "Yeah, good to see you too. I'm actually here about the Rose Festival," I squeaked out.

His brow wrinkled. "You look like you ran here. Is everything okay?"

Great. I'm so glad you noticed, I thought to myself, but forced a smile and wiped a bead of sweat from my brow with my coat sleeve. "Is Tomo around? I need to tell him about something I just witnessed. You're familiar with Dark Fusion and everything that's been going on with them and the festival, right?"

"Some greeting. I thought you stopped by to see me. Make good on my promise to take you out for dinner, but, nope. You just want to see Tomo." Pete's tone was light.

I was happy to hear that he remembered our dinner date. We were interrupted by an investigation the last time we had tried to have dinner together. Pete had promised a raincheck, but I'd been so busy preparing for the Rose Festival that I hadn't had a spare minute to even consider it. And, if I was being honest with myself, I hadn't pressed the issue because I was nervous about jumping into something so soon after leaving Chad.

"So, what do you say, dinner soon? Or if not dinner, a latte?" Pete raised his coffee cup in a toast.

"Sure. Yeah. Either would be great." My words sounded mumbled. I hoped that my cheeks weren't on fire.

"Excellent. I'll set something up." Pete motioned toward the doors next to the reception counter. "About Dark Fusion, let's talk in my office."

The downtown precinct was impressive, with a glass atrium and large windows allowing for ample natural light. Pete greeted at least a dozen officers, all outfitted in standard blue uniforms, on our way to his office on the second floor. I'd never been inside his office and was surprised to find it decorated with potted peace plants, bamboo, and a fern. I took it as a good sign that he appreciated green, living things.

"Wow, this bamboo is lovely," I said, running my hands along the spine of one of the stalks.

"I've had that for years." Pete pulled out a chair next to his desk. "Please, sit. Can I get you something to drink? I'm afraid the precinct coffee isn't as good as Demitasse, but it's fully leaded."

I chuckled and took a seat. "No, I'm fine. I don't have a lot of time. I need to get back to working on our float, but there was an incident last night and I wanted to check in with Tomo to see if he knew anything more."

"You mean the fireworks?" He propped on the edge of his desk.

"How did you know?" I tried not to stare at Pete's angular face with his russet-colored hair and square jawline. A narrow scar stretched from the corner of one eye to his lips.

"I'm the detective in charge. It's my job to know." His eyes, which in this light looked as if they were speckled with amber and copper, gave off the slightest hint of enjoyment. Otherwise his face was completely neutral.

"Well, in that case. Did they catch whoever ran away from the scene?" My foot tapped on the floor.

He picked up a file folder and leafed through it. "Yeah, Zigs. One of the key players in Dark Fusion."

"I know Zigs." I went on to fill him in on what I had seen last night. "That's one of the reasons I ran here now. Dark Fusion is at the waterfront again and it sounds like they're planning something big." I proceeded to tell him everything I had just heard.

Pete tapped his fingers on his chin when I finished. "Thanks for the intel. I'll send a couple of squad cars now." He excused himself for a minute.

I couldn't sit still. I wandered to a bookcase near the window, where there were dozens of framed awards for Pete's years of service in the Los Angeles Police Department, as well as a few photos. I picked up a photo of Pete and a woman who I assumed was his mother. They posed in front of the ocean on a dreamy summer day. Waves crashed behind them. Children splashed in the surf. Their faces were bright and happy. I returned the photo to its spot on the bookshelf and picked up another. The photo was of Pete and a woman about our age. They wore matching police uniforms and stood shoulder to shoulder in front of a squad car. Was she Pete's former partner?

"I'm back," Pete's deep voice sounded behind me.

I nearly dropped the photo. "Sorry," I said, placing the frame on the shelf. "I'm kind of spooked."

He gave me an odd look, but sat at his desk and motioned for me to do the same.

"Do you think the firecrackers last night were a warning? Could they be plotting something bigger?" I didn't want to voice my growing concern that the float barn could be Dark Fusion's next target. Every Grand Floral float was stored in the barn. If Dark Fusion wanted to make a statement, blowing up the barn would an easy way to do so. I shuddered at the thought. "Tomo said that this is almost exactly what happened with his parents' ramen shop. It started with protests, and then escalated."

"Britta, if I thought you or any other civilians were in imminent danger, I would shut the float barn down immediately." The sincerity of Pete's tone and his intense gaze made my neck start to feel hot.

He ran his index finger along the edge of his scar. "This is between us, but I'm worried about Tomo. He's too connected on a personal level. On the force we learn from day one that you have to keep your emotions in check. Personal attachment leads to clouded vision and bad decisions."

I got the sense that we weren't talking about Tomo any longer. Pete stared out the window for a moment, and then cleared his throat.

"However, this is an anarchist group we're talking about. We haven't been able to get a good read on the group. We're working hand in hand with a special operations unit, our counterterrorism team, and our hate crimes department. Dark Fusion is a bit of an anomaly. Some of their past members have turned to violence, but the only things we've seen from them in recent days are verbal threats. I know that doesn't make it any easier, but typically with situations like this the violence escalates at a pretty steady rate." He made the motion of a steep curve with one hand. "There's no evidence of that here. I don't get it, but for the moment I'm leaning toward the belief that Dark Fusion gets satisfaction from scaring people with empty threats."

I felt a slight sense of relief at Pete's reassuring words.

"But what about the volunteer yesterday, and Sham and Ted?" I asked. "They looked like they were about to punch each other."

"But they didn't. Did they?" Pete pressed his lips together. "That's the thing that doesn't add up. The kind of threats that they've been spewing haven't re-sulted in anything that we can hold them for. Maybe that's their plan—to try to be a nuisance and disrupt the Rose Festival enough to scare off tourists."

"You think so?"

"I don't know." He sighed. "At this point every theory is on the table, but we need tangible proof that they're plotting something bigger—like attempting to detonate a bomb at the float barn. Don't get me wrong, we're taking this threat seriously. We have teams positioned throughout the city. We've called in extra reinforcements for parade day, and we're following up on every lead." He drank his coffee. "Your intel is a good enough excuse for me to take a walk and come keep an eye on things over there. Are you headed back? I'll walk with you."

"That would be nice, but I was going to grab some lunch for Elin and me." Why did I say that? Pete was offering to escort me and I turned him down. *Not a smart move, Britta.*

Pete looked at the clock on the wall. "Lunch. I could go for lunch. Mind if I crash your party?"

There was something about his stare that made me feel off balance. "Sure, that would be great."

He tossed his coffee cup and grabbed his suit jacket. "Let me text Tomo and tell him to meet me at the float barn, in what? An hour?"

"Oh, no, sooner. I was going to grab something from one of the food carts. We have hours of work left on the float."

Pete texted as we walked downstairs. Then he tucked his phone in his pocket. He opened the front door and placed his hand on the small of my back, sending a jolt of electricity through me. "How is the float? Are you almost ready for the parade?"

I bit my bottom lip. "I hope so. Gloria, our crew chief, who has been a volunteer forever, assures me that the last couple of days are always a mad dash. I think a better description might be semi-organized chaos."

Pete laughed. "That bad?"

"You'll have to come see for yourself." I held out my hands, which were dotted with tiny cuts from sewing strands of garland and poking myself with metal wire.

"They're working you to a pulp." Pete reached for my hand and flipped it from one side to the other.

His touch sent another bolt up my spine. I wanted to freeze the moment, but it was over in a flash. He released my hand and motioned to a bike messenger who darted between traffic to get in the bike lane.

Had he felt a spark too? I could never exactly tell what he was thinking. Pete was a man of mystery, which made him even more intriguing.

"Battle scars," I said, trying to keep my tone light. "Every self-respecting float designer's hands should be bruised and bloodied."

"That sounds more like my line of work." Pete pressed the button on the crosswalk.

"Have you ever seen the parade?" I asked, waiting for the light to change.

"Nope. I've heard that it's a big deal. The mounted force is riding, and of course our patrol cars will be leading the procession. And then we'll have a large presence throughout the parade route. We do anyway, but like I said, the chief called in reinforcements in case the Dark Fusion threat amounts to anything."

The "walk" sign flashed. "What about you? Are you on duty?"

"Yeah, but detectives don't get the cool jobs. No waving and handing out silver police-badge stickers to the kids, for me." He winked.

We arrived at a food cart pod. Portland's street-food scene was legendary. Cart pods had popped up in practically every neighborhood in town, offering everything from exotic fare to good old-fashioned American cheeseburgers and fries. The downtown pod was one of the first in the city, with over twenty-five unique food stands. My stomach rumbled in response to the assortment of delicious smells wafting together. There were so many choices I wasn't sure how I was going to decide.

"What are you in the mood for?" Pete asked.

I scanned the busy outdoor lunch trucks where people were queued up for Asian fusion, barbecue, and hand-thrown pizzas. Finally, my eyes landed on a cart with a fake bamboo roof and pineapple twinkle lights. "How about pad thai noodles?"

"Thai and Stop Me?" Pete pointed to the food cart's clever name. "That's a good one." He moved toward the cart. I watched as people subtly moved out of his way. There was nothing about his attire that revealed he was on the force, and yet his posture and stance exuded a natural confidence.

We ordered chicken and shrimp pad thai, along with spicy noodle soup and an order of cream-cheese wontons for Aunt Elin. I hadn't realized I was so hungry. Waiting among the delectable, savory smells was torture. When our food was ready, Pete carried the bag and we made our way back across the Hawthorne Bridge. Dark Fusion had taken up camp in their usual spot on the riverfront path. Their familiar chants echoed along the river. Two teams of police officers were stationed in the parking lot—one protecting the front entrance and the other the back. These must have been the reinforcements Pete had called in. I felt better knowing that there were officers on-site.

"Stay here, Britta." Pete handed me our lunch bags and removed his badge from his jacket pocket.

I watched as he went to speak with his fellow officers and then approached the protestors, flashing his badge and holding his tall body in a commanding position. He singled out Sham, who motioned for his crew to quiet down. I couldn't tell what they were saying, but when Pete finished and headed back toward me, Sham forced everyone to spread out and clear space on the walkway.

"What did you say?" I asked Pete.

He took the bags again and walked me to the front. "I reminded them of the fact that if they're gathering to protest without a formal permit, I could arrest them."

"Looks like it worked." I shot a final glance at Sham before following Pete inside the float barn.

"Whoa, this is massive." Pete's awed expression made me smile.

I showed him each float, and gave him a brief introduction in the art of floral design, explaining how every artist had layered together different textures and color palettes to give their floats a cohesive esthetic. He listened and took it all in as we made our way through the barn.

Elin was sawing birch branches when we arrived

at the Blomma float. Sawdust particles floated in the air, making Pete cough.

"Hungry?" I asked, when she paused with the saw in her hand.

Pete held up the bag of food.

"Detective Fletcher, nice to see you. I promise this is not a weapon." Elin placed the saw on the float and wiped her hands on her smock. "That smells divine. I didn't realize that our wonderful men and women in blue delivered."

Pete handed her the bag. "At your service, Ms. Johnston." Elin, like my mother and a long line of women before them, had opted to keep her maiden name. Swedish women often maintained their own identity when entering a marriage. My mother had been so attached to her name and Swedish heritage that my parents had opted to give me my mother's last name instead of my father's. I had followed suit when I married Chad, and I was very thankful that I didn't have to go through the messy process of changing my name in addition to navigating our divorce settlement.

Elin laughed. "Are you joining us?"

"I'd love to, but first Britta's promised me a personal tour of your float."

"Excellent. You show Detective Fletcher the float, and I'll get our lunch set up." Elin took the takeout to the pigpen.

"This is incredible." Pete sounded genuinely impressed when I showed him how we had engineered the base of the float and constructed the arbor.

I picked up one of the strands of violets. "Each of these will be weaved through the arbor and some will hang loose to give the effect of a forest canopy dripping with flowers."

"Yeah, I can see it." Pete ran his hand along a section of the float that had been covered with moss. Then he glanced around us. "You have the best float here, by a mile."

"Thanks." I felt my cheeks warm. "There are some pretty incredible designs. You should go check them out. When you're up close you can really see the detail."

"I don't need to. Blomma has my vote."

"Too bad you don't get a real vote."

Pete caught my eye and held his gaze steady. "Honestly, Britta, this is spectacular. You have nothing to worry about."

I gulped. "Thanks. Should we eat?"

"Sure." Pete shook his head. "You have to learn how to take a compliment, Britta."

"I can take a compliment," I protested.

Elin overhead us. She looked at Pete. "No. She can't. She is the most wonderful floral designer and every time I say this, she turns bright red."

"Exactly." Pete gave me a look to say *I told you so.*

"Hey, I'm right here. You guys are talking about me like I'm not in the room."

"Are we?" Elin smiled. She handed us each a paper plate loaded with spicy pad thai noodles, and a plastic fork. "Dig in while it's still hot."

We gathered around the makeshift table. Pete filled Elin in on what he'd told me about Dark Fusion. I was pleasantly surprised by his easy rapport with my aunt and how forthcoming he was about his take on the anarchist group.

She twisted noodles around her fork. "I agree. I have been thinking that something seems quite off about this entire situation, but haven't been able to put my finger on what. You've spoken with Ted, I assume?"

Pete dug into his steaming plate of noodles. "We have, and we're aware of his stance, but again there's been nothing to back up his claims. As I mentioned to Britta, we intend to have a strong show of force for the parade. We'll be setting up checkpoints along the route where spectators will have their bags searched, but unless some concrete evidence comes in, there's not much more we can do."

"It's true," Elin agreed. "We can't live our lives in fear or let people who promote hate win. If anything, we as flower workers should spread more light. The parade is a celebration of our wonderful city and we must keep that as our focus."

"Well said." Pete smiled.

We chatted about other things as we finished our lunch. Pete left to check in with the team outside and Elin and I busied our fingers with more garland strings. I took my aunt's words to heart. Flowers were a way of spreading joy and light. That was our mission, and we couldn't let Dark Fusion, or anyone else, distract us from sharing such a wonderful celebration.

Chapter Eight

I lost track of time as the day and evening progressed. Tension ran high in the float barn. Every time someone dropped a hammer or a chainsaw revved up, I flinched. Whenever the doors would open, the sounds of Dark Fusion's threats wafted inside. Nicki scurried around the barn, running back and forth between floats, warning decorators that we were entering the point of no return. Twice she came by our area to access the locked warehouse, and disappeared for long stretches. She directed a group of high school students to help her set up plastic folding tables, chairs, and portable heaters in the parking lot for the volunteer dinner. Every year designers, volunteers, the Royal Rosarians, and the Rose Court celebrated weeks and months of hard work with a special dinner. I was surprised that the dinner was going forward outdoors, given the fact that Dark Fusion was camped less than a hundred feet away.

My eyes were grainy by the time Elin left to pick

up Eric at the airport. She kissed both my cheeks. "Have a wonderful evening. You'll have to tell me every single detail in the morning. The dinner is supposed to be one of the highlights of the festival."

"You have a wonderful time with Eric," I replied, giving her a hug.

She zipped her knee-length rain jacket and squeezed my hand. "Thank you. Do I look nervous?" Her eyes were bright with anticipation. She smoothed her hair and tied on a creamy pale blue cashmere scarf.

It was strange to see my aunt show vulnerability. Her Swedish temperament often gave her a more reserved appearance. I knew that she cared deeply for friends and neighbors, as they did for her. She expressed her love by delivering surprise bouquets to neighbors' doorsteps and inviting friends for elaborate midwinter feasts. Seeing Elin pinch her cheeks and ring her hands together like a nervous schoolgirl, made me feel even closer to her.

"You look wonderful," I assured her.

"*Tack*, my darling." Her eyes misted.

"Go." I nudged her toward the front. "Have fun." She flashed a smile and left.

Gloria and I packed away supplies and prepped for the next day. Sometime after six, Nicki hollered into the bullhorn, "Dinner time! Put down your shears and paintbrushes."

Everyone shuffled outdoors. The folding tables had been lined with rose-red butcher paper. Each place setting had a white paper plate, napkin, plastic silverware, and a gorgeous sugar cookie in the shape of a rose, covered with thick red buttercream. This year's theme, Shine, was written in white frosting. It was a beautiful sight, with one glaring exception—the line of temporary barricades and police officers that formed a blockade along the pathway.

"Do you think this is a good idea?" I said to Gloria, noting the officers standing at attention, as if waiting for an attack.

"It's tradition." Gloria pulled a pair of fluffy red gloves over her hands and zipped up a matching red parka. "Ted refused to budge."

How were we going to enjoy a wonderful dinner while under the watchful eye of the police? I stood on my tiptoes to see over the barricade. The crew of Dark Fusion members who had been camped out earlier were gone. Hopefully that was a good sign. Maybe the police had forced them to move out.

"Come this way," Gloria said, pulling my arm. "Let's see if we can get a seat near the princesses."

Four tables closest to the waterfront had been reserved for the Royal Rosarians and the Rose Court. Gloria nudged her way to a nearly full table directly across from the princesses. "There's room," she said to me, sticking out her elbows to block another volunteer hoping for a seat.

I gave the volunteer a sheepish smile and sat next to Gloria.

"Aren't they wonderful?" Gloria's eyes landed on the princesses. She seemed oblivious to the fact that we were under police protection. I wished I shared her obsession with the Royal Court.

They wore matching white dresses that hit just below their knees, and red cardigan sweaters with name tags cut in the shape of a rose. Each princess had a single white rose pinned to her cardigan.

Priscilla sat at the head of the table, wearing the same dress but in the opposite color scheme. She wore a red dress with a white cardigan, and a red rose. She exuded queen-like elegance with her flawless skin and perfect posture. Ted, who was seated next to her in his royal cape, shot her a look of approval when she scowled at one of the princesses who reached for a piece of pizza. "Not yet." She slapped the girl's hand. "A lady—a princess—waits until everyone has been seated before serving herself."

The princess blushed and dropped the slice of pizza.

Nicki was handing out boxes of pizzas to the tables. There were huge bowls of green salad, salad dressing, bottles of wine, soda, and sparkling water for everyone to share. Ted stood. He clapped his hands together for attention. Everyone stopped talking and turned to listen. I kept checking over my shoulder, anticipating Dark Fusion's arrival any minute.

"Thank you all for your incredible effort," he said, offering the crowd a bow. His Royal Rosarian's cape fell over his head. He had to pause to untangle himself. A few people chuckled. "This has certainly been a memorable year in the festival's long and revered history." He glanced to the spot where Dark Fusion had been protesting, giving a long bow to the uniformed officers. "Portland's finest is out tonight. We won't be silenced. We won't allow Dark Fusion to rain on this parade! Please join me in giving our men and women in blue a round of applause for their support and protection."

Everyone clapped.

"It's in times like these, in times of adversity, that

we come together as a city. I know that you have risked life and limb to be here and to ensure that our most beloved parade goes on as planned."

His use of *life and limb* might have seemed like an exaggeration a few days earlier, but I couldn't shake the unsettled feeling in my stomach.

Ted was just warming up. "This alfresco dinner is a highlight for our decorators. Isn't it wonderful to have a twilight view of our lovely Willamette River?" Ted swept his arm toward the river.

Except for the wall of police officers, I thought to myself.

"We will not bend to the threat of violence. We are here to celebrate our Rose City tonight. We will not let outcasts and criminals taint our parade. We will march through the streets on Saturday morning as a symbol of good. As a symbol of justice, and a reminder of the power of community. Our message is one of unity. We will come together as one. This will be the best parade Portland has ever seen."

His impassioned words were met with cheers and applause.

He picked up a wineglass. "A toast to you, our wonderful volunteers, my fellow Royal Rosarians, and our lovely Royal Court."

Everyone raised a glass. Ted took his seat.

Gloria dabbed her eyes with her napkin. "Isn't he wonderful? He's the best grand marshal we've ever had."

"He's definitely passionate about the parade."

She wrinkled her brow. "Of course he is. That's his job."

A woman across from us handed me a box of

pizza. I took a slice and passed it on. My mood lightened a bit as we ate. Volunteers swapped stories of their time in the float-barn trenches and showed off their battle scars. I kept catching Priscilla nag at the princesses. She reprimanded them for everything from their posture to checking their smartphones during dinner. Maybe her role was to instruct them on etiquette, but she seemed to be taking things too far. After all, we were noshing on pizza on paper plates in a gravel parking lot. This was hardly a three-star Michelin restaurant.

I devoured my pizza, and enjoyed people watching. The crowd was very diverse. Volunteers of all ages and demographics chatted amicably with one another as the sun set on the opposite side of the river. The air grew chilly. Someone lit the portable heaters and a band appeared from out of nowhere.

Nicki introduced them. "We thought everyone could use a happy surprise tonight. For your enjoyment, we give you Portland's oldest brass band."

A twelve-piece brass band in tuxedos paraded down the path and began belting out toe-tapping tunes. The princesses shot up from their table, ignoring Priscilla's commands to maintain their composure. They twirled around and snapped selfies. Other volunteers joined in. I wished Elin were here. Hopefully she and Eric were having a wonderful reunion. Maybe Nicki and Ted had been right to stage the dinner outside. Maybe this was exactly what we needed, a reprieve from worry and to reclaim the space.

The band played for about an hour. They were halfway through their final number when the sound of drums thundered.

"Is this part of it?" Gloria asked.

The drumming become louder and louder. It was completely out of tune with the band's music.

I shook my head. "I don't think so." A sick feeling swirled in my stomach. Where were the drums coming from?

I stood. Other people had stopped dancing and were looking around for the source of the sound. Soon the sound became deafening.

Dark Fusion marched into sight. Their members had doubled in size. I estimated at least fifty, maybe closer to sixty. Half of those were pounding drums hanging from straps around their shoulders, with such force it made my hands hurt.

The band stopped playing.

Nicki and Ted sprang into action. The police officers tried to hold the marchers back, but they were no match for Dark Fusion's numbers. There was no chance that the dozen or so officers could hold the barricade, given the sheer force of Dark Fusion.

Gloria stuffed her fingers into her ears. "What are they doing here?"

"Trying to get a reaction," I replied, hoping that was the extent of their mission. The pounding sound of drumbeats reverberated in my head. I plugged my ears, which just made it worse.

Ted stormed to the front of the group. Nicki ran over to the police officers, who appeared to be calling for backup.

"Out!" Ted tried to shout over the sound of the reverberating drums, but it was futile.

Zigs led the march. He smacked his drum with force and ignored Ted. I scanned the group, dressed in black with bandanas masking their faces, to see if I could spot Sham, but it was too dark.

"This is terrible. Make them stop." Gloria clenched her jaw.

Ted attempted to block Zigs with his body. He held his cape out to one side. Zigs laughed in his face and walked around him. Ted then waved for his Royal Rosarians to join him. No one moved. I couldn't blame them. The frantic, rapid drum beats were ominous.

What else did Dark Fusion have planned?

I couldn't be sure because my head was pounding, but I thought I heard the familiar wail of sirens over the drums.

Ted was undeterred. He caught Sham, who brought up the rear. They came face-to-face. Was this déjà vu? I wished I could hear what they were saying. Ted's arms flew as he spoke. Sham stayed rigid. He wasn't carrying a drum. In fact, his bulky body and posture reminded me more of a Buddhist monk. He held his hands clasped in front of him and planted his combat boots on the pathway.

"What's taking the police so long?" Gloria shouted.

"I don't know," I shouted back. "I guess it's kind of hard to get down here. There's no easy access."

"Should we go?" Her face was filled with concern. "What if this is the start of something bigger? They've been threatening us for days."

She had a point. I didn't want to panic. If we started to freak out, likely other people around us would too.

One of Dark Fusion's drummers lunged at a princess. Priscilla screamed at him and raced to join Ted, who was still arguing with Sham. I had to give her credit for protecting her young protégée. Sham and Ted came nose to nose. It looked as if Sham was about to take a swing, but Priscilla stepped in between them.

Sham motioned for her to get away. The cops tried to break Sham and Ted apart, but before they could, Ted threw a punch that landed directly in Sham's gut. He stumbled back and looked shocked. I couldn't see Priscilla's face, but the way she lurched backward made me think she was equally stunned or worried that Sham might come after her.

It took two officers to hold Ted back. He was surprisingly strong for someone his age. Then again, he was obviously fuming with anger.

Sham pulled Priscilla closer and whispered something into her ear. Was he threatening her?

"We need to get out of here," Gloria said. "I don't like this one bit."

"I agree, but I don't know where we would go right now." I pointed to each side of the waterfront path. Dark Fusion members flanked the exits. "Our best bet is to wait for more police to arrive."

Gloria shook her head. "What if they start shooting? What if they have a bomb?"

"They have a bomb!" the woman across from me shrieked.

"No." I shook my head. "You misheard."

But she was already waving wildly and shouting for everyone to run. "Bomb! There's a bomb! Run!"

Panic ensued. Pizza boxes flew through the air as volunteers and Royal Rosarians stampeded. This was a disaster.

I sat and watched as little old ladies and men in regal uniforms ran in every direction. Dark Fusion continued to thud on their drums. Everything felt surreal.

More police poured in. They were dressed in riot gear and holding riot shields in front of them. They were able to hold Dark Fusion back enough to allow volunteers to escape on the east side of the pathway.

I sat, feeling dumbfounded. Maybe I should have made a break for it too. Not long ago I had been wishing that Aunt Elin were here with me; now I wished I was anywhere but here.

Chapter Nine

More officers arrived on the scene. Strobes of police lights flashed off the warehouse and above my head. A trucked marked ATF UNIT rumbled into the parking lot and officers wearing bomb detection gear unloaded a robot. Sirens stabbed the air. I sat in stunned silence, as a team of officers with bomb-sniffing dogs raced into the float barn. Some members of Dark Fusion began to disperse, but others started pounding on the police shields and tossing smoke bombs. Chaos erupted in every direction. I didn't know where to look. It was like a bad dream. I wanted to pinch myself.

My fingers were numb. I wasn't sure if it was from cold or fear. I tried to shake them to get blood flowing again, but it didn't work.

I shivered and moved closer to one of the portable heaters. A couple members of Dark Fusion hurled pinecones and rocks at the police. I ducked just in time as a three-inch rock landed next to my feet.

It was like a war zone. Everything seemed to be happening in slow motion through a hazy lens.

"This is nothing!" Zigs's familiar voice cut through the swirling violent activity around me. "Portland is ours! And we will fight!"

Sham's heavy frame appeared like a shadow behind Zigs. He extended a burly arm and pushed Zigs and a dozen other members away from the police. "Prepare for change!" He raised a fist in the air.

What did that mean?

I had to get out of here.

I glanced behind me. My things were inside the float barn, but the bomb squad had the entire warehouse closed off. Was there a bomb in there? If Dark Fusion wanted to send a message, blowing up the float barn would certainly do just that. There would be no way to recover if they destroyed every float tonight.

I rubbed my shoulders, imagining all our hard work and beautiful floats going up in flames.

"Britta, what are you doing?" Tomo's voice sounded behind me. "You have to get out of here!"

"Thank God." I threw my arms around him. "Tomo."

He hugged me back. "It's okay." Releasing me, he stepped back and studied my face. "Britta, maybe you should sit down. You look like you're going to pass out."

Words stuck in the back of my throat. I could feel every muscle in my body begin to twitch.

Tomo guided me to a nearby table and forced me to sit. "Breathe, Britta. It's okay. You're safe. There's no bomb."

My body trembled. I wrapped my arms around

me and tried to rub my shoulders to stop the convulsions. What was wrong with me?

"That's it. Slow and steady. Keep taking nice deep breaths." Tomo's voice had an easy lull to it, but I could see the concern in his eyes.

"I can't get warm," I managed to mumble. "What's wrong with me?"

"You're experiencing a mild form of shock, but you're going to be fine." Tomo reached for his walkie-talkie. "Do you want me to call over the medic?"

"No." I squeezed my arms tighter. "No, I'm okay."

He kept his walkie-talkie in one hand and sat next to me. I caught a faint hint of garlic. He must have been helping at the ramen shop. Instead of his standard blue uniform he wore a pair of skinny black jeans, an untucked flannel shirt, and red Chuck Taylors. A black stud earring dotted his left ear.

"You're sure there's not a bomb?" My teeth chattered.

"They haven't given the official all-clear yet, but one of the guys told me the dogs didn't find anything."

I told him about dinner and how Gloria had mentioned a bomb and then paranoia had spread like wildfire.

"It's like a game of telephone," Tomo said with a half chuckle. "Do kids still play that anymore?"

"No idea." I breathed into my palms to try to warm them. "What's going to happen? Will you arrest everyone?"

Tomo shook his head. "No. I wish. DF's leaders are smart. They know the law and are tiptoeing right on the line. I think this is all part of their master plan. If you watch closely you can see that they're being very strategic tonight. None of their leaders have done anything other than shout a few threats. We can't arrest anyone for that. They've sacrificed a handful of guys—the ones throwing things and actually coming into contact with us—but if you pay close attention it's like a choreographed performance. They want us to think this is pure chaos, but, Britta, it's not."

His words sent a new round of chills through my body.

"I don't know what their end game is yet. I'm convinced that they want us to think that they're trying to cause as much disruption as they can. They want everyone to think that this is a battle with the badges." He placed a hand over the silver badge pinned to his chest. "It's not. I'm telling you, something else is going down. I just wish I knew what, and how to prove it."

We both turned as one of Dark Fusion's members lit a T-shirt on fire and flung it toward the river.

"Like that." Tomo sighed.

Within seconds the police had the guy in handcuffs.

"And now he gets to spend a night in jail," Tomo said. "But look. See that guy with the mohawk and the other huge dude? They're not part of any of the action."

Tomo was right. Sham and Zigs were watching everything unfold from a safe distance.

"It's crazy," I agreed. "And so sad. Do you think the parade is going to even get to go on?"

Tomo shrugged. "It's too soon to know."

"Some of my favorite childhood memories are of

watching the Grand Floral Parade with my aunt. I don't understand their motivation." My eyes drifted along the waterfront. At least ten men and women had been arrested and were lined up, awaiting transport to the police station. A few protesters were still hurling insults at the police, but otherwise it did appear that the situation was under control. I spotted Ted. He was standing next to one of the officers and pointing at Sham.

What if Dark Fusion's obsession with the parade wasn't about the parade, but was about the parade's most prominent member? What if it was personal?

I started to say as much to Tomo, but at that moment Pete appeared. He had ditched his suit jacket for a navy-blue windbreaker with the word *Police* on the back. He paused and stared at us for a second. "I'm not interrupting something, am I?" His tone was cold.

"What?" Tomo scowled and looked at me. "No, why?"

Pete gave me a strange look and then turned to Tomo. He spoke as if I wasn't there. "I want Miss Johnston out of here, understood?"

I pointed behind us to the barn. "But my things are inside."

"Tomo, escort her inside to retrieve her things." Then he gave me a hard look. "After you get your things, go straight home. Understood?" There was no mistaking the commanding tone in his voice.

I nodded. Why the shift in attitude? Pete didn't crack a smile. Our flirty banter earlier had evaporated. Without another word he left us and went to confer with a team of officers.

Tomo stayed close to my side while I gathered my

things. Police blocked each exit and were combing over every float. If they weren't worried about a bomb threat, their actions showed otherwise.

"Are you sure there's not a bomb?" I asked Tomo after I snagged my stuff.

He led me out the back entrance. "Yeah. If there was even a slight chance of an explosive they would have cleared a five-mile radius."

"That's a relief." I zipped up my jacket. My pulse had returned to normal.

"It doesn't mean you're out of danger, Britta." Tomo glanced around us. "I wouldn't put it past DF to vandalize the floats tonight. I'm sure we'll have a team here twenty-four-seven from now on, but be careful and stay vigilant, okay?"

"You don't have to ask me twice." I checked behind us and spotted Pete huddled with a group of his colleagues. "What's the deal with Detective Fletcher?"

Tomo shrugged. "I think he's mad at me. He thinks I'm too connected because of what happened at the Happy Spoon. The man is a conundrum. Sometimes I think he thinks I'm rocking it, and other times I think he thinks I'm an idiot. But you know, he is from LA." The path was dimly lit by glowing yellow street lamps, but I didn't have to see Tomo's face to know that he was rolling his eyes. California transplants had been a bone of contention with Northwest natives for many years. Many Portlanders resented the fact that Californians had moved north, scooping up property, sending housing costs soaring, and contributing to overcrowded freeways and schools. Much like everything else in life, it was a complicated issue, and just one facet of Portland's current growing pains.

I didn't care where Pete was from, but I was bothered by his 180-degree shift in personality. Was he worried about Tomo's attachment to the investigation, or was he upset with me?

We arrived at the base of the Hawthorne Bridge. "Where's your car?" Tomo asked.

"My aunt took the Jeep. I'm going to catch the streetcar." Since I'd returned to Portland I hadn't seen a need to invest in a car. Riverplace Village was walkable, and Elin's house was conveniently located just a couple blocks away from a streetcar stop. Portland's public transportation system was inexpensive and easy to navigate. Between the streetcar, Max trains, buses, and miles and miles of biking trails, a car wasn't necessary.

"Are you sure?" Even in the dim light I could see Tomo's eyes cloud. "I don't think Detective Fletcher will be cool with that. I can go grab the squad car and give you a ride."

"No, that's not necessary. I know you have your hands full tonight. I enjoy walking over the bridge." I pointed above us where a few cars and buses rolled overhead. "It's not that late."

Tomo hesitated. "I don't know, Britta. Are you sure? It's late and things are pretty tense down here."

"I'll be fine." I pointed to a group of twentysomethings who were dressed like they were ready for a night of bar-hopping. "I'll follow them."

"Okay, but promise me that if you see anyone who looks like they're associated with DF that you'll ignore them and keep walking."

"Will do." He didn't need to warn me. After what

had just transpired, there was no chance I would initiate contact with any of the anarchists. I waved and followed after the partygoers before Tomo could change his mind.

"Be careful, Britta," Tomo cautioned.

The twentysomethings were completely oblivious that anything was amiss in our fair city. They linked arms and laughed.

I was struck by the contrast. Portland was alive with activity. Tourists in town for Rose Festival packed into pubs and queued up at dance clubs. There was a vibrant energy mixed into the crisp night air. This was how things were supposed to be. Dark Fusion might have been successful in their attempt to unsettle the volunteers and Rose Festival insiders, but no one else in the city was any the wiser.

I took relief in the thought as I parted ways with the group of pub-hoppers and climbed aboard the streetcar. It rolled past the waterfront village, where kids with giant wands of cotton candy, up way past their bedtimes, raced through a maze of carnival games. A band played on the main stage, serenading hundreds of people dancing to its vibrant beat. Teenagers screamed from the top of roller coasters. How strange that two sides of the river could have such different vibes.

When the streetcar arrived at my stop, I prayed internally that Pete, Tomo, and the rest of the police force could contain Dark Fusion's negativity.

The house was dark and cold, fitting after what I had just experienced. Elin had texted that she and Eric were having a cocktail and not to wait up. I wasn't sure that I would be able to sleep, but I must

have crashed the minute my head hit the pillow, because the next thing I knew my alarm was sounding.
I fumbled in the dark bedroom to find the off switch.

What time was it? It felt like the middle of the
night, but my alarm read seven a.m. I bolted upright.
I really must have crashed, because I had slept in my
clothes. I tossed off the covers and hurried to take a
quick shower. The hot water revived my senses. Last
night felt like a blur. I wondered what today would
hold. We had so much to finish—or did we? Would
the parade even go on?

I dressed in a rush, tossed a change of clothes
into my bag, and headed downstairs. The house was
quiet. Elin must have overslept too, I thought. I
started a pot of coffee. Then I went to wake her.

"Elin." I knocked on her bedroom door. "It's after
seven. We need to go."

No answer.

I knocked again.

"Elin?"

On the third attempt, I opened the door a crack.
Elin's bed was still made. The pillows and sheets had-
n't been disturbed.

She must have stayed at Eric's hotel.

I returned to the kitchen, guzzled a cup of coffee,
and went to catch a train. Portland was in a sleepy,
dusky haze. The train rumbled along the waterfront
and came to a stop not far from the Hawthorne
Bridge. Unlike last night when the streets had been
packed with people, at this early morning hour it
was like a ghost town.

A thin layer of fog hung above the river, giving it
an eerie, otherworldly glow. I quickened my pace.

Every few minutes a car or bus would pass through the middle of the bridge, but otherwise there weren't even any early morning joggers out yet. Twice I stopped and checked behind me because I could have sworn I heard footsteps.

Stop, Britta, I chided myself.

When I arrived at the float barn there was a single police car parked in front of the entrance to the parking lot. Otherwise the place was deserted. Tomo had said that the police were going to stay to protect the floats all night. I was surprised that they'd only left one squad car. I continued on to the front doors, which were unlocked.

"Hello! Am I the first one here?" I called. My voice echoed in the empty space.

Nicki must be here. Otherwise how were the doors unlocked?

An uneasy sensation swelled through my body as I walked with trepidation toward our float. Something about the huge, cavernous space felt foreboding.

"Hello!" I called again.

The only answer was the sound of my own voice bouncing off the walls.

Shouldn't the other decorators and volunteers be here by now? We were supposed to report by seven thirty for the morning meeting. Had I missed a message? Was the parade canceled?

I thought about turning around, but I willed myself forward.

Bad choice.

When I made it to our float I looked up in horror. Our float had been destroyed. The arbor and grapevines that we had meticulously secured had been torn apart and were scattered in broken pieces throughout the floor.

I stepped forward and let out a scream.

Sham's body was sprawled among the ruins. A noose of purple violets twisted around his lifeless neck.

Chapter Ten

I screamed again and dropped my bag on the ground. This couldn't be happening. Was it some sort of a prank? Was Dark Fusion trying to scare us?

Through one eye I glanced at the floor again. Sham's head hung to one side like a rag doll.

I covered my mouth with my hand. I knew I should move, but I stood there frozen, unable to act.

"Britta!" a woman yelled behind me.

It felt like I was swimming upstream as I turned toward the sound of her voice. It was Nicki. She raced toward me with a look of concern. "How did you get in?"

Words wouldn't form in my mouth. I managed to mumble something incomprehensible and point to the float.

"How did you get inside?" Nicki repeated, without looking at the float.

I swallowed hard. "Sham." I point again in the direction of his body.

Nicki scowled. "What has he done now?" Then her eyes finally landed on the floor. She recoiled. "Oh my God! Oh my God! Is he dead?"

"I think so." I nodded, finding my voice.

"What happened? I don't understand. How did you get in here?"

"The door was unlocked. I got here a few minutes ago. I thought it was weird that no one was here, and then I came back to get started on the float and found Sham, like that."

Nicki blinked twice as if trying to un-see Sham's body. "Where are the police?"

"I don't know. I only saw one car in the parking lot."

Reality was beginning to dawn on me. One of us needed to go get help.

"That doesn't make sense. They've been here all night. Multiple teams. Multiple sweeps of the barn." She stuffed both of her pinkies into her mouth and gnawed on her fingernails. "This is impossible. Impossible. How could this have happened?"

"We need to get the police," I said, starting to move.

Nicki grabbed my arm. "Wait."

"What?"

She walked closer to the float.

"What are you doing?" I asked.

"There could be a bomb. Maybe Dark Fusion rigged the entire float."

"Why would they do that?" I stared at her in disbelief. "And all the more reason to get the police. We shouldn't touch anything."

She paused in mid-stride. "You're probably right."

"I'm going to get the police." I left, but checked over my shoulder. Nicki was acting strange. She paced back and forth in front of the float, chewing on her fingernails like they were candy.

I ran to the parked police car and rapped on the driver's side. "Come quick. There's a body in there."

Two officers sat in the parked car. The officer sitting in the driver's seat looked at me like I was speaking a foreign language.

"A man is dead inside," I repeated with as much composure as I could muster. "I think he's been murdered, but maybe it's a suicide."

His partner got out of the car. "Miss, we've been here all night."

"Well, there's a dead body in the float barn. I don't how long he's been there, but he's definitely dead."

The two officers looked at each other and shrugged. I could tell they didn't believe me. It didn't take long to change their minds. Everything happened in a blur once they confirmed that Sham was indeed dead. They called in reinforcements, cleared me and Nicki out of the barn, and began assessing the crime scene.

Swarms of police cars and an ambulance arrived. I kept hoping that I would wake up. The Grand Floral Parade was doomed.

"Do you think it was murder?" I asked Nicki.

She paced in a small circle. Creating a ring in the gravel. "It had to be. Did you see how the vines around his neck were tied like a noose? No one could have done that to themselves."

"But who would want to kill him?" I regretted the words the minute they escaped my lips. Nearly everyone involved in the Rose Festival had a motive to kill Sham.

"Who?" Nicki's face flamed with color. "Where should I start? I can rattle off a list of about a hundred people who would be happy to hear that that criminal is dead. Everyone at the party he ruined last night. Ted, for sure."

Yes, Dark Fusion had disrupted our parade preparations and made things stressful for the organizers, but that didn't make me *happy* that Sham was dead. I hoped that Nicki hadn't considered her words in the shock of the moment. I agreed with her that it appeared that Sham had been murdered, and with our imported African violets. My body let out a shudder. A feeling similar to what I had experienced last night began to well inside. *Keep it together, Britta.*

Who could have killed Sham? He was a big guy. It would have taken strength and power to bring him down. My mind immediately flashed to Ted. He was a strong man. Could he have killed Sham? Nicki was right. He had been fuming about Dark Fusion's protests and threats. Not once, but twice I had watched him have it out with Sham. The Grand Floral Parade was his pride and joy. Had he taken matters into his own hands last night? What if he had stuck around after the drumming incident? Could he have lured Sham into the float barn and then murdered him?

My mouth felt dry.

Ted was a former mayor and a revered member of Portland's business community. Would he risk that for murder? Then again he was the parade's staunchest supporter, and Dark Fusion had threatened to destroy it. That could be motive for murder.

I licked my lips and tried to swallow. My throat was scratchy and rough like sandpaper. Volunteers and designers began to arrive. They congregated in the parking lot. Everyone assumed that the police presence was because of Dark Fusion. When word spread of Sham's death, a strange lull came over the crowd.

Time passed in a fuzzy haze. I couldn't believe that Sham was dead. Yes, he and his band of anarchists had stirred up trouble, but he didn't deserve to die.

Had Ted killed him? I didn't want to consider the former mayor as a possible suspect, but after their altercation last night and Ted's parting threat, it was hard to rule him out either.

Nicki's sole focus was on the parade. She kept pestering the police for an update and answers.

"They won't tell me anything. What am I going to do? I have volunteers waiting to get in. The Royal Court and our corporate sponsors will be arriving any minute. They are expecting to see the floats." She yanked a strand of hair from her head.

Ouch. Instinctively, I rubbed my scalp.

"Try to relax." I was going to say more, but she threw her arms in the air.

"Relax? We have thousands of people arriving. As we speak, tourists are pouring into the city. They'll be expecting to start staking their spots for the parade. The princesses and corporate sponsors are going to show up and I don't have a single float to show them. How can I relax?" Her voice was shrill.

"I know." I reached for her arm. "I understand the gravity of the situation, but a man has died. The police have to close off the space until they've completed their search."

"They should be able to make an exception. This

is the biggest event of the year in Portland. The Grand Floral Parade brings in millions of dollars, and if we don't get in there now, we'll never get everything done. My God, imagine the disaster if we have to cancel the parade."

I considered telling her that I didn't think there were any exceptions made for murder, but given her fervid attitude and constant pacing, I was fairly confident that she wouldn't respond well.

In addition to the volunteers and growing crowd of spectators, more police continued to arrive on the scene, as did members of Dark Fusion. Zigs bellowed profanity through a megaphone. He had obviously learned of Sham's murder, because he was on a warpath, vowing to avenge their leader's death and blow up the entire city if necessary.

I wondered if the police would call in reinforcements.

"Britta, what's happened?" Elin's voice pulled me away from the mayhem. She looked confused and worried.

"Elin." I kissed her on the cheeks. "You have no idea. I don't even know where to start."

She peered from me and then back to the police. "What is it? Did Dark Fusion make good on their threats?" She held on to my arms and studied my face.

I filled her in on everything that had happened last night, and then told her about finding Sham's body. She scooped me into a huge hug. "Oh, my, *lilla gumman*. I'm so sorry. I should have been here."

"It's not your fault." I brushed a tear from my eye.

"Yes, but had I been here, at least you wouldn't have had to go through something so awful alone."

I pulled away. "Elin, I'm fine. I'm just shaken, that's all."

She frowned. "Britta, I know you. Finding a dead body has to have you more than *shaken.*"

I couldn't argue with that, so I changed the subject. "How was the reunion with Eric?"

"Good." She pressed her lips together. I knew that she wanted to say more about Sham's body, but there was nothing else to say at the moment. Talking about it wasn't going to erase the image of his neck wrapped with our lovely violets. I wondered if I would ever be able to see a violet in the same way again or if they would forever be tainted.

Elin must have sensed my unease. She shifted the conversation, speaking in a gentle, calm tone. "Should I tell you about Eric?"

"Yes, please. Any distraction would be most welcome."

She wrapped her hand over mine. "We had a wonderful dinner. Then we went for a moonlight stroll along the river. It was magical to see so many families camping out. It was very festive. Then we ended up at a midnight dance party and danced until after two a.m. I can't remember the last time I was up that late, let alone out that late."

I kissed her cheek. "I'm so happy."

"Me too." She returned my smile. "It's as if no time has passed. I feel like I'm twenty again. I hate to say this in light of the tragedy here, but I feel as if I'm as light as a bunch of fluffy cotton. And Eric can't wait to meet you. I gushed on and on about how wonderful it's been to have you home again and about everything you're doing for Blomma."

"Is he coming today?" I was glad that she was floating on air, and equally glad for any distraction from seeing Sham's body again and again.

Elin looked to the float barn. "Will they let us inside?"

I shrugged. "Good question. If Nicki has her way she's going to force the police out, but I don't know."

At that moment, Detective Fletcher walked over to greet us. "Miss Johnston, we need to stop bumping into each other like this." He winked, but his face was heavy. The scar running the length of his cheek appeared deeper than usual. Dark circles masked his eyes, and yet there was something in his smile that made my stomach flop.

Why did he have the ability to make me weak in the knees with one look? Tomo was right, Pete was impossible to read. Last night he had sent me away without a word, and now he seemed to be flirting again.

He removed a notebook from his suit jacket. "I hate to ruin your morning, but I'm going to need to get an official statement, Britta."

Elin stepped away. "Of course. You go. I'll wait here." Then she stopped Pete. "Is there any update on the parade?"

He lowered his voice. "Not officially, but I will tell you that we are doing everything in our power to get the crime scene tightened up and documented as quickly as possible. We don't want to have to call off the parade, but I do need to warn you that since the victim's body was found near the Blomma float, and due to the damage your float incurred, I can't guarantee that you'll be allowed to continue working anytime soon. Full disclosure: Depending on how long our investigation takes, your float might not be accessible at all."

"I understand," Elin replied. I knew what she was thinking. Hours and hours of hard work, potentially wasted. I felt terrible. Sham was dead. That should be the only thing that mattered. Maybe Nicki wasn't so far off base after all. The thought of the parade continuing without our float was a major blow.

"I really am sorry, Britta. You know if there was anything I could do to speed things up, I would." He strummed his fingers on his reddish stubble. I got the sense that he wanted to say more, but was holding back.

"Yeah, I get it." I didn't trust myself to speak more.

Pete got torn away from our conversation by a police officer. I tried to disguise my disappointment. If Pete was right, Blomma had just lost our chance to shine.

Chapter Eleven

The police worked in record time while Zigs led his crew of anarchists in mounting howls. Their chants grew more urgent and disorganized, almost like an outward expression of their grief over losing their leader. It was impossible to think. I tried to ignore their bellows and insults. Everyone did. Volunteers huddled together near the entrance to the float barn, safely behind a line of police officers responsible for securing the scene. Fog hung low on the river, shrouding the rioters in a thin veil of mist.

Zigs raced from one side of the group to the next, riling up the crowd. His hands flew in the air. "They killed Sham!" He sounded frenzied, almost manic. "He's been murdered by fascists! Now the fascists must die!"

The rioters roared in response.

"Get out your helmets and gas masks! We're going to war! We are the new face of activism! This is a revolution. We will weaponize! We will take up arms.

For Sham! For all the disenfranchised people living on the streets!" He paused and spiked up his mohawk.

A volunteer standing next to me tapped one of the police officers on the shoulder. "Why aren't you doing anything? They're going to attack us!"

The officer who was outfitted in riot gear tried to calm her. "Ma'am, trust me, you don't want us to intervene at the moment. They want us to initiate a fight and the minute we do, we jeopardize your safety."

She wasn't satisfied with his answer. "So, you're just going to let them take over our streets?"

He held his police baton at the ready. "No. We have a specific tactical plan to follow in situations like this. Dark Fusion might look unorganized, but they aren't. They train their members in first aid and self-defense in anticipation of hand-to-hand combat. They are taught to take an offensive stance. These aren't peaceful protesters—their entire goal is political violence."

Zigs continued to fire up his followers. "We will never bow down to a single fascist, we will never bow to a cop in a uniform." He flung his skinny arm toward the police. "We will destroy the status quo by any means necessary."

I stuffed my hands in my coat pockets. When would this ever end? And worse, how would it end? The police were in an impossible situation. I understood why they were waiting it out. If they began trying to move the group off the pathway or attempted to make an arrest, there was no doubt in my mind that Dark Fusion would react, putting all of us right in the middle of a war zone.

I wished there was something I could do. Instead I waited, along with the rest of the volunteers, in a weird limbo. When the coroner wheeled Sham's body out of the warehouse, wails and profanity sounded from the protesters. I wondered if this would be the point that would send them over the edge, but nothing changed.

Detective Fletcher emerged not long after, looking haggard. His charcoal-gray suit jacket was slung over one arm. The other held a bullhorn. He commanded silence as he put the bullhorn to his lips. To my surprise, even Dark Fusion quieted.

"Ladies and gentlemen, we've concluded our initial sweep and will be allowing you inside the float barn, under police escort. Once inside, we ask that you stay in your assigned area. Keep clear of the crime scene."

"What about the parade?" someone shouted. "Will it go on?"

One of the rioters responded before Pete. "It's going down in flames, you corporate fascists!"

Pete ignored the comment and addressed the volunteers. "Our investigation shouldn't change the parade. Teams will be interviewing you, and your help is going to be essential. If anyone witnessed anything you think could be connected or of any significance, we ask that you come forward immediately."

He cleared his throat. "At this point there's no reason that the Grand Floral Parade won't proceed; however, some floats have been impacted. Our team will advise you on whether you're able to access your entire float, and of areas that are currently off limits. We understand that you're under a tight time

limit and will do our best to make what accommo-
dations we can. Thank you."

Zigs stuck two fingers in his lips and whistled.
"You heard him. The parade is on. You know what
you need to do. Let's roll out! For Sham! Let's do
this for Sham!"

"For Sham!" they shouted in unison.

Drums thudded as they marched down the pathway toward the Hawthorne Bridge. What were they
planning? I didn't like the sound of Zigs's words or
how quickly the members of Dark Fusion fell into
line behind him.

It was looking more and more like Tomo had been
right.

As Dark Fusion marched out of sight, Priscilla
rounded the corner. She wore an ankle-length red
ball gown, her tiara, and a white sash that read:
QUEEN. An entourage of princesses in tea-length
matching red dresses huddled together at the end
of the float barn, near where I had found the firecrackers last night. Priscilla swept over to them, I
guessed to reprimand them about the way they
were carrying themselves.

However, she fell to her knees after one of the
princesses said something and pointed inside.

What was that about?

Without thinking, I headed straight for her. Other
volunteers had begun to stream into the float barn,
under the watchful eye of Detective Fletcher's team.
I moved against the tide, relieved to have something to focus on.

Priscilla had regained her composure by the time
I made it through the crowd. She smoothed out her
dress and adjusted her sash.

"This is crazy, isn't it?" I had no idea what to say to her, I just knew that I needed to do something, and since I hadn't yet been formally introduced to the Rose Queen, there was no time like the present.

She curled her upper lip. "Have we met?"

"I'm Britta, one of the float designers." I pointed toward the float barn.

Priscilla straightened her sash. "Oh. Nice to meet you." She extended a smooth hand. Her nails were painted in a French manicure with tiny red roses adorning each finger. A massive princess-cut diamond ring devoured her ring finger.

"Did you hear the news?" I felt self-conscious about my appearance as Priscilla stared at me.

She exuded a sense of nobility. "Are you talking about the murder?"

"Yes. It's terrible, isn't it?"

Her expression didn't change, but upon closer inspection I noticed that a single tear had run down the left side of her face, leaving a streak in her perfectly applied makeup. "Terrible?" She sounded detached and disinterested.

"I can't believe that someone actually died inside." I felt like I was annoying her.

She stared at her fingernails as she responded. "Wasn't it one of the anarchists? I say good riddance."

Did she mean that? An image of Sham's face flashed in my head. I blinked twice to try to force the picture away.

"What these anarchists don't understand is that they'll never succeed in their mission." Priscilla didn't make eye contact as she spoke. "There is no place in the Rose Festival or in the business world for their violence. They can scream and shout as much as they like, but they'll never achieve their goals with their lewd behavior and destruction."

I was about to point out the fact that Dark Fusion's intent was exactly that—to cause chaos and try to shake up the status quo—but Ted swept over to us. His cape brushed across my shoulder. "Sorry to barge in, ladies."

He greeted each of us by kissing our hands. "Wonderful news this morning. Simply wonderful, isn't it?"

"What?" I wrinkled my forehead. He couldn't be serious.

"Not about the murder, of course." He must have read my facial expression because he puffed up his shoulders and tried to appear solemn. "The fact that someone . . ." He trailed off for a moment.

I got the impression that he couldn't bring himself to say Sham's name.

He coughed. "That someone was killed is most unfortunate. However, we have a clean slate to work with this morning. The police assure me that the parade will go on as planned, and the long-term forecast is calling for sunny skies on Saturday. I would say that things are coming up roses, aren't they?" He smiled broadly.

I wasn't sure how to respond.

"Priscilla, might I beg a word?" He gave her a strange look, and then gave me a half bow. "There have been some new parade developments that we must discuss. Please excuse us, Britta." With that he flung his cape behind him and took Priscilla by the arm.

Obviously he wasn't the slightest bit shaken about

Sham's murder. My mind immediately flashed to last night. Were Priscilla and Ted sneaking off for a private discussion about the parade, or could they be in it together? What if they had killed Sham? Both of them had longstanding attachments to the Rose Festival. Sham had threatened to ruin everything the festival stood for. Was that motive for murder?

Stop it, Britta. I tapped myself on the thigh. What was wrong with me? I had to stop worrying about who had killed Sham. I needed to leave the investigation to the police. They were the experts, and I had other things to focus on—like our float.

I headed for the entrance, where Tomo spotted me and waved. "Over here, Britta." Like last night, he wasn't dressed in uniform, but rather a weathered pair of skinny jeans, intentionally ripped at the knee, and a black flannel shirt. I wondered if his wardrobe consisted of anything other than flannels and skinny jeans. Tomo was a Portlander through and through. He wore his hipster "uniform" with pride.

"Hey, how are things going?" I asked, getting a first glance into the float barn, where dozens of police officers were positioned like guards at each float.

He frowned. "You're in the clear. I just saw your aunt. She's on her way to take a look at the damage to your float. Man, I'm sorry to hear that you guys got the worst of it. I don't know anything about flowers, but if you need help, my fingers are yours." He wiggled his fingers as an offering.

"Thanks." I chuckled. "I appreciate it, but I'm sure you have better things to do than snip violets."

Tomo looked to the left, then right. He motioned

for me to come closer and then spoke in a low whisper. I could barely hear him. "Look, Britta, Pete wants me to keep an eye on your float today."

"Why?" I kept my voice low in response.

"Let's just say that I've been assigned to 'watch' you today."

"Watch me?" I nearly shouted. "You mean as in undercover? Is that why you're dressed like that?"

Tomo held out both his hands and motioned for me to keep it down.

"Watch me?" I repeated. "Why? Am I in danger?"

"We don't know yet." He glanced around us again. Why was he being so cautious? "Look, I'm not supposed to say anything. Detective Fletcher assigned me to stick next to you for the next couple hours." He paused and checked to make sure no one was listening again. "I'm really not supposed to be telling you this, but they're looking into one theory—that your float could have been a target. It's the only float in there that was damaged."

"What?" I couldn't believe it. "Why would anyone target us?"

He shrugged. "We don't know. And like I said, it's just one of the many theories that are floating around right now. This is how investigations work, especially in the beginning. It's probably kind of like creating a flower arrangement. You have to stick a bunch of ideas out there and see which one comes together."

I wasn't sure there was any connection between murder and flowers, but I waited for him to continue.

"It could be a coincidence, but we can't rule out the possibility at this point. Can you think of anyone who might have been hanging around your float? Did you see anything suspicious last night when the chaos broke out?"

I'd been so caught up in finding Sham's body earlier that I hadn't thought about the fact that our float had been damaged while none of the others had been touched. Was it intentional? Could someone have it in for us? I didn't want to think so, but when I returned to Portland earlier in the spring, I had learned that Aunt Elin had an archrival. His name was Darren and he owned a gag floral shop— Drop Dead, Gorgeous—that delivered bouquets of dead black roses. He had been leaving black roses on Blomma's front porch as a way to try to scare Elin after she had made public comments about his tasteless business. Darren had been quiet as of late, but maybe he had been waiting for an opportunity like this. Although he had no connection to the Rose Parade. I hadn't seen Darren in months. Why would he go silent and then strike now? Or for that matter, how would he have gotten access to the float?

No way, I thought to myself. *Strike that theory.*

I couldn't believe that we were the target. What was more likely was that the killer and Sham had had an argument and we were the unlucky site. Maybe the damage our float had incurred had nothing to do with us, and everything to do with Sham. Perhaps the killer ripped everything down in a violent rage.

The thought made me twitch. What if one of us had been there?

"Britta, you good?" Tomo's calm voice brought me back to reality.

"Yeah. Sorry. Thinking about the . . . the . . . murder."

He placed a hand on my forearm. "I know. As much as they try to prepare you for the real world at the police academy, it's impossible." His eyes glazed. I wondered if he was thinking about his dad.

"Right."

Tomo held the door open for a group of women wearing matching T-shirts with silhouettes of a wine-glass that read: STOP AND SMELL THE ROSÉ.

I smiled at the clever pun, in spite of my fear and the general feeling of unrest.

"I'm going to keep an eye on you," Tomo assured me as we went inside. "And if you're stuck with me for a while, you might as well put me to work."

"Okay." I was glad that Pete had assigned Tomo to keep watch over us. If we had to have police protection, I was glad it was my friend. We made it to the float. I put my hand to my chest and let out a groan. In my panic earlier, I hadn't really taken the time to assess how much damage had been done. The entire arbor had been destroyed. Hundreds of shattered branches, twigs, and vines littered the floor.

Elin and Gloria were gathering pieces.

"It's bad, isn't it?" Tomo asked, twisting the black stud in his ear. "Can you salvage anything?"

"I don't know." I stared at the fragmented remains of our float. "You should have seen it last night. It looked amazing. We were almost done. Short of stringing up the violets." The thought of violets sent a shiver down my spine.

Elin held up a snapped bundle of grapevines. "We didn't know where to start. The police said it was okay to salvage anything that isn't marked." She motioned to the team of men and women in blue who were scanning our float for any visible evidence. Yellow markers dotted the floor where Sham's body had been.

I stood back to study the float. "We'll never have time to rebuild the arbor. That's out of the question."

Tomo frowned. "I don't know that you'll be able to get up there, for a while anyway."

"Right." Given the swarms of officers and the state of disarray our float was in, I was starting to doubt that we would even be ready in time for Saturday's parade.

Elin scrunched a bunch of the branches in her hands. It reminded me of a tree in the dead of winter.

"Hey, do that again. Grab more branches," I said, as an idea began to form.

"What—this?" Elin asked, fanning out the grapevines.

"Yes. What if we tie them together like trees? It won't be as tall or impressive as our arbor, but we can still create your concept of the first flowers of spring by twisting violet garlands from the roots of the grapevine. Maybe we can glue leaves to the end of each branch? What do you think?"

Gloria cracked her knuckles. "I heard that zoo float has an overstock of Japanese maple leaves. Would those work?"

"Yeah. They would be perfect." I felt lighter. We could work on building the trees in the pigpen, out of the way of the investigation. They might not have the same architectural effect as our original designs, but we just might be able to pull them together in time for the parade.

"Good idea. The contrast of the vines with the

delicate flowers and feathery leaves will work well."
Elin's face flushed with excitement. "But the challenge will be getting them to stand. There's not near
enough time to build a base, especially since we can't
get on the float at the moment."

Gloria picked up a galvanized-tin bucket. "I have a
few more of these on the supply cart. We can weight
them down with sand and pebbles and stick the
branches in. Then we can hide them under greenery.
I'll go ask around and pilfer whatever supplies and
materials I can from the other floats. I'm sure that
given the circumstances, the other designers will
gladly lend us anything they're not using. I've already had at least five crew chiefs come by to offer
up extra volunteer hands."

"Yes!" Elin clapped.

I tossed Tomo a spool of twine. "How are you
with knots?"

He flexed his muscles. "They used to call me
'knot man' in high school."

"Sure they did." I laughed.

"Hey!" He pretended to be injured by my words.
"I'll have you know that I was on the varsity crew
team three years in a row."

"Well, knot man, I stand corrected. Let's see you
put those tying skills to the test. We have work to do."

For the next hour we worked without speaking.
Everyone concentrated on the task in front of us.
Not only did each of us have days' worth of intricate
floral arranging to pull off in less than forty-eight
hours, but it was easier to keep our focus exclusively
on creating grapevine trees and ignore the chatter
of police officers nearby.

Pete's voice shook me from the task. "Miss Johnston,

I need a minute of your time to take your official statement." His tone was all business. He motioned for Tomo to come join us, and pulled out one of the folding chairs in the pigpen. "Have a seat."

Tomo whipped out a notepad and ballpoint pen and stood next to Pete.

Pete waited for me to sit. Then he removed his suit jacket and hung it on the back of a chair before taking a seat. "Walk us through exactly what you saw this morning."

"Don't leave any detail out," Tomo added, his pen eagerly awaiting my words. "We find that it's most beneficial to include anything and everything you remember. You never know what might be important or will trigger another memory."

"Got it." I nodded and repeated everything that had happened since I arrived at the float barn. Nothing new popped into my mind, but I was careful to tell them about Nicki's reaction and the fact that she had been the only other person at the scene.

"What about violets?" Pete asked, staring at our float. "Do they have special meaning? Could the string of violets around Sham's neck have significance?"

I thought for a moment, trying to pull up a mental picture of the violet section from my flower bible. A flower bible is an essential guide for any florist. Mine contained notes on growing conditions, rare stems, and photos with extensive research on the history and various meanings for each flower. In Victorian times, nearly every household kept a guidebook for the language of flowers. Understanding the symbolism for each stem became a popular pastime. From the color of a particular varietal to how bouquets were delivered (handing flowers to someone with the right hand meant giving the recipient a yes answer, whereas handing them from the left meant no) was well studied and thought-out. How a ribbon was tied, or the fullness of the bouquet could convey well-wishes or profess love. Flowers had their own secret code, like the bitterness of an aloe plant or rejection sent in the form of a yellow carnation.

"Violets, like all flowers, have a variety of meanings," I said to Pete. "White violets represent innocence, and purple violets are often given as a token of love. Folklore offers many interpretations though. Violets have been used to express devotion, loyalty, and faithfulness."

"Hmm." He considered my words.

Was he on to something? Could Sham's killer have been sending meaning through flowers? The violets around his neck were purple. Maybe his death wasn't connected to the parade. Maybe it was motivated by a lover scorned?

Pete cleared his throat. "Thanks, Miss Johnston. I appreciate the insight. If you think of anything else that might be helpful, please let us know. Otherwise, we'll be in touch if we need anything further." A hint of a smile tugged at his cheeks; otherwise he had treated me with the utmost formality. Trying to figure out what he was thinking was making me dizzy.

While I returned to my work, they called Elin and then Gloria over for questioning. I knew that it was standard protocol to interview as many potential witnesses as soon as possible. People tended to forget details or have their memories altered by other people's stories the more time elapsed.

I watched Pete question Gloria and noticed that she appeared nervous. She kept removing her reading glasses and cleaning them on a tissue.

I shrugged it off to the stress of the fact that a dead body had been only a few feet away from where we were working only a short time ago. If we wanted to participate in the parade, we were going to have to work around the clock to redesign our float. After tying dozens of branches together and intertwining them, with twelve-inch dowels to hold them in place, we were ready for the ultimate test—would the grapevine tree stand in Gloria's bucket of sand?

Once Pete finished his interviews, Elin and Gloria filled the galvanized tin halfway with sand. Tomo and I lifted the prototype tree into the bucket.

"Here goes nothing," Gloria said as we placed the end into the sand. The tree stood at nearly twenty feet.

I held my breath and bit my bottom lip, fully expecting that the tree might topple over in the process of trying to hoist it upright. Tomo held one side and I secured the other while Gloria and Elin poured sand and heavy rocks up to the lip of the bucket. Once we were allowed onto the float again, we would have to cinch the tree to the base of the float with heavy fishing line.

"What do you think?" Elin asked, camouflaging the tin with bows of evergreen branches and pinecones. "We can hide the buckets with organic material that you find on the forest floor."

"Definitely." Gloria arched her back. "Let's drag it to the far wall. We don't want it to topple over on someone."

Elin and Gloria steadied the bucket. Tomo and I

shuffled toward the wall. The tree was surprisingly heavy. Once we had propped it against the wall, we stood back to get a better look.

"What do we think?" I asked.

Tomo shot me a thumbs-up. "Honestly, Britta, it looks great. If I didn't know otherwise, I would have thought you had planned it this way."

"You're just saying that to be nice." I nudged him in the arm.

He shook his head and crossed his finger over his chest. "Scout's honor. I swear it looks awesome. No one will ever know."

The top of the tree began slipping to the side. Tomo raced over and caught it before it crashed on the ground.

"I think we better tie it off," I said. Elin was one step ahead of me. She was digging through the supply shelves.

"The last thing we need today is to take someone out with a fake tree," Tomo agreed.

Elin tossed me the fishing line. I was about to cut off a ten-foot piece of the translucent line when I noticed a thick black smudge on the bottom of the spool. It was a fingerprint.

"Elin, do you have glue or anything on your hands?" I called, careful not to touch the bottom of the spool.

"No. Why?"

I held it out for Tomo. "You better take this."

He kept one arm on the tree. "What is it?"

"Look at this smudge." I pointed out the spot on the bottom of the plastic spool. "That's a fingerprint. A very clear print."

He nodded. "Yeah, it is."

"Maybe it's nothing. We've used fishing line for other things, but what if the print belongs to the killer? I don't remember seeing a smudge like that last night. Sham had a string of our violets around his neck and we used this exact line to tie the violets together."

Tomo glanced around the float and waved to one of the police officers. "Do you have a paper towel or napkin?" he called to Elin.

"We have napkins. One minute," Elin replied.

Gloria came up to my shoulder and stared at the spool of fishing line. "That print could be from anyone. These spools have been used by half the volunteers in here."

Elin handed Tomo the napkin and took his spot, holding the tree to the wall.

Gloria scowled. "I wouldn't get your hopes up. Dozens of volunteers have used fishing line in the last few days. There's no way to know who that could have been from."

"True, but forensics can run it through the system." Tomo wrapped the spool of fishing line in the napkin. "You never know. It's worth a shot."

"But my prints will be on it, and Elin's and Britta's," Gloria said, tugging on the strings to the hood of her faded Rose Festival sweatshirt.

"We can cross-check prints with the people assigned to your float." Tomo waited for one of the officers to get an evidence bag. "I better take this to Detective Fletcher."

Gloria shook her head. "Waste of time, if you ask me."

I wasn't sure why she was so against having Tomo run the print. She did have a fair point that any of our fingerprints might show up, but what if it matched the killer's print? This could be a major clue in the case. Could there be some other reason Gloria didn't want Tomo to take the spool? Did she know that the only thing he would find would be her fingerprint?

I found myself watching her as we finished potting the trees. What would her motivation for murder be? She was one of the Rose Festival's most dedicated volunteers. Like Priscilla, Nick, and Ted, she had a deep affection for the parade. Could sweet little Gloria have killed Sham? I couldn't imagine it, and yet I couldn't rule it out either. Everyone associated with the parade seemed to have a reason to want the leader of Dark Fusion dead. I hated considering my fellow volunteers, but I had to face reality. I could be working side by side with whoever had killed Sham.

Chapter Twelve

As I returned to work on the trees, I couldn't get the image of Sham's purple face out of my head. Why did it have to be violets? Our violets. Violets were known to represent innocence. I felt as if my innocence had been shattered. This should have been a time of celebration with the frenzy of last-minute preparations, but instead the float barn had become a crime scene. We had to work around caution tape and evidence markers. Police milled around the float barn, keeping careful watch and casting an aura of tension.

Our float remained off-limits until the police finished their examinations. Gloria and I worked to secure our test tree with a new spool of fishing line.

I noticed that Detective Fletcher had pulled Ted aside near the cutting station. He stood with his one arm casually resting on a sawhorse while Tomo stood next to him with a pen and notebook in hand. I turned to Gloria, who was gluing striated yellow and green Japanese maple leaves onto the tips of a branch with a hot glue gun. "Do you think that Ted could have done it?"

"Done what? Killed Sham?" She looked up from her work and stared at Ted. Did he ever leave the house without his Royal Rosarian's cape?

"Yeah. After last night, I just keep wondering if he could have reached his limit with Sham and Dark Fusion. The police seem to be pretty focused on him."

She nodded. "I suppose it's possible. But I can't imagine Ted risking his reputation. He's been in constant contact with the authorities. He told me that he was close to getting Sham tossed in jail. Ted is a former mayor and the leader of the Royal Rosarians. He wouldn't do something that drastic. He would, and has, followed the necessary steps through the proper channels to bring justice to these radical groups." She pressed a tube of glue into the gun.

"True." Fishing line dug into my skin as I tied a long string to the edge of the pigpen. "But what if the police told Ted there wasn't anything they could do? Like you said before, he's taken this personally. It's almost as if he believes it's his quest to ensure that the parade goes off without disruption."

"It is his responsibility. He's the grand marshal." Gloria gave me a strange look. "Britta, why are you suddenly fixated on Ted?"

I could feel my cheeks begin to warm. "I'm not. I mean, I'm not focused solely on Ted. Maybe it's because I'm the one who found Sham. I guess I feel responsible for wanting to know who killed him."

Gloria's face slackened. She put a sticky hand on mine. "I understand. I'm sorry that you had to witness something so awful."

"Thanks. I'll be okay once this is all over."

"You are Elin's niece. I don't doubt that you'll come out of this just fine." She returned to gluing leaves on the grapevines. "You know, if you're looking for suspects, I would suggest that you look elsewhere."

"What do you mean?" Was she protecting Ted?

She nodded toward Nicki, who was showing one of the volunteers how to use the industrial shop vac in the wood shop. The wood shop housed a variety of power tools, including chainsaws, Dremel rotary tools, and sanders for cutting larger tree limbs and more refined wood-sculpting. "I'm not convinced that Ted had anything to do with Sham's death," Gloria said, lowering her voice. "However, I wonder about Nicki."

"Really? Why?"

Gloria's demeanor had shifted. She set down the hot glue gun. "I saw them together last night."

"Who? Ted and Nicki?" I snipped off the end of the fishing line.

"No. Nicki and Sham." She raised her eyebrow.

I nearly dropped the spool. "When?"

Gloria glanced around us to make sure that no one was listening. "Near the end of the dinner. I was going to go inside to get my things, but then, as you know, everything exploded into chaos. I saw Sham and Nicki sneaking off down the riverfront. It wasn't long after Ted and Sham exchanged, well, shall we say, *heated* words."

Heated was an understatement. But I nodded for Gloria to continue.

"You're going to think that I'm a nosy little old

lady, but I followed them. I didn't set out to follow them." Her tone was sheepish.

"Since I'm peppering you for information about Ted, I can't really blame you for following Sham and Nicki." I offered her a look of solidarity. Apparently I wasn't the only one snooping.

"True." Gloria smiled. "Does that mean we're both nosy sleuths?"

"Guilty as charged." I raised both hands in the air.

"In any event," Gloria went on in a conspiratorial tone, "at first there was nothing interesting. They walked about a half mile down the waterfront path together. Past the Hawthorne Bridge. I thought that Nicki was telling him off, but then they got to the point where the path splits. Right before the Steel Bridge."

"I know the place you mean."

Gloria nodded. "They stopped. Again, I thought that Nicki was trying to get Sham out of the float area and had walked him as far away from the barn as possible. But then something strange happened."

"What?" I was holding my breath with anticipation.

"Sham yanked a large envelope from his leather jacket. He thrust it at Nicki and then he ran off."

"Really? Any idea what was in the envelope?"

Gloria shook her head. "I wasn't close enough to see, and after Sham gave her the envelope, Nicki turned around and headed back my way. I didn't want her to think that I had followed her, so I ducked behind some trees and waited for her to pass. Whatever it was, it must have been important, because she read it quickly and then stuffed it into her purse. I tried to follow her back to the barn, but she was too fast for me. By the time I returned she was gone."

"I wonder what it could have been?" Suddenly my fingers felt tight. I looked at my hand. While we had been talking I had unknowingly wrapped fishing line around my fingers. They were turning blue at the tips. I quickly unwound the line.

Gloria shrugged. "Your guess is as good as mine, but there was something very suspicious about their exchange."

"Right. Why would they walk half a mile away to have a conversation? Or for Sham to give her the envelope?" I thought aloud.

"I have no idea."

My mind tried to connect the dots. Nicki had been frantic since the first time I met her. I had assumed it was because she was frazzled by a myriad of details organizing the parade, but what if I had pegged her wrong? Maybe she'd been working in conjunction with Dark Fusion. Could she be a double agent? What if Dark Fusion had planted her as an insider and she was actually working with them? What if she had set off the firecrackers last night and been responsible for the float damage? She was the only person who had full access to the float barn twenty-four hours a day, except maybe Ted. She had been the only one here this morning when I arrived.

As I considered the possibilities, my throat began to tighten. Had I been alone with a killer this morning? What if the envelope was payment? Had Sham paid Nicki to sabotage the Grand Floral Parade?

"That reminds me. In all of the craziness this

morning, I forgot to tell you that I brought in my old Rose Festival scrapbooks for you," Gloria said, pointing to the rolling cart. "They're in a bag marked with your name. I thought you would enjoy looking through them."

"Thanks."

Gloria continued to glue golden-toned leaves onto the grapevine. I tried to concentrate on bundling a new set of branches, but my thoughts kept returning to Nicki. If she had secretly been working with Dark Fusion, what would her motive be for killing Sham? Had he not paid her enough? Or could he have been blackmailing her? Maybe he had something on Nicki and had forced her to work with him. What if she refused? Could she have lured Sham into the float barn alone? Called a private meeting and then killed him?

I thought about it for a minute. Gloria's information had definitely set me on a new course of questioning, but there was only one problem. Did Nicki have the physical strength to kill Sham? Could she have tied the noose of violets around his neck? Yes, I had heard that in times of intense stress, humans could perform otherwise insurmountable tasks. But Sham was a big guy.

Maybe there was another possibility. What if they were having an affair? Nicki could have arranged a secret meeting and then taken him by surprise. But that didn't explain the envelope. I had to find out what the envelope contained.

A plan began to formulate as I tied the last bunch of reedy grapevines together. The float barn was a swarm of activity. Nicki was still helping in the wood shop and the police were going from float to float, questioning volunteers. I knew what Nicki's purse looked like. If I could sneak into the break area where I had seen her store her purse earlier, maybe I could take a quick peek inside.

That's a crime, Britta. I scolded myself for even thinking about it, but then another part of my brain took over. This was also a murder investigation. That envelope could contain a crucial piece of evidence. It might be tangible proof that Nicki had killed Sham. I had to at least try.

"I'm going to take a quick break," I said to Gloria.

She was immersed in a conversation with a group of volunteers sent over from the Oregon Zoo float about the best way to secure wooden dowels into our grapevine trees. "Go ahead."

The break area was located near the front entrance. It consisted of a few folding tables, plastic chairs, a coffeepot, electric teakettle, small fridge, and shelving for coats and purses. My pulse thudded as I made my way around one of the chairs. The question was how to be discreet. I glanced around to make sure that no one was watching.

Float production was in full swing. The camel float was nearest to me. A team of hockey players were on the scaffolding tying four-foot stalks of wheat to the camel's shaggy mane. They didn't notice me as I tiptoed to the shelves.

Rows of purses and lunch sacks lined the temporary shelving unit. I remembered seeing Nicki with a black leather purse with a gold handle. I scanned the shelves.

This is stupid, Britta. Really stupid.

My own words didn't sway me. I scanned the shelves,

finally spotting a purse that looked like the one I had seen Nicki holding.

It's now or never.

I bit the inside of my cheek and reached up toward the black leather purse handle. Just as my hand skimmed the soft leather surface, something crashed.

The sound made me abandon my mission and whip around. A two-by-four had fallen off the top of a stack of lumber in the wood shop. No one had been hurt, and luckily Nicki was in the center of the action. She yelled at a volunteer for being careless. "People, people, this is why we tell you time and time again—safety first."

This is your chance, Britta.

I stood on my tiptoes to reach the purse, which was tucked into one of the cubbies near the top of the temporary shelving. My heart pounded faster.

I did a quick check and snagged the purse. Then I hurried over to one of the tables and tried to slide the zipper open.

It was stuck.

I tugged as hard as I could. It wouldn't budge.

My sweaty fingers trembled as I tried to massage the zipper and squeeze both sides of the purse together. With one more tug the zipper broke free.

Whew.

I did another look to make sure no one was coming over for a cup of coffee or a snack. Nicki was helping a group of older ladies use the handsaw. I opened the purse, not even realizing that I was also holding my breath.

Inside there three boxes of mints, a tube of lipstick, a wallet, sunglasses, and a small umbrella in a black case. No envelope. I wished I had asked Gloria how big the envelope was. Could Nicki have folded it and hidden it inside her wallet? I had assumed that Gloria meant she had seen Sham hand Nicki a large manila envelope.

There was only way to know.

I reached inside with clammy, sweaty hands and took out Nicki's wallet.

This is crazy, Britta. How would you feel if someone went through your purse?

Violated, I answered back internally.

But you're not a suspect in a murder case, I rationalized, and started to open the wallet. It was overflowing with receipts and credit cards.

The sound of footsteps crunching through scatted twigs, seeds, and dried leaves sounded behind me. *Uh-oh.*

My heart rate spiked. I shoved the wallet back into the purse and was about to zip the purse shut when I heard Nicki's voice.

"Britta? What are you doing?"

I gulped. Then I turned around and smiled. "Oh, I'm looking for Tylenol or Advil. I have a killer headache and Gloria mentioned that she had some in her purse."

Nicki stared from me to her purse and then back at me again. She didn't look convinced. "That's not Gloria's purse. That's my purse."

She ripped it from my hands.

I tried to sound as innocent as possible. "Really. I'm so sorry. Gloria told me that her purse is black with a gold handle. This is the only purse I saw that matched her description."

I willed Nicki not to look in the cubbies. I had no idea how many black purses might be on the shelves.

"If you needed Advil, why didn't you just take some from the first aid kit?"

Why did she have to be so smart? "I didn't even think about it. I just happened to mention that I have a headache." I paused and massaged my temples for effect. "Gloria said she always keeps Tylenol on hand and offered it to me." Was I talking too much? I felt like I was making it worse.

Nicki looped the gold handle over her arm and walked away without another word. I wasn't sure if she believed my spur-of-the-moment lie. I doubted it. Lying isn't my skill set, especially on the spot.

Despite being caught by Nicki, I was more determined than ever. I had to find the envelope.

Chapter Thirteen

After my first (and hopefully last) foray into snooping—or should I consider myself a purse snatcher?—I decided that it would be a good idea to take a break from the float barn and get some fresh air. What was wrong with me? I had gone through a stranger's purse. Yes, I knew that things were off-center with Sham's murder and the ever-present threat of violence from Dark Fusion, but that didn't give me the right to violate Nicki's privacy.

Elin had left before lunch to check on Blomma and work on the centerpieces and gifts for the dignitaries' dinner. I needed to get some distance and clear my head.

I left Gloria in charge of our volunteers and headed across the river. The sky continued to drizzle, although the fog that had hung heavy on the river earlier had vanished. Families had gathered along Portland's sidewalks. People staked their claims for the parade with duct tape, chalk, and even crime-scene tape stretched from trees to utility poles along the route. Anyone showing up the morning of the parade was going to be out of luck. Nearly every square inch of grass and sidewalk had already been accounted for.

The atmosphere was alive with activity. Kids wearing bright red and yellow rain boots and jackets, splashed in the Salmon Street Springs fountain, oblivious to the rain falling overhead. Partygoers queued up for carnival rides and to try their luck at duck hunting and the ring toss. I took in the scent of grilling hot dogs and caramel corn wafting from the inflatable circus tents. Yet again I was struck by the dichotomy of this morning's brutal murder and raging protest and the joyful atmosphere along the waterfront.

When I turned into Riverplace Village, I breathed a sigh of contentment. The cheery Rose Festival banners hanging from the antique lampposts that lined the cobblestone streets, waved in the gentle breeze. A couple strolled arm in arm, stopping to peer into the inviting window displays. At the far end of the village, near the Riverplace Inn a crew of sailors in crisp navy whites posed for pictures.

I smiled, feeling more normal and centered than I had all day.

Elin was at the wine bar packing up bottles of Oregon rosé that would be packaged along with our succulents as parting gifts for each dignitary. "Britta, you're here." She said it more like a question. "I'm so glad. Tomo and I both agreed that you looked a bit harried earlier."

"I know. I was planning to stay and try to finish the rest of the trees, but I needed a break from the drama. I needed to clear my head."

Placing the pretty wine bottles on the edge of the counter, Elin pointed to an open bottle of the light pink wine. "Would you like a glass?"

"No, I'm fine. I just thought a little space might help." Oregon didn't produce large amounts of rosé. Those fortunate enough to score a bottle of the pink-hued wine would find their palates treated to a complex flavor of nectarines, grapefruit, and strawberries, with a custardy finish. The sweet yet minerally blend that we had selected for the gifts was sure to be a purely Oregon experience.

She nodded. "Any new developments after I left?"

We walked to the workstation where an assortment of glass and ceramic vases, potting soil, gravel, and pebbles, along with creamy ivory roses, light peachy and pink miniature roses, and succulents sat, as if waiting to be made into masterpieces. Flowers have the ability to evoke emotion and transform our feelings. Every bouquet, whether it be a simple bedside vase with garden mums and leafy ferns or a stunning wedding arrangement dripping with jewel tones, can remind us to slow down, breathe deeply, and surrender to their beauty.

Flowers set the tone and the stage. Suddenly I found myself almost desperate to dig my hands into the earthy, grainy dirt and create something beautiful.

I rested my coat on a stool and reached for a chunky ceramic vase. As I massaged dirt into the pot, I found my breath returning to its natural rhythm. Working with dirt is like a form of meditation for me.

"Dirt is magic." Elin's eyes glinted as she used a thorn-stripper on the ivory roses.

I told her about Gloria's input. Although I left out the part about rummaging through Nicki's purse. Somehow I didn't think she would approve.

"Hmm. And what about the other Dark Fusion members? They've gone silent." She filled a twelve-inch clear glass vase with water.

"Yeah. They left this morning and haven't been back. It's worrisome. Zigs said something like, 'You know what you need to do.' I can't help but wonder if they're planning to retaliate." I patted the dirt and sprinkled on a fine layer of gravel. Succulents store water and nutrients in their leaves, which means they don't require a lot of root space like traditional potted plants. The gravel would aid in the drainage process and help the arid, drought-resistant plants avoid root rot. Next, I blended the soil and gravel together with my hands, like kneading bread dough.

"It is odd that they've vanished, especially after weeks of escalating protests." Elin trimmed the single-stemmed roses into varying heights for the centerpieces.

"Right." I paused for a minute, brushing dirt from my hands. Then I filled a bucket with water and worked it into the mixture. When first planting succulents, it is imperative to give them plenty of water. "Hey, do you know why Nicki has the warehouse next to our float blocked off?"

"No. Why?" She tucked a handful of luscious, fragrantly sweet peach-colored roses into the vase.

"I saw her in there earlier. She said that it was off-limits—still being used by the carnival company. I just thought it was kind of strange that she would be going back and forth." Now that the water had absorbed into my soil-and-gravel mixture, I removed a minty blue-gray echeveria from its nursery container and placed it on the left side of the pot. I would start with the largest plant and cluster smaller plants—sedum, fleshy agave, aloe, and lovely lemon-yellow aeonium—around the edges.

"That is odd." Elin added rough pieces of bark and billowy pussy willows to her arrangement. "Although I'm sure she has keys to the entire building. It could be nothing. She might have stored extra supplies in there."

"Right." I wasn't convinced. I wished there was a way I could get in there.

What was wrong with me? First, I'd snooped through Nicki's purse, and gotten caught. Now I wanted to try to get into an off-limits area of the float barn.

"Where's Eric?" I asked, changing the subject.

"He's meeting with a writer who does some freelance work for him." She stared out Blomma's cheery front windows with a starry-eyed look. "I can't wait for you to meet him."

"I'm beginning to think that he's a figment of your imagination," I teased. "He's a man of international mystery, who evidently vanishes anytime I'm around."

Elin's smile was wide. "Stop. You know that he's eager to meet you. Once I finish these centerpieces for the dinner, I'm bringing him to the float barn and putting him to work." She finished the bouquet with strawberry moon sedum, chocolate sunflowers, and touches of moss. The design was unique, woodsy, and captured Portland's spirit.

"What do you think?" She twisted the arrangement around to showcase each side.

"It's wonderful." I knew there was no doubt that our flowers would add an elegance to the stately dinner. "How about something like this for each of them to take home?" I showed her my potted succulent garden.

"*Ja*." She slipped into Swedish for a moment. "I think these will be beautiful and impossible to kill."

"Exactly." I brushed my hands on my jeans. "You should bring Eric by, but please don't feel like you need to work. We have it covered. The grapevine trees turned out great. In fact, in some ways they're even more striking than our original arbor. I think we'll be done with time to spare. You and Eric should go enjoy the night out. Join in the Rose Festival fun."

She nodded, but I could tell that I hadn't swayed her. "We'll see."

"I should get back. I know that Gloria has it under control, but I want to be there when the police give us the all-clear, to help make sure that the trees get tightly secured to the float. I'll come back later tonight and finish the rest of the potting. See you soon." I left to gather more twine and fishing line. Then I decided to stop at Demitasse, the artisan coffee shop two doors down from Blomma. I could use an afternoon pick-me-up.

Ancient oak trees flanked the cobblestone streets. A crowd had gathered at Gino's, an Italian restaurant with old-fashioned red-and-white awnings. I smiled as a violinist serenaded the waiting guests. He wore a black-and-white striped shirt and black pants with a red scarf tied around his neck and a red rose tucked in his teeth. The sandwich board in front of the restaurant invited visitors inside for a three-course lunch, wine, music, and dancing.

The thought of hearty pasta and tiramisu was tempting, but I wanted to check in with Nora, the owner of Demitasse and Elin's best friend. The coffee shop's wall of windows was nearly always fogged over from the constant steam of the espresso machine. Today was no exception, as I pushed open the door and stepped inside.

Sticks, the coffeehouse mascot and Nora's beloved pug, ran up to greet me by licking my toes. He had a black leather collar around his neck.

"Hey, Sticks." I bent over to pat him on the head and he nuzzled my hand.

"Britta, come in, come in! You're here for *fika*!" Nora called from behind the counter. Elin had taught her just enough Swedish to be dangerous. She was short and petite with funky, spiked platinum hair and a distinct rocker-chick style.

Her black V-neck T-shirt made me chuckle. It read: A Yawn Is a Silent Scream for Coffee.

"Good one," I said to Nora, approaching the coffee bar.

"Right? It's true. Every yawn just begs for a cup of my deep, dark heaven. Have we finally converted you to a coffee girl?" she asked with a wink. "That didn't take long."

"I know. I must not have an ounce of willpower. I've only been home a few months, and yet here I am, jonesing for an afternoon fix."

Nora's bright eyes sparkled. "Don't sweat it, girlfriend. You didn't stand a chance. Not with your aunt and working in the village. It's impossible to resist the sweet nectar of the coffee gods." She opened a canister of espresso beans.

The scent immediately hit my nose. "That smells amazing."

"This is a dark roast from a vendor here in town. They delivered these beauties less than an hour ago. Let me make you a cup. You're going to go weak in the knees."

I didn't doubt that was true. I reached down to pet Sticks, who yapped happily when Nora tossed him a dog biscuit from a bowl she kept stocked for any four-legged friends who happened into the shop.

The pastry case had a tantalizing collection of rose-inspired sweets, from almond shortbread cookies to rose-infused chocolate truffles. The one that really caught my eye was a tea cake. I read the description—vanilla sponge cake layered with basil rose buttercream and fresh strawberries.

"Yum, right?" Nora's thick black eyeliner gave her eyes the appearance of racoons. Yet she pulled off the classic rock look with her youthful energy.

"I might have to try it. For the sake of the Rose Festival, after all."

"Girlfriend, it is yours. On the house." Nora put the cake on a plate and handed it to me. Next, she ground the beans and within a few minutes thick, rich espresso dripped from the stainless-steel machine. "Have you met Eric yet?"

"No." I pursed my lips together. "Have you?"

"They came by earlier. Hand in hand. Like two young lovebirds." Nora grinned. "He's as handsome as ever. It's no wonder that your aunt has never considered anyone else after all of these years."

Nora had been the one to fill me in on Elin's heartbreaking past. She had also been the one who encouraged Elin to pursue love. I was glad that my aunt had a friend like her.

"He's nervous to meet you," Nora continued, pouring steaming milk over the black espresso. "Must have asked at least a dozen times while they were here what you were like and whether you harbored any ill will toward him."

"Why would I?"

She topped the coffee off with a fluffy cloud of foam and handed me the drink. "Because he deserted her after your parents died." She waved at one of her employees to take over. "Come sit."

We walked to a table near the steamy windows. "Don't just sit there, girl. Eat. You have to try that cake and tell me what you think."

I wanted to get back to the topic of my aunt, but I knew from Nora's expectant gaze that I had to try the cake first. My fork cut through the fluffy pink buttercream. I took a bite and was greeted by an unusual yet delightful flavor. The sweet strawberries mingled with hints of rose and the flavor was balanced by a savory finish of basil. "This is amazing," I said through a mouthful.

Nora kicked her ankle-high black booties onto a chair and clapped. "Rockin', isn't it? The pastry shop that I wholesale from baked an entire line of desserts for Rose Festival. I told them they had better bring me double tomorrow, because with the crowds in the village I'm not going to be able to keep anything in the case."

She tossed Sticks another biscuit. "Speaking of romance. How is Mr. Suit?"

Mr. Suit was Nora's semi-affectionate nickname for Pete. She was convinced that Pete had a secret inner-rocker streak. But then again, Nora was sure that everyone was a closet rock-and-roll lover. I had tried to tell her that classical music was my style, but she refused to listen.

"He was in here asking about you. Wondering why Blomma was closed and whether you were going to be around soon." Nora gave me a knowing look.

I felt a blush creep up my neck. "Yeah. I saw him."

"And?" She leaned closer. "Dish, girl. You can't leave me hanging like that."

"There's nothing to tell. He's really hard to read."

She waved me off. "Please, honey. There's nothing hard to read about Mr. Suit. He's totally into you, and if you can get him to loosen up, I guarantee you that he's all rock and roll under that buttoned-up shirt and tie. I see it every day."

Nora catered to Portland's business crowd. Demitasse served artisan coffee and pastries. She played classical music overhead, with one unique twist. All of the songs were actually rock-and-roll favorites, like AC/DC's "You Shook Me all Night Long," played on the cello. Nora claimed that her business clientele were lawyers and doctors by day and rockers by night. One of her daily customers apparently had tattooed every inch of his body, except for his hands and neck. He wore a suit to cover up any evidence of his "inner rocker," as Nora called it. Pete's tiny tattoo on his forearm didn't exactly qualify, but I enjoyed Nora's carefree attitude and insistence that everyone could rock if they wanted to.

I savored another bite and steered the conversation back to Elin. "What happened between Eric and Elin was years ago. Why would he think that I would harbor a grudge? If Elin has forgiven him, I do too. Plus, I can hardly judge him. I didn't make the wisest choices in my twenties. Think of the years I wasted with Chad. Maybe this is how their love story was supposed to play out. They spent years apart, growing, creating independent lives, only to come together now. Isn't love sometimes about timing?"

"You are wise beyond your years, Britta." Nora snapped at Sticks to stop licking the floor.

I took a sip of the espresso, tasting buttery notes. "This is just what the doctor ordered."

"We heard about the incident this morning. Your aunt said that you found the body?"

I had almost momentarily forgotten about Sham's murder. "Yeah."

"Was it terrible?"

"Yeah." I couldn't think of more to say. No words did justice to seeing death firsthand.

"I'm sorry, honey. If there's anything I can do, let me know." She reached across the table and squeezed my hand. "I told Elin that I'm a terrible designer, but I'll put my coffee hands to work however you might need."

"Actually, I might have to take you up on that." I told her about how Elin was planning to bring Eric to work on the float. Then I polished off the rest of the rose basil cake.

"Count me in. I'll drag Jon over too."

Jon owned Torch, the candle shop, across the street from Blomma. He, Elin, and Nora were a fierce threesome. They sent customers to each other's shops, and filled in whenever and wherever necessary. I loved the community spirit in Riverplace Village. "Great. Maybe we can boot Elin out of the barn and send her and Eric on a romantic date."

Nora fist-pumped me. "Consider it done." She scooped Sticks onto her lap. They looked like quite the pair, with Sticks's leather collar and Nora's leather boots. "And, girl, I want an update on Mr. Suit. Deal?"

"I can't promise there's going to be anything to update you on, but deal." I thanked her for the cake and left with my coffee. The paper mug warmed my hands as I headed for the bridge. The rain had stopped and a sliver of sun poked out from behind the clouds. I was about to cross up toward the Hawthorne when I spotted Priscilla sitting on a bench that looked out onto the Willamette River. A blood-red umbrella rested by her feet and she had her face buried in her hands.

Was she crying?

Without thinking, I walked straight to her and asked, "Priscilla, is everything okay?"

Priscilla snapped her head in my direction. She was still wearing her tiara. Her eyes were bloodshot, with huge puffy circles beneath them. She had laid a plastic poncho on the damp bench to protect her dress. "What do you want?"

The sun glinted on her tiara. I had to shield my eyes. "I just wondered if everything was okay. You look like you're upset."

"What are you talking about?" She brushed a tiny wet leaf from the bench. "You asked me that earlier and I told you I was fine. I'm still fine. Why do you keep asking me?"

"I guess because I'm upset. I think everyone involved with Rose Festival is upset. Sham's murder has us all on edge."

She frowned. "Why? He was a menace. There are proper channels to get things done in a civilized society. I have no respect for someone who smashes windows and vandalizes mom-and-pop shops. For what? What kind of a statement is that? Sham should have known better."

"I agree, but he didn't deserve to die."

Priscilla didn't respond. She simply shrugged and flicked another leaf off the bench. "I had forgotten how horrendous Portland is in the spring. My allergies are killing me." She reached into her purse and removed a package of expensive tissues. Then she dabbed the corner of her eyes. "I've been miserable since the moment my plane landed. People think that LA is smoggy, but so what. I can deal with that, but the pollen here is like soup. I don't know how I'm going to manage to keep my composure in the parade tomorrow if my nose is running and my eyes are watering. It's not very regal."

I was surprised that her allergies were flaring up in the rain. Although Portland was notorious for its spring allergy season. One of the gifts of living through dreary wet winters were the flowers and trees that burst to life in springtime. Unless you suffered from allergies. For weeks in the spring, pollen fell like snow. During the height of the blooming season, thick, yellow pollen coated cars and sidewalks. Puffy, marshmallow tufts of pollen floated through the air and gathered in dense clumps on street corners. I was fortunate. I had never suffered from allergies, but I knew that some Portlanders had to take drastic measures—like leaving town—once the trees began to bud.

Was Priscilla really suffering from allergies, or was she lying? She didn't appear to be shaken up about Sham's death, but then again, her icy exterior didn't give much away.

Priscilla folded her tissue and placed it back in her purse. She stood. "I'm due to meet the princesses for high tea."

"Enjoy." I kept my tone light.

She gave me a strange look and then clicked away on her heels. There was no reason not to believe her, but I didn't trust her. I couldn't imagine what motive she would have to kill Sham, other than maintaining a certain level of posh exclusivity with the festival. Yet, her tears seemed like more than just allergies. When I got back to the float barn, I would have to ask Gloria more about the former Rose Festival Queen. Could she have fled to LA for other reasons? Maybe she'd left skeletons in her Portland closet, and being back again had opened up her past.

Chapter Fourteen

"Britta, welcome back. What do you think?" Gloria asked when I returned. She and the other volunteers had finished three trees. They stood nearly twenty feet tall from the base of the float. Draped in greenery and budding with colorful Japanese maple leaves, it looked like a scene from a fairy tale.

"Amazing. I love them!" I walked around the float to admire it from every angle. Talk about happy accidents. The float had turned out even better than our original sketches.

"There's good news and bad news." Gloria pointed to the float. "Which do you want first?"

"I'll take the good."

"The police have finished their investigation and given us permission to start working on the float again."

"That's great news." I realized the yellow evidence markers had been removed. "What's the bad news?"

"We have five more trees to construct, position,

and secure on the float, and then *only* a few hundred strands of violet garlands to create."

"Only?"

I wasn't immune to hard work or long hours. If I had to stay through the night and the next night too, I would.

"Is there anything else you want us to add to the trees before we start trying to haul them up onto the float? We're in the zone here with tree construction, so if it's okay with you, I'd like to get these done before we move on to anything else." Gloria clutched a pair of shears.

"You're the boss." I grinned. "But no, I think they're good to go. And I don't want you doing that work. I'll climb up on the scaffolding when we get to that point."

"My creaky knees thank you for that." Gloria smiled. She and the crew of volunteers continued bundling the trees. Since everyone was occupied and there wasn't anything for me to do, I decided to go see if I could get a peek inside the adjacent warehouse. Maybe Nicki had stashed the envelope somewhere. She acted strange every time she went back and forth between the float barn and warehouse, constantly warning me to keep out. I had assumed that was because she took her responsibility seriously and was concerned that one of the volunteers might accidentally damage the carnival equipment. But what if I was wrong? Maybe Nicki didn't want anyone going into the warehouse, because she was hiding evidence.

A heavy steel door had a sign posted that read: AUTHORIZED PERSONNEL ONLY.

Did I count as authorized personnel? Probably not, but I turned the cold handle anyway. To my surprise, the door opened.

The warehouse was pitch-black and freezing cold. Keeping a hand on the wall, I fumbled along it until I found a light switch. I flipped on the lights. They slowly hummed to life. A low buzzing sounded from the warming lights. I hoped that it wasn't loud enough to arouse suspicion, but then again, the main warehouse was a frenzy of activity. No one would notice the sound of industrial lights, right?

Right, Britta.

My eyes adjusted to the dim light. There were huge wooden crates stamped with the carnival company's logo, a disassembled Ferris wheel, and dozens of carnival rides. I walked around the carnival equipment, noting boxes of giant stuffed animals and dismantled arcade games.

Where would Nicki have hidden an envelope?

The space was massive. Cardboard boxes and plastic storage tubs stretched the entire length of one wall. This was going to be impossible. It was like looking for a needle in a haystack.

I did find the buckets of black dahlias. They were sitting next to something covered with a large blue tarp the size of Elin's Jeep. Without considering the consequences, I walked toward the tarp. Whatever was underneath was big. Really big. Like the size of a float.

Just as I started to lift one edge of the tarp, the steel door thudded behind me. I dropped the plastic tarp and ducked behind whatever was underneath it.

"How did these get turned on?" Nicki's voice echoed through the cavernous space.

My stomach flopped. Had she seen me? How was I going to talk my way out of this one?

I glanced around. Was she headed toward me? There was another exit about two hundred feet away. If I was quiet and careful I could probably reach it without her seeing me. Of course any sound I made would be impossible to mask in the empty space.

I kept my body low and inched toward a crate. The sound of Nicki's feet tapping on the floor made the hair on the back of my arms stand at attention. There was something ominous about the way she kept stopping abruptly. I had a feeling she was checking each area to see if someone was hiding out.

I needed to get out of here—now.

The warehouse smelled rusty, like the weathered rides had been subjected to years and years of rain.

I raced toward a Tilt-A-Whirl and waited, breathless, until I saw Nicki's backside. She was looking inside one of the crates. I tiptoed toward the exit door.

Please let it be unlocked.

My hand clutched the door. At first it wouldn't turn. Panic pulsed through me. What was I going to do? Nicki would surely find me. How was I going to explain this? She had already caught me digging through her purse. If she was the killer, there was no chance she would let me go this time.

I tried again. The door swung open. I ran outside and headed straight for a clump of spiny bushes clustered together on the waterfront path. I landed hard on the dirt, leaping behind the spiky bush just as Nicki stepped outside.

Thorns dug into my hands. I didn't even care.

The next thing I knew, Nicki twisted her head from side to side. "Who's there? I know someone's out here!"

I gulped. A cut on my hand started to bleed. *Don't move, Britta.*

"Zigs, is that you?" Nicki kept glancing in every direction. I prayed that I was hidden well enough in the bushes. I could make out Nicki through a small gap in the bushes. Did that mean she could see me too?

"Zigs, I told you to stay away! You step one foot on this property and I'm calling the cops." Nicki waited for a minute and then returned inside. She slammed the warehouse door shut.

That was close. Way too close.

Zigs? Nicki thought I might have been Zigs. My God, was my far-fetched theory right? Were Nicki and Zigs working together? And if so, what were they hiding under the tarp? A giant bomb?

Everything about this day was getting weirder by the moment. What was Nicki hiding in the warehouse? Why was she adamant that no one could go in there? And why did she think Zigs had been in the bushes?

"Britta? This is getting ridiculous." I heard a familiar voice. "What are you doing in the bushes?"

Uh-oh! I looked up to see Pete Fletcher staring at me.

He extended a hand. "Want some help up?" His crisp white shirt brought out flaxen tones in his eyes.

My cheeks flamed with heat. "Thanks."

I let Pete help me to my feet and then pulled a thorn from my palm. Blood trickled down my hand, staining my jeans.

"You're hurt?" Pete reached for my hand. The twinkle in his eyes disappeared and was quickly replaced by a look of concern.

"It's nothing. Just a scratch. I landed wrong. That's all." I pointed to the thorny bushes.

He caressed my wrist. "You need to get that cleaned. I have a first aid kit in my car. Come on."

"Really. It's no big deal. I'm fine." I didn't want to have to explain that I had been snooping. Given the weird and ever-changing energy between us, I had a feeling Pete wasn't going to be thrilled to hear that I was meddling in his investigation.

He took me to his squad car without saying a word. I could tell that he wasn't happy to have found me hiding the bushes. His touch was gentle as he dabbed my palm with rubbing alcohol and covered the cut with a bandage. He gave me a quizzical look. "Now, do you want to tell me what you were doing in the bushes, or am I going to have to interrogate you?"

Recounting my snooping made me feel even more sheepish. Pete listened with a half smirk at first. He made a few notes in his spiral notebook. "Thanks for the intel. I'll have my team check it out, but, Britta, I don't want to have to remind you again that this is a dangerous situation. Please don't get yourself in the middle of it. I know that Sham wasn't exactly an upstanding member of the community, but he was brutally murdered. There is a killer among us and I don't want you involved. Got it?"

"Got it." I nodded. Thankfully, Pete didn't seem as angry as I thought he might be. Then I decided to share my theory that Nicki and Zigs were hiding a bomb in the warehouse.

Pete's jaw tightened as I spoke, filling him in on how skittish Nicki had been about locking the warehouse. When I finished, he frowned. "Listen, Britta. This is off the record. We're working some intel about potential explosive devices. This is not public information, understood?"

I nodded.

"I'll relay this to the team, although given the thorough sweeps they did last night and this morning, it's doubtful there's an explosive on-site here, but we're at a high threat level at the moment. We're not sharing that information with the general public and I'm not sharing it with you to freak you out, but I want to reiterate how important it is that you stay out of this, okay?"

I couldn't think of a worthy response, so I nodded again.

"Good." He closed the notebook. "Now, on to better topics. About our dinner date. Do you have plans tonight?"

More heat crept up my neck. "No."

"Excellent. Would you care to join me at the Riverplace Inn, at seven? It just so happens that the fire chief offered me a window table for the show tonight. Apparently, it's quite a production. The fireboats put on a water show on the Willamette, followed by a display of actual fireworks."

"That sounds great."

He glanced at the clock on the dashboard. "I need to get back to work. Meet you there at seven?"

"Sounds great," I repeated. Pete had a knack for making me lose my ability to formulate a complete sentence.

"See you then." He sauntered away.

I heeded his advice. Pete had confirmed my worst fears—there was a bomb threat. Regardless of how much I wanted to know and help figure out who had killed Sham, I didn't want to have any involvement with a potential explosion.

On my way to the float barn, I noticed a happy couple holding hands and laughing. They stood shoulder to shoulder with their hands clasped together. It was evident from their body language that they were meant for one another. Upon closer inspection I realized it was Elin and Eric. I practically sprinted over to greet them, momentarily forgetting about a secret bomb.

"Here she is." Elin broke away from Eric and kissed both of my cheeks. "Eric, meet my dearest niece, Britta."

"Finally. I was beginning to think you were a figment of your aunt's imagination," Eric said, embracing me in a giant hug. He was tall and thin, with kind eyes and a warm smile. His salt-and-pepper hair gave him a distinguished look, as did his tailored khaki slacks, sleek navy button-down shirt, and brown leather loafers. A canary-yellow pocket square finished his outfit with a pop of color. "But here you are in the flesh."

He turned to Elin. "Should I pinch her to see if she's real?"

Elin swatted him playfully.

I instantly felt at ease.

"Funny. I said the same thing earlier. I think Elin is trying to keep you all to herself." I winked and nudged my aunt.

Elin pressed her hands together. "Nothing makes me happier than seeing two of my favorite people together."

"How are you liking Portland thus far?" I asked Eric as we continued together along the riverfront path.

"It's wonderful, as always. There's no place more vibrant than Portland in the spring." He paused and held up his index finger. Then he let out a sneeze. "My apologies. This bounty of gorgeous flowers certainly has flared up my allergies."

My thoughts went to Priscilla. Maybe she had been telling the truth.

"This year is absolutely one of the worst," Elin said to Eric. "I have friends who can't go outside. It's terrible."

He waved her off. "Not to worry. A bit of pollen won't keep me down. Now, Britta, tell me about you. I'm eager to hear your thoughts on the Rose City. Elin tells me that you have big plans for Blomma and are ready to take the flower world by storm."

"I don't know about that." I chuckled. I liked Eric's playful spirit and the way he hadn't let go of Elin's hand since we had started walking.

"She showed me some of your designs at the shop. They're magnificent. You have a natural talent." He removed the pocket square and dabbed the corner of his eye.

"Thanks. Everything I learned is from Elin."

Eric's smile widened. "That I don't doubt. Your aunt was crafting unique arrangements and creating flower fashions long before the trend started." He hadn't taken his eyes off of her for one second as he spoke. He went on to tell me about their earlier years in Portland. I watched Elin's face grow lighter as they recounted happy memories.

"Of course, then I went off and ruined it all." Eric's voice was thick with emotion.

"Nonsense." Elin leaned into his shoulder. "We took different paths."

Eric's eyes misted. This time I could tell that the moisture from his eyes had nothing to do with allergies. "And wasted years."

Elin kissed his cheek. "We have each other now. That's all that matters, *ja?*"

I felt tears beginning to form in my throat. This is what I wanted. My life with Chad had been dull and lifeless, like a stale, unscented flower bought at a supermarket. I wanted a love that made my eyes sparkle like Elin's.

We arrived at the float barn. "Just wait until you see the finished product," I said, holding the door open for them. We gave Eric a brief tour of the other floats. He oohed and aahed at the sheer scale of the designs and stopped to admire the detailed craftsmanship and fine flower work at each of the floats. When we arrived at the Blomma float, Eric's enthusiasm was palpable.

"This is incredible! It's the best float by far," he gushed, running his arm over the towering grapevine trees popped on the wall.

Elin and I shared a look.

"It's not even close to done," I said, with a laugh.

"I can completely picture it my mind," Eric said with another sneeze. His eyes dripped. He kept dabbing them with his yellow pocket square to no effect. The flower-laden barn triggered a sneezing fit. He pressed the square to his nose, as if trying to stop his sneezing by force.

"We need to get you out of here," Elin said with a look of concern.

Eric started to speak, but sneezed again.

Elin turned to me. "Is there anything else that needs to be done?"

I shook my head. "As long as you're happy with the final design, we're going to start securing the trees to the base, and then the only thing left will be stringing up the violets." The word *violet* gave me a moment of pause.

"It's perfect." She patted my hand. "Pass on my thanks to the volunteers. I'm going to take Eric to his hotel room and give him a heavy dose of Benadryl."

"Good plan." I gave Eric a hug. "Feel better."

He sneezed three more times before being able to say thanks.

I felt terrible for him. If the Benadryl didn't help, there was no way he could attend the parade tomorrow morning.

"What did Elin think, Britta?" Gloria asked, appearing behind me. Where had she come from? I hadn't noticed that she had returned. I glanced toward the pigpen and noticed that the door to the adjoining warehouse was propped open.

"She loves it," I said, distracted by the open door.

Were Pete and his team scouring the area, searching for a bomb?

Gloria followed my gaze. "Oh dear, how did that get open?" She shuffled to the door and tugged it shut.

"Were you just in there?" I asked.

She shook her head, but her cheeks were splotched with color. "No. I was sending the final crew of volunteers home."

I got the sense she was lying.

"Shall we call it a day?" Gloria said. "We have an early start tomorrow. Need to get those trees on the float and then start fingers flying on the violet production line."

"Yep." I decided not to press it after Pete's warning.

She pointed to the rolling cart. "Don't forget the scrapbooks I brought for you."

"Oh, right. Thanks again for bringing them and for your help. We couldn't have done it without you."

"It's a team effort." She shrugged off the compliment. "See you bright and early tomorrow." With a half wave, she hunched her shoulders and headed for the front.

I watched her leave. Was there a chance she could have killed Sham? I wished that I knew the official cause of death. If the killer had strangled him, that all but took Gloria off my list of potential suspects. With her creaky knees and arthritic fingers, how could she have strangled the burly resistance leader?

I pushed the thought aside, gathered my things and Gloria's scrapbooks. I had a couple hours before I was due to meet Pete for dinner. I knew exactly what I was going to do. I would head to Blomma, pour myself a glass of vino, and plant more succulents. There was no point in going all the way home and then back to the village for dinner. A respite at Blomma from the float activity sounded like perfection. The flower shop was my happy place, and after finding Sham's body this morning, I could use a heavy dose of happiness.

Chapter Fifteen

It didn't seem possible, but even more parade-goers had crowded onto the waterfront since lunchtime. As dusk began to settle over the city, the party atmosphere grew. A band had struck up a spontaneous concert at the edge of Waterfront Park. People danced the beat. The scent of grilling smoked salmon, hamburgers, and sausages filled the warm evening air. Street vendors peddled light-up balloons, glow sticks, and ice cream. I almost considered finding a tiny square of sidewalk and watching the action, but I needed some alone time.

I passed through the lively crowd and turned onto the cobblestone streets of Riverplace Village. The trees twinkled with tiny white lights, and sidewalk boards sat in front of nearly every business, announcing a variety of Rose Festival sales and specials. Navy and coast guard ships had docked along the water, inviting visitors aboard for tours. A group of young women had gathered near the gangplank, hoping to catch a glimpse of the men in uniform. To their delight, a crew of sailors disembarked and stopped to chat with the women.

Kids raced past in paper sailor hats. Jet boats zoomed on the river below—passengers squealing as the boats skimmed the surface and spun in crazy circles. The earlier rain had given way to clearing late-afternoon skies.

A mariachi band in bright costumes and sombreros played on the riverfront deck at La Comida, a Mexican restaurant famous for their hand-rolled tamales and spicy guacamole. Every shop and restaurant in the village had gone the extra mile to welcome visitors and guests to our little corner of Portland.

"Afternoon, Britta," called Jon, the owner of Torch, the candle shop across the street from Blomma. He was making a few adjustments to his front window display. The bay window had been illuminated with dozens of shimmering stained-glass lamps, giving it an aura of moving color. Almost as if it was floating on the sea.

"How's the shop?" I asked, crossing the cobblestone street.

He polished a smudge on the window and then folded an expensive silk handkerchief and tucked it into the pocket of his taupe overcoat. Jon won the award for best-dressed business owner in Riverplace Village. He had a regal air about him, without being snooty. It was one of the reasons that he and Elin had been friends for so many years. They shared a common love of beautiful aesthetics. Elin's in the form of flowers. Jon's in the form of light. "The crowds are picking up," Jon commented.

"Have you seen how many people are lining Naito Parkway?" I asked.

"It's like this every year." Jon held the front door open. "Care to come inside? I've put the finishing touches on my rose display."

"I'd love to see it." Stepping inside the candle shop brought an instant smile to my face. Torch was intentionally low lit to allow the candles and lamps to shine. Jon had created a hazy ruby dome of rose light near the front window. There were antique Tiffany lamps with bronze bases and clumps of roses on alabaster bell shades, and table lamps with tiled roses. Rustic tins of rose-scented candles, and pink, red, and white wax candles in the shape of delicate roses had been lit and flickered on beds of silver platters. If I closed my eyes, I would have thought I was inside Blomma. The smell of sweet, subtle flowers was so authentic it was hard to believe these were candles.

"Jon, this gorgeous." I picked up a plum-colored votive.

He ran one of this long, slender hands along the base of a Tiffany rose lamp. "Glad you approve. Now if I can only convince one of my customers that they *need* this on their coffee table, I'll consider the display a success."

I glanced at the price tag on a pendant Tiffany lamp: three thousand and fifty dollars. "I see why you say that."

Jon smiled. "That, my dear, is the price we must pay for those of us with exquisite taste. Maybe I'll have to offer an incentive in the form of a matching Blomma bouquet to whoever walks out the door with this gem."

"Consider it done." The idea of matching flowers to the etched beige and blood-red rose lamp would be a unique challenge.

Jon walked to the back of the shop. "Can I interest you in a cup of tea or a rose wafer?" he asked when we arrived at the vintage cash register, where galvanized tins were overflowing with impulse buys—miniature tea rose candles and strings of LED rose-leaf lights.

"A rose wafer?" I asked.

He removed a leather box from under the counter. "I had these imported from Paris. I thought they would be a perfect accompaniment to the Torch rose experience this week."

I helped myself to a thin, pale pink wafer. The creamy, not-too-sweet wafer melted in my mouth. I tasted white chocolate, vanilla, and the slightest hint of rose. "This is delicious."

Jon's ebony cheeks expanded as he smiled and nibbled on a wafer. "Nothing but the finest for my Torch customers. These pair beautifully with the rosehips tea I have steeping."

"You really have gotten into the spirit." I bit into a second wafer.

"Rose Festival comes but once a year and it's our grandest parade. Riverplace Village is the epicenter." He paused and poured us each a cup of tea. "Have you noticed the dashing sailors in uniform strutting around the waterfront? It's making me swoon." He pretended to fan himself. Then he winked and handed me a delicate teacup.

"It would be hard not to notice the sailors," I bantered back.

"Speaking of swooning. Give me the dirt on Elin.

She's been mysteriously absent as of late, and Nora tells me that Eric is in town."

Elin didn't stand a chance between Nora and Jon. They were relentless in their quest to help her find love again.

"I finally met him," I said, sipping the tea. The refreshing rosehips tea had an almost tropical flavor with an aromatic, flowery finish.

"And?" Jon raised a groomed brow.

"He seems great, and he obviously adores Elin."

"Most excellent." Jon tipped his teacup toward mine. "A blooming romance in the midst of Rose Festival. How perfectly Portland."

I sighed. "Yeah, as long as there's not a disaster at the parade."

"Why?" Jon's expression turned to concern.

I filled him in on what had transpired with Dark Fusion and Sham's murder.

Jon adjusted his deep burgundy tie. "I heard rumors about Dark Fusion, but I wasn't aware that the violence had escalated. One of my most loyal customers is a lawyer, and he was in the shop yesterday. He mentioned that there's a bit of a legal scuffle brewing."

"That's what I heard too." I told him about Ted.

"I'm familiar with Ted." Jon looked pensive for a moment. "Did you know that he used to work in the village years ago?"

"No. Really?"

"Indeed. He began his early career—long before he became involved in politics—at the Riverplace Inn."

"What did he do?"

"He worked in the corporate offices. If memory serves, I believe he was in marketing, but perhaps it was finance. He made the bulk of his money in real estate. In the eighties he snatched up dozens of duplexes and small apartment units. Made a fortune once the housing market began to boom in the late nineties, and then went on to invest it in his political career."

I wasn't sure if Ted's financial background could tie into Sham's murder, but it was good information to log.

"Rumor in the village is that he had intended to run for another mayoral term, but that his opponent dug up some dirt on him that he didn't want to come to public light, so he declined to throw his name in the hat for another term."

"Really?"

Jon finished his tea. "I never heard more or if there was any substance to the rumors. You know how it is being enmeshed in a tight-knit community like ours—rumors swirl and then fade into the ether."

"Right." I handed my teacup to Jon. "Thanks for the tea and the yummy wafers. I should check on Blomma."

He walked me to the front and kissed my cheeks. "Tell Elin to stop being so secretive and to bring her dreamy gent this way so that I can give her my seal of approval."

I laughed and waved. Once I crossed the street, and flipped on the lights inside the flower shop, I couldn't help but wonder if Ted's past was somehow connected. Could Sham have been the person who "found dirt" on him? And if so, what was the dirt? If Ted had something to hide and Sham knew it, killing him would ensure that Ted's secrets would never come to light.

Ted had a long-running reputation as one of Portland's most revered mayors, not to mention his status as grand marshal. If Sham had uncovered something from Ted's past, could Ted have gone to drastic lengths to keep it buried?

I shuddered at the thought and set Gloria's scrapbooks on the workstation. As of this afternoon, I had decided that Ted might not be the most likely suspect, but after my conversation with Jon, I was going to have to put him back on the list of potential killers.

Chapter Sixteen

Before I got my hands dirty potting succulents, I checked out the stunning assortment of arrangements that Elin had stored in the refrigerated case. Each bouquet and arrangement had its own unique construction. Some had spindly designs allowing for neutral space between the lush blooms, while others were tightly packed, as if the flowers were bursting from the earth. Every creation was one of a kind, and yet Elin had kept the same tones—chocolates, peaches, creams, with touches of pink and dark, woody greenery. She was a master. I knew that regardless of what happened with our float, Blomma's flowers would shine at the dignitaries' dinner.

The dinner was being hosted at the Riverplace Inn. Getting an invite to the exclusive six-course feast was nearly as impossible as scoring seats to *Hamilton*. Portland would roll out the red carpet for the night, treating dignitaries to cuisine prepared by award-winning chefs and entertainment by the city's top talent. As the official florist for the event, Elin and I had both received formal invitations. I couldn't wait to have a chance to watch women in elegant ball gowns and men in tuxedos sweeping across the dance floor.

The smell of roses lingered in the shop. I set Gloria's scrapbooks on the edge of the concrete workstation and turned on classical music. I thought of Nora. She would be disappointed that I opted to listen to Bach as I immersed myself in the meditative process of arranging succulents, instead of the Rolling Stones or Jimi Hendrix. Within an hour I had fifty containers lining the counter. Each gift would last for many years to come. I hoped that each time the dinner guests watered their potted plants it would trigger fond memories of their visit to the Rose City.

I had time to kill before dinner with Pete, so I decided I might as well thumb through Gloria's scrapbooks. She wasn't exaggerating when she said that she had saved every newspaper clipping, brochure, and program from over three decades of the festival. Leafing through the yellowed pages was a reminder of the Grand Floral Parade's storied history. Dignitaries from around the world had attended the festival, as had presidents and celebrities. Styles and fashions had evolved over the years, but the parade itself stayed true to its roots, with a focus on Portland's finest blooms and elaborate organic floats.

I found myself feeling slightly nostalgic as I remembered past parades where I would munch on caramel corn and watch clowns whiz by on unicycles. In addition to newspaper articles and Rose Festival advertisements, Gloria's memorabilia also included a box of hundreds of old pictures. They were categorized by year with hand-written notes on the back. Gloria was a super fan. I couldn't believe how much Rose Festival material she had garnered. There was enough in each scrapbook to fill a small museum.

A nagging internal voice urged me to look closely at each picture. What if there was a clue to Ted's past hidden in the stacks of old photos? I spread them out on the workstation in piles. Then I began methodically scanning each picture. I wasn't exactly sure what I was looking for, but I had a feeling I would know it when I saw it.

I was so lost in the process that I almost forgot about my dinner with Pete. The clock on the wall announced the top of the hour. I looked up and realized I was due at Riverplace Inn, so I set one pile of pictures that I had already reviewed back in the box and the rest I left for later. Then I went to the bathroom to assess my appearance.

My hair needed attention, as did the rest of me. A frantic day in the float barn had my fingers stained and my jeans sticky. Fortunately, my purse was always stocked with hair clips, lip gloss, and a brush. I splashed water on my face and applied a layer of shimmery peach gloss. Then I brushed my hair and pulled one side back with a silver barrette. I dusted my cheeks with blush and ran a little bit of matching peach powder on my eyelids. The light makeup helped warm up my pale skin. Elin and I kept a change of clothes in the cottage. Long days in the flower shop meant that we typically worked in jeans, boots, and warm sweaters. We usually delivered bouquets in our work clothes, but some occasions (like weddings) required more professional attire.

I slid the barn door open and entered the cold cottage. Despite the fact that we hadn't hosted a workshop in the past week, the minute I turned on the overhead iron chandeliers the cottage immediately felt cozier. I found my clothes hanging in the closet near Elin's wooden desk. Tugging off my jeans and boots, I pulled on a knee-length red flare skirt and a simple black sweater. I found my favorite pair of faux-fur-lined black boots at the back of the closet, and finished my transformation with a simple necklace. It had been a welcome-home gift from Elin. The necklace was carved from wood in the shape of adjoining roses, half that had been left natural and the other half that had been painted red with deep green stems. The necklace was incredibly light, and anytime I wore it, it became a conversation starter.

Before I left to meet Pete, I took one final glance in the mirror. I was happy with the change. The soft black sweater matched my hair and made my eyes look especially blue. My cheeks had a touch of a glow from the blush, and the funky rose necklace accentuated my narrow neckline. *Thank goodness for wedding clients*, I thought as I locked up the shop and headed down the sidewalk toward the hotel.

The Riverplace Inn was one of Portland's swankiest hotels, with six-paned windows, a collection of red bikes in the front for guests to use while touring around the village, ornate wood-burning fireplaces, and an inviting lobby complete with complimentary wine-tasting and appetizers each night. The east side of the hotel offered guests iron-balcony suites with river views and red Adirondack chairs. The restaurant where Pete and I were meeting had a wall of windows that were nearly eye-level with the Willamette River. Tonight we would be treated to views of the fireboats. It was an annual tradition for the fireboats to put on a colorful show. Red, white, and blue streams of water would shoot from the boats, like fireworks. I couldn't wait to have a front-row seat for the action.

I passed through the lobby with its golden-yellow lamps and huge potted ferns and made my way into the dining room. The space was aglow. Hand-loomed Pendleton blankets hung from the walls. Edison-style bulbs cast a romantic soft light across the room.

Pete was already seated at a window-side table. He pushed out his chair and stood to greet me. "Britta, you look lovely." He held my gaze for a moment. Then his eyes traveled to my necklace. "Is that made of wood?"

"Yeah, isn't it cool?"

He stared at it for a minute. "Is it heavy?"

"No." I took off the necklace and handed it to him.

He lifted it with ease. "Very cool." He gave me back the necklace and pulled out my chair.

I sat down. There was an open bottle of red wine and two glasses waiting.

"I hope you don't mind, I went ahead and ordered a bottle." Pete almost blushed. Was he nervous too?

"No. That's great."

Pete poured the light pinot into our glasses. "I remembered that you like pinot. I hope this is a good choice. Our waiter recommended it."

"I'm sure it will be great. I'm not a wine snob." The aromatic wine reminded me of wild vine roses.

Pete's eyes twinkled. "I've seen the wall of wine at Blomma, and beg to differ." He held my gaze for a moment, making me fight to keep my feelings in check. "It's a lot of pressure trying to impress the woman who knows everything about wine and roses."

"Hardly." I shook my head.

"Well, I say let's toast to the Rose City." He held his wineglass.

I picked up my glass and clinked it on his.

"And to you." Pete's eyes made me want to leap into his arms.

"How about to us?" The words fell from my mouth before I could stop them. I wished I could hit rewind. *Brilliant, Britta.* I kicked myself under the table, as an uncomfortable warmth spread across my chest.

"I'll drink to that." Pete tipped his glass. He looked as handsome as always, in a well-cut black suit. The glow of candles from the black iron chandeliers overhead flicked off his head, making his auburn hair appear almost red.

The briefest frown clouded his face for a moment. "Britta, there's something I want to ask you."

"Okay." I clutched my wineglass. That didn't sound good.

"It's about Tomo."

"Tomo?" I expected Pete to launch into an explanation about why he was pulling Tomo from the investigation, but he took me by complete surprise when he continued.

"I've noticed that you two seem close. And, well, I don't want to interfere with your relationship with him." Pete sounded uncomfortable.

Was he implying that I had romantic feelings for Tomo? I nearly spit out my wine. "Wait, what? Tomo? He's nearly ten years younger than me."

Pete looked relieved. He chuckled. "I can think of a dozen celebrities in LA who have twenty-year-plus age gaps between them."

"Maybe, but no. Tomo and I are good friends. He's like a brother to me."

"You're sure." Pete swirled his wineglass. "I don't want things to be weird."

I couldn't believe we were having this conversation. Maybe Nora was right about Pete's interest. But why would he think I had feelings for Tomo? "Nope, no weirdness."

"Good." He raised his glass. "To first dates."

"To first dates." I smiled and changed the subject. "Any update on the case?" I glanced out the window. The dragon boats were circling in the river below us. I wondered if they were practicing for Saturday's race or the opening act for the fireboat show.

"Any news on the"—I paused and mouthed—"bomb?"

Pete frowned. "Way to kill the vibe. I thought we were having a romantic evening. I'm here on the waterfront with a gorgeous woman, toasting with Oregon's finest wine, and you want to talk murder." His tone was playful.

"I don't want to talk murder, but I can't stop thinking about it. After finding his body . . ." I trailed off, not trusting myself to say more.

Pete reached across the table and covered my hand with his. "I understand."

We stayed locked in the moment, until our waiter came by to tell us about the specials. Pete released my hand and studied the menu.

"What sounds good?"

You holding my hand again, I thought internally. "Everything." I glanced at the menu.

Our waiter suggested their signature Rose Festival dinner that included a crisp salad with pears, walnuts, and an apple vinaigrette, a creamy chicken-and-leek puff pastry, and a pistachio rose cake. The three-course dinner was a fundraiser for the parade. In addition to scholarship money for the royal court, the Rose Festival Foundation supported a variety of causes and outreach throughout the city.

"That sounds great," I said.

Pete nodded. "We'll take two."

The waiter left. "When I moved to Portland, some of my colleagues told me that the Rose Festival was a big deal, but I had no idea quite how big. I don't think you can go anywhere in the Portland vicinity and not be bombarded with roses. From rose doughnuts to one of the gas stations near headquarters that is advertising rose-scented oil changes."

"What?" I nearly spit out my wine. "A rose-scented oil change. That has to be a joke."

"Maybe." Pete shrugged. "But I wouldn't be surprised if people lined up for rosy oil."

"Gross."

Pete took a drink. "True."

I stared outside for a second. "I can't get over how many people are already staking their claims along the parade route. The sidewalks look like they're being held together by duct tape."

"I know." Pete chuckled. "One of the guys at head-quarters gets so riled up about it. Technically it's a violation. People aren't supposed to stake their spots until twenty-four hours before the parade, but we don't have the staff to enforce it, and frankly everyone else is cool with it. It seems like a rite of passage that most Portlanders agree is tradition."

"Yeah. I remember camping out one year for the parade when I was twelve or thirteen. It's a favorite memory." I thought back to sleeping out under the stars with Elin and thousands of our "neighbors." Elin had loaded up a picnic hamper with a thermos of hot chocolate and enough sandwiches and cookies to feed a small army. We shared our feast with the people camped around us and were treated to new culinary delights—like American potato salad and baked beans. Pete was right. I was glad that the police weren't intending to put the kibosh on the tradition. "Not to shift the conversation again, but is there any news about the murder?"

He cleared his throat. "We're not going to talk about anything else tonight until we've hashed out the investigation, are we?"

I gave him a sheepish smile. "Maybe."

"Listen, Britta, you know that I'm not at liberty to discuss with a civilian the details in an ongoing investigation."

"I know. I just wondered if you learned anything

new. What about cause of death? And did you find anything in the warehouse?"

He shook his head. "Not anything dangerous." Pete cracked his knuckles. "I'll tell you what little is public record. This is information that our communications department released to the media about an hour ago. We have brought Ted Graham in for questioning."

"You think Ted is the killer?" I couldn't contain myself. My foot tapped on the floor.

"Slow down. I didn't say that. I said that we brought him in for questioning. We bring lots of people in for questioning. That doesn't mean that an arrest is imminent."

"But it does mean that Ted is on the suspect list, right?"

Pete moved his head from side to side. "It means he's a person of interest in the case right now."

"You should talk to Jon, the owner of Torch. I was over there earlier and he told me that one of his clients is a lawyer who is working with Ted on legal action against Dark Fusion. He also said that there were rumors during the last election that Ted wasn't running again because his opponent was going to go public with damaging information."

Pete didn't look surprised. He nodded. "Yes, we've been pursuing that. At this point it's merely circumstantial. There's nothing to back it up, but my team is following every possible angle."

"Do you really think Ted could have done it?" I told him about my initial response and how I had been sure that Ted was the killer, but now I wasn't as sure.

When I finished, Pete leaned back in his chair and linked his fingers together behind his neck. "What am I going to do with you, Britta?"

"Sorry. I have a tendency to spiral sometimes. Honestly, I think I feel connected to wanting to know what happened because I was the one who found the body."

"Yeah." Pete frowned. Then he scooted his chair closer. "This is off the record, okay?"

"Okay." I felt a rush of excitement. Was Pete going to divulge insider information?

"Ted is the easy answer. It would be a quick case for me if he's the guy, but I don't think he is."

"You don't?" I took a sip of my wine. The smooth cherry and oaky flavor warmed my throat.

"No. He doesn't fit the profile. He has too much to lose, and he has power. This killing was impassioned. That's not Ted."

"How so? What do you mean by impassioned?"

"You asked about cause of death earlier?"

I swirled my wine and nodded.

"Sham wasn't killed with your violets. He wasn't strangled. He was clubbed on the base of his skull. The killer wrapped the violets around his neck after he was already dead."

"Oh." I was thankful that Pete trusted me enough to share this information, and relieved in a strange way to know that our violets weren't the cause of death.

"Ted has already opened up the proper legal channels," Pete continued, topping off his wine. "He has influence. He likely has a good case against Dark

Fusion. It doesn't fit. Why would he go to an extreme like murder? He's the kind of guy to go to the DA."

Pete was right. His theory validated the conclusion I had come to earlier, before talking to Jon. However, it also meant that I was no closer to figuring out who the killer was.

Chapter Seventeen

"Britta? You still with me?" Pete asked.

"Huh? Oh, sorry." I shifted in my chair.

"You know, I should really hire you. You are as wrapped up in this case as any of my team." Pete winked.

Our food arrived. We dug into the three-course meal as the conversation shifted to Elin and her budding romance with Eric. Pete hadn't been very forthcoming about his past. Thus far I was content to keep things on a more casual level. We were still getting to know one another, and quite frankly I had more work to do on myself before I was ready to pursue a new relationship. However, at some point I wanted—I needed—to understand his history. Was there a reason he was so guarded? Leaving Chad had taught me that I deserve to be in a relationship with someone who cares deeply for me and is willing to share his secrets. I got the sense that

Pete could be that guy, but as I regaled him with the saga of Elin and Eric keeping the home fires burning low for decades, I noticed a sadness wash over him. He kept his eyes focused on his plate and didn't say much.

"Did I say something that upset you?" I asked, polishing off my chicken-and-leek puff pastry.

Pete started to respond but our waiter arrived with the dessert course. He waited for the waiter to leave. I thought that maybe he was finally going to confide in me, but we were interrupted again. This time by Tomo.

He looked out of place in the fancy restaurant in his hipster jeans and knit cap. He approached the table and stopped to catch his breath. Had he run here?

"Sorry to break up what looks like a great dinner. I know you're off duty," he said to Pete and then looked at me. "But there's been a development with Dark Fusion. We need you."

What did that mean?

Pete folded his napkin and placed it next to his uneaten pistachio rose cake. "Apologies, Britta, but duty calls."

"I understand. Go."

"Please box this up and take it home for your aunt," Pete said, standing. "I'll be in touch when I can."

Tomo mouthed "Sorry," and they left together.

My pistachio rose cake was lovely, with six deca-dent layers of pistachio cake sandwiched with rose-infused buttercream. I picked at it but had lost my appetite. If only I could have tagged along with Pete

and Tomo. What could the development have been?
Had they made an arrest? Did they think that someone from Dark Fusion killed Sham?

When the waiter returned I had him box up both
pieces of cake and left. So much for a romantic dinner. I had had visions of Pete and I strolling hand in
hand along the waterfront, stopping to watch the
fireboats in action. In my daydreams I had imagined him leaning in to kiss me under the moonlight. Instead I was walking home with uneaten cake
and more questions than ever.

I decided to call it a night. I could have stayed to
watch the fireboats, but it didn't feel the same without Pete. There wasn't anything else that could be
done, and I knew that if I returned to the float barn
or Blomma I would spend hours spinning on my
thoughts. Plus, tomorrow we had twenty-four solid
hours to re-create a float from the ground up. I
needed to be as rested and refreshed as possible.

Alas, nature had other plans for me. My sleep was
sporadic. I kept waking through the night with
dreams about Sham's purple face and being chased
by strands of violets. I finally gave up sometime before six and padded down into the kitchen. Elin
hadn't returned home again, so I used the quiet
time to savor my coffee and try to focus on the parade.

Around seven I left the house in a pair of jeans, a
sweatshirt, and my rain boots. A light drizzle fell
from the low-lying clouds. Portlanders nervously
obsessed over the forecast for weeks before the parade. The current forecast called for intermittent
showers and clouds with potential clearing overnight.

Everyone in the city was likely crossing their fingers and toes in hopes of a dry morning for tomorrow's parade. June in the Rose City can be brilliantly blue with Mother Nature welcoming guests with a show of spring sunshine. Or it can be miserable and gray. Locals often deem the month—Juneary.

I returned inside and grabbed a rain jacket. My morning walk was uneventful. For the first time in recent memory there was no sign of protest activity. Not a single member of Dark Fusion waited to hurl insults or pinecones at me. The parking lot was void of police cars. There were no drums or rioters dressed in black. It was almost surreal. I hoped that it was an omen of good things to come, but I couldn't help worrying that Dark Fusion's disappearance signaled something much more sinister.

The princesses stood in single file outside of the float barn. Priscilla walked from the front to the back of the line, reminding them to maintain perfect posture and asking to see their royal waves.

They reminded me of schoolgirls, with their matching pink-rose raincoats and boots.

"Ladies, remember, all eyes will be on you tomorrow," Priscilla said in a commanding tone. "No slouching. We want your shoulders and heads held high."

"But my raincoat is dripping," one of the princesses said, holding her hood over her head to try to stop the rain from falling on her face.

"It doesn't matter," Priscilla scolded. "You are Rose Festival princesses. It is your royal duty to remain regal at all times. Understood?"

The girl nodded and tilted her head back.

"We will have ponchos to cover your dresses should it sprinkle tomorrow, but under no circumstances should the ponchos go over your heads. People want to see your smiling faces."

"What if it pours?" another princess asked.

"Then you'll just have to smile broader and wave more." Priscilla stopped and flicked one of the girls' jacket sleeve. "This is one day. One magical day in your lifetime. You won't ever have another experience like tomorrow. Rain or shine, I want to see your pearly whites."

I felt sorry for the princesses. Priscilla obviously took her duty seriously, but I couldn't imagine anyone complaining if the princesses had to wear raincoats. There had been many years when the skies unleashed on the parade. In fact, last night when I was looking through Gloria's scrapbooks, I had seen evidence of umbrellas and raincoats throughout the Grand Floral Parade's history. I shrugged and went inside.

Nicki was in the process of organizing the floats. "No, no, I need the dragon boat first," she huffed to one of the volunteers who had opened up the wrong bay door. "You must follow the exact order for the procession, got it? If we don't, the entire parade will be thrown off."

She walked over and yanked the cord to open the bay doors for the dragon boat. I headed for the Blomma float. We were last in line.

Nicki grabbed my arm as I walked past. "Britta, where's Gloria? I can't find her. She was supposed to be here an hour ago. She's the only other person who seems to understand the processional order."

"She's not here?" I glanced around the bustling warehouse.

"No." Nicki lifted her arms in disgust. "Why would I be asking you where she is if she's not here?"

It wasn't like Gloria not to show up.

Nicki waved me off. "Just get to your float. We're going to be ready for you in about three minutes."

I continued to our float. Gloria was nowhere to be found. Had she overslept? It seemed doubtful. She had been volunteering for years and had never missed a day. Nicki blared out orders on her megaphone. I had to prepare the Blomma float for the processional and inspection, but I was worried about Gloria. Had something happened?

What if that's why Tomo had come for Pete last night? Could Gloria be hurt? But why would anyone from Dark Fusion want to harm a sweet grandmother?

As promised, three minutes later Nicki was rolling up the door and ushering me out of the way. The dress rehearsal didn't take long. Each float took a turn around the parking lot. It was an opportunity for the drivers to practice steering and for the judges to observe the floats from each angle. Unfortunately, in our case the judges had nothing to critique us on. There had been discussion yesterday about making a special accommodation for us, since no one could have predicted that a murder would occur.

Nicki then had us all wait next to our floats so that the judges could ask us questions while they took a closer look at each float. I wished that Elin or

Gloria were here. I could talk to the judges about our vision and show them the original sketches, but otherwise, until we finished constructing the new design, there wasn't exactly anything compelling for them to see. My stomach began to swirl as Royal Rosarians checked boxes on clipboards and pressed their faces as close as possible to the fine seed-work on our float.

I led them inside to see the grapevine trees that were propped against the wall. One of the judges asked me about the trees and what they represented. I was happy to answer and felt relieved that Elin had had such a strong vision from the start. It wasn't hard to explain her vision, and while I knew that I was biased, I could tell that the judges were pleased with the esthetic. I didn't know if we would be granted an opportunity to be judged on a completed float, but I knew that we had managed to pull together a magnificent testament to Portland's lush, vibrant forests.

"What is this material?" another judge asked, inspecting the twine.

I assured her that everything we had used in construction was in line with the Grand Floral Parade's requirements. After what felt like an hour, the judges left to confer.

It was odd not to have Gloria in charge of volunteers. I found myself being constantly bombarded by questions and frazzled by the amount of work we had to do. Sweat dripped from my brow as I directed a crew of high school football players whom Nicki had recruited for their brawn. They weren't exactly gentle with the trees as we hoisted them up the scaffolding and onto the float. But any help was welcome at the moment.

My knuckles ached as I yanked the fishing line as tight as possible. "Secure it with at least three or four knots," I called to my helpers.

Positioning and tying the trees down took longer than I expected. Gloria was sorely missed. I realized just how critical the role of crew chief was. Her expertise and years of experience had made things at the Blomma float run effortlessly. Without her I was floundering. I scurried between projects, trying to keep the volunteers on task, answer their questions, and ensure that the trees were solid and sturdy.

I mopped my face with a hand towel after cinching the last tree into place. The cut from yesterday had reopened. Dots of blood trailed from the float to the pigpen and back again. I stopped to catch my breath and apply a new bandage. The trees were impressive. They gave off the impression of towering giants—much like the hundred-year-old evergreens in Portland's Forest Park.

Not bad for two days of work, Britta. I would feel proud to have the Blomma name attached to the float, and there were still plenty of final touches— like the garlands of violets that would breathe even more life and color into the finished design.

My football players had to return to school, and there was a break between the morning and afternoon volunteer shifts. I knew what I needed to do— go check on Gloria. The question was how? I had no idea where she lived. I texted Elin to see if she had Gloria's contact information, but she didn't get back to me. I figured she and Eric were probably

enjoying a leisurely brunch or hiding out due to his
allergies. Hopefully the rain would temper them.
Priscilla had appeared to be okay while she was outside imparting her vision for how the princesses
were to behave tomorrow.

I had seen Nicki with a stack of volunteer files.
Gloria's address must be in one of the files, so I
made my way to the break area and found a plastic
tub labeled VOLUNTEER INFO: PRIVATE.

This was a special circumstance, right? Gloria
could be in danger.

I leafed through the files until I found Gloria's
address. She lived in an older apartment complex
not far from Blomma. Perfect.

I snapped a picture of her volunteer information
sheet and was just about to return to the file when
Nicki appeared out of nowhere.

"What are you doing?" She folded her arms
across her chest.

This felt like déjà vu. Yesterday she had caught me
snooping through her purse. Now going through private volunteer files.

I held up Gloria's file. "I wanted to check on Gloria, but I don't have any of her contact information."

Nicki didn't try to mask her displeasure. She
took the file from my hands. "These are confiden-
tial. They have people's personal information on
them."

For a moment, I considered asking her why she
kept them in an unlocked plastic tub in the middle
of the busy break area, but I decided it was probably
better to keep my mouth shut.

"Sorry. I'm worried about her. She's always here."

Nicki stuffed the file into the tub and snapped on the lid. "Me too, but please ask me next time before you go through private files."

"Absolutely." I backed away.

Armed with Gloria's address, I planned to go straight there. I wasn't sure if Nicki knew something about Gloria that she wasn't telling me, but I had a sinking feeling that something terrible might have happened to the Rose Festival's most dedicated volunteer.

Chapter Eighteen

"Tomo, it's Britta. Call me back when you get this. I'm on my way to Gloria's. She's a volunteer with the festival and didn't show up this morning. I know it probably sounds crazy, but I think she might be in danger." I left him the address and hung up. In hindsight I could have called Pete, but Tomo was less likely to tell me to stop meddling.

Gloria's apartment was ten blocks northwest of the waterfront, tucked into a hillside. The complex was small, with eight individual cottage-style units that opened to a shared grassy courtyard. I had walked by it dozens of times but never knew that Gloria lived there. New developments—sleek, modern condos—rose in every direction, but the quaint complex had remained a final holdout from Portland's past. Constructed of brick and wood, each cottage was self-contained with a small green yard and white picket fence. There was a courtyard in the center of the complex surrounded by snaking rose vines and potted palms. No wonder Gloria had chosen the apartment. It felt like a nature oasis in the center of the city.

As I turned onto her street, I stopped dead in my tracks. The sound of fire trucks wailed nearby. Neighbors in bathrobes and pajamas huddled together at the end of the curb. Two firetrucks and an ambulance with their lights flashing were parked in front of the complex.

My heart lurched.

Gloria.

"What happened?" I asked a woman whose hair was soaking wet.

She pointed to the apartments. "Can't you smell it? There's a gas leak. One of the units was damaged earlier."

The smell of odorous gas hit my nose. It smelled like rotten eggs. I followed her finger to one of the cottages. Sure enough, the doorway was marked with yellow police tape and the back windows and doors looked as if they had been blown out.

"They evacuated everyone. I was about to blow-dry my hair when the place a couple doors down went up in flames," the woman continued, scrunching her wet curls.

A terrible feeling of dread hit my body. Could the gas leak be why Gloria hadn't shown up this morning? What if it was her cottage?

"How long have you been outside?" I asked, rain splatting at my feet. I pulled my hood over my head.

She glanced at her naked wrist. "I don't know. My watch is inside. Maybe a half hour or so."

That didn't make sense. Gloria was supposed to be at the float barn a couple hours ago. If the leak was from her apartment, could she have inhaled the fumes in her sleep? I felt sick. I wasn't sure if was from the thought of Gloria being hurt or from the noxious smell of gas.

"Is everyone okay?" I asked the woman.

She shook her head. "I don't think so. My neighbor said that they took an older couple and two others to the hospital, but I don't know for sure. The police aren't telling us anything."

"What about the ambulance?" I nodded to the ambulance parked on the street nearby.

She shrugged. "I saw them wheel a woman on a stretcher earlier, but it hasn't moved. I don't know if that's a good thing or bad thing."

I caught her meaning. If whoever was in the ambulance was already dead, there would be no need to rush the body to the hospital. I had to get closer.

I made it about thirty feet before a firefighter pushed me back. "You can't come any closer, miss."

"But I think I have a friend inside."

He turned behind him. "We've swept the entire complex. Every resident has been accounted for."

"Is everyone safe?"

"Everyone has been evacuated." His tone was calculated. "We're about to push the boundary back a few blocks. This entire place might blow. You really need to move away—now."

I stepped back. The complex could blow?

A rush of panic hit me. There had to be a connection. What were the odds of Gloria's apartment complex having a massive gas leak? Was this the work of Dark Fusion?

"Britta!" Tomo raced toward me, clasping his badge onto his uniform. His face was ashen.

"Where did you come from?" I asked.

He pointed to his squad car on the opposite side of the street. "I got your message about the same time I got the call about the gas leak. I was supposed to be on duty at the waterfront in a little while, but they've called everyone here. As in the entire force. It's bad." His dark eyes were wide with worry. "The fire chief thinks this entire block could be in danger. You've got to get out of here! They're saying this explosion might be felt a half mile away if the whole thing blows."

"But what about Gloria?" I pointed to the complex. "I haven't been able to get any information about her. I don't know if she got out, or if her cottage is the one that already sustained damage."

"I don't know. I'll see if I can find out anything, but I wouldn't count on it. I know I've only been on the force for a few years, but I've never seen anything like this, Britta." He stopped and motioned to the sea of emergency responders and flashing lights all around us. "This is serious. They don't send in these kinds of numbers for nothing."

A group of firefighters approached the crowd. "Everyone back up! This area is not safe. Back away!"

People began to panic. There were piercing screams. "My house! Everything I own is inside."

Someone else yelled, "There's a dog in there!"

Tomo pushed me into the throng. "Britta, get out of here."

I started to respond.

"Hey, you!" One of the firefighters motioned to Tomo. "We need an extra hand here."

Tomo jumped into the line of firefighters and

helped secure a broader perimeter. I stood on my tiptoes and watched as he raced with the rest of the crew toward the cottages. First responders never ceased to amaze me. While we moved away from danger they ran into it.

I held my breath, in part from the rotten egg smell, and due to my growing fear not just for Gloria but also for Tomo. I lost sight of him in the flurry of activity.

Everything went eerily still for a moment. It was as if every sound around me had been amplified. I could hear each individual drop of rain hit the pavement and the rustle of each leaf in the trees sounded in my ear. Then, suddenly a massive explosion rocked the ground so hard that I almost fell over. Flames and shrapnel shot out of the apartment complex. The violent sound of the blast muffled the noise around me and sent a high-pitch ringing through my ears. Everything seemed to be happening in slow motion. People ducked and screamed. First responders fled from the flames. I tried to focus on my feet, but my eyes weren't tracking.

A firefighter was running toward me waving his arms in the air. It took a minute to process what he was saying. He was shouting for us to get back. "It's going to blow again. Get back!"

I ran away from the cottages with the crowd, just as another blast reverberated and I hit the pavement.

Chapter Nineteen

A huge cloud of dense, acrid smoke erupted where Gloria's complex had stood. I was six blocks away and could feel the heat from the blast. The drizzly skies didn't damper the billowing smoke. Pandemonium broke out around me. A woman nearby dropped to her knees. Apparently her dog was still inside her apartment. I tried to comfort her as other residents begged the police and firefighters to let them closer to see what was left of their homes.

The smoke burned my eyes and made my throat scratchy. Sirens wailed as more fire trucks arrived on the scene. My jeans were soaking wet. I kept my arm around the woman with the missing dog while we waited on the damp sidewalk for any news.

A cheer spread through the crowd as a firefighter emerged from the blaze holding a golden lab. The woman cried out in happy relief. "That's my dog!" She ran to be reunited with her hound. Tears slid down my cheeks. At least there was one piece of good news amidst so much destruction.

What about Tomo? Was he okay? I searched in every direction but couldn't find him. Then again it was a mob scene of activity between the first responders, displaced residents, and the ever-growing gawking crowd of bystanders.

Please let him be okay.

The rain began to seep into my jacket. I rubbed my hands together to keep them warm. Glass shards covered the street and sidewalk from nearby windows that had been blown out.

I thought I saw Pete's car pull up near the barricade but I couldn't be sure. There were so many squad cars and unmarked vehicles that identifying Pete's would be nearly impossible. Firefighters doused the flames with water, causing plumes of gray and white smoke to fan out like a thick fog. The smell made my lungs burn. There must have been at least a hundred firefighters attempting to quell the flames. Residents walked around like zombies, the shock of losing their homes and possessions beginning to sink in.

After what felt like hours, I spotted Tomo through the crowd. He was covered in ash and dust.

Thank goodness. A wave of relief washed over me. I hadn't realized that I had been clenching every muscle in my body.

"Tomo, how are you?" I threw my arms around him when he made it to me.

He patted my back. "Careful, I'm a mess."

"It's okay. I'm soaked. I'm just so glad that you're okay."

"A couple bruises and some buzzing in my ears, but otherwise I'm good." He brushed thick, wet soot from his uniform.

"What about the other residents?"

"The building was clear except for a dog, and fortunately the fire crew was able to make a rescue. It could have been so much worse, Britta. If a resident hadn't called in the smell of gas, we could be talking about multiple casualties."

I gulped. "What about my friend Gloria? Any news on her?"

Tomo shook his head. "No. She could be at the hospital. The ambulance transported three residents before the blast."

"Do they know what caused the explosion?"

"It's too early to say what the cause of ignition was. Officially it's a gas leak, but one of my colleagues said that the fire inspector thinks it's arson. That's not public info, okay? The fire chief said it's a miracle that no one was killed, and he's never seen anything like this in his twenty-eight years. The two explosions were only thirty seconds apart. The device they use to measure gas didn't indicate that an explosion was imminent. The fire chief is asking for anyone who might have caught an image of the blast on their phone to come forward. They'll start reviewing surveillance cameras in the area. They're not officially saying it's arson yet, but, Britta, I'm sure this was intentional."

I wanted to ask Tomo about a potential connection to Dark Fusion, but he got called back to the scene. The smoke was giving me a headache. I didn't want to stand around in the rain breathing in the fumes, so I decided to head over to the hospital to see if Gloria was one of the residents taken by ambulance.

The hospital was located at the top of Portland's southwest hills. It was too far to walk, but if I returned to the waterfront I knew that I could take the sky tram. I had a hard time catching my breath as I wound my way through the ever-growing crowd. Parade-goers who had been camped out on the surrounding streets had gathered to get a look at the action.

I felt like I was a fish swimming upstream. Everyone was racing toward the blast zone as I was hurrying away. I made it to the tram in record time, and climbed on board. The view from the sky gave me a greater appreciation for the danger I'd been in, and how right Tomo was that the explosion could have been disastrous. Smoke fanned out in a quarter mile radius. Plumes still rose in the air near the site of blast, like an erupting volcano. I caught a brief glimpse of what was left of the complex—which looked like nothing. Brick rubble and exposed cottages had been reduced to nothing. I couldn't imagine that the residents would find anything left of their valuables and possessions once they were able to return.

When the tram arrived at the top of the hill, I went in search of the emergency department. At the nurses' station I asked if Gloria had been admitted. A young nurse stared at me. "Are you family?"

Without thinking, I nodded. "I'm her granddaughter."

Yet another lie. What was wrong with me?

The nurse typed something into her computer.

"Yes, she has been admitted, but I can't let you see her."

"Do you know if she's okay?"

The nurse looked at the computer again. "You'll have to wait to speak with the doctor, but she is in stable condition."

I figured pretending to be family with Gloria's doctor might be pressing my luck, so instead I asked the nurse if I could leave her a note. Then I wrote a brief note telling Gloria that I was sending her healing vibes and that I would be back later to check on her. I had to get to the float barn to meet the afternoon crew.

Word of the gas leak had already spread. Nicki ran over to me. Twigs and branches stuck out from her frazzled hair. Her khaki pants were stained with dirty splotches and her white tennis shoes looked as if they had been dipped into a vat of mud.

"What happened to you? Did one of the volunteers accidentally mistake you for part of a float?"

She wasn't amused. She ignored my questions and folded her arms across her chest. "Where have you been? I've been searching everywhere for you. You have ten volunteers waiting and no crew chief. I had to pull the crew chief from the Royal Court's float to oversee work on the Blomma float."

It wasn't as if Gloria's disappearance was my fault. I glanced to the Royal Court float, which was in the next stall. The simple tiered design was nearly finished. Volunteers were trimming red, pink, and white roses to add to tin buckets lining each side of the float.

"Thanks for sending over extra help." I wanted to point out that I thought that was Nicki's job as float

barn director anyway. Not to mention that every
decorator had offered their services after our float
was destroyed. "It wasn't as if I was off taking carnival rides. I was visiting Gloria at the hospital." I went
on to explain how I had seen Gloria's cottage explode, but Nicki stopped me in midsentence.

"Yes, yes. I know. We've heard the news and it's
terrible, but I can't think about that for the moment. There is way too much work to do." She
scolded me like a child, pointing her index finger
at me and then to the back of the float barn. The
tip of her finger was stained black. "They need you
at Blomma, like forever ago."

She shoved me toward the Blomma float stall.
Come to think of it, how did Nicki know about Gloria? I stopped and turned around. She had set her
sights on a poor volunteer who was holding a pair
of shears upside down. I watched as she snatched
them from the unsuspecting volunteer's hands and
stormed away.

Had she finally snapped?

I tried to put her out of my head as I met with
our new crew chief and examined a strand of violets. They had been done perfectly. The buttery
white and purple leaves offered a soft, springlike
compliment to the rustic trees. I set my things in
the pigpen, rolled up my sleeves, and climbed onto
the ancient scaffolding. It buckled as I lifted one
knee, then the next, onto the top level. The view
was spectacular. Floats that had been patchy and
full of empty, blank sections were now flush with
color. The camel's mane looked so real, I wanted to
run my fingers through it. The flamenco dancers

appeared larger than life, swirling in beautiful blue-bells, yellow daisies, and pure red roses.

I set to work twisting strings of violets in between branches and through the Japanese maple leaves. I wanted it to look natural, as if the violets were wild vines, and yet I needed them to hold. It was a tedious and slightly scary job. I had to balance with one foot on the scaffolding while reaching above my head to secure the flowers onto the tops of the trees. We found a rhythm after a while. As soon as the volunteers finished a new strand of violets, one of them would climb onto the first level of scaffolding and place it at my feet. I clipped a plastic tub of twist ties, twine, and scissors to my waist so that I didn't have to keep climbing up and down the rickety steps every time I needed supplies.

We had to repeat the process around the entire float. It took the majority of the afternoon. Twice I spotted Nicki sneaking into the warehouse. Both times, she unlocked the door and glanced around skittishly before opening it. Pete had assured me that there was no bomb tucked away in the cavernous space, but that didn't explain Nicki's actions. What was she doing?

And where were Dark Fusion? Again they were eerily absent. Not that I wanted the rioters protesting outside, but I couldn't believe that they had just given up. The odds were slim to none that they had decided to go quietly into the night. There had to be a connection with Gloria's housing-complex explosion and whatever Nicki was doing in the barn. I knew I was missing something, but I couldn't figure out what.

As the afternoon wore into the evening, volunteers trickled out. Every float except for Blomma's was complete and ready to roll out. A handful of volunteers agreed to stay late and help me finish hanging the violets. My fingers were raw with tiny cuts and sticky with sap when we wrapped the final strand around the base of the last tree. I climbed down from the scaffolding to survey the float. If I never had to use the sketchy ladder system again, that would be absolutely fine by me.

We gathered together and appraised our work. The float took my breath away. It felt like something from the pages of a fairy tale, with its towering forest landscape and wispy, iridescent violet vines. They shimmered like magical pixie dust from every handcrafted branch. I thanked the volunteers profusely for giving up their Friday night to help me finish. There was a sense of accomplishment and relief in the air.

I wanted to get into the warehouse, but Nicki ushered everyone out, claiming that the police had insisted the float barn be locked up by midnight. I wasn't sure I entirely believed her, but she escorted us to the parking lot and yanked the door shut behind her.

Oh well. I was exhausted. A hot cup of tea and a handful of Elin's cookies were calling my name. Before returning home I stopped by Blomma to get my things, and grabbed Gloria's scrapbooks too. I doubted that I would be able to sleep knowing that the parade was first thing in the morning, so I decided that I might as well keep looking for any clue that Portland's past parades might offer.

Elin called to check in on me. She had heard

about the explosion and gotten my message. I assured her that I was okay, and made her promise to enjoy her time with Eric. Once he returned to London, we would have plenty of time to hash out the last few days' events. I made sure to downplay how close I had been to the explosion, and tried to keep my tone upbeat.

After we hung up, I took a long, hot shower, then I made myself a strong pot of tea and returned to my search. Thankfully, Gloria had been meticulous in her organization of each year's Grand Floral Parade scrapbook. I went decade my decade, scrutinizing each photo and newspaper article for anything that might shed light on this year's debacle.

I was about to call it a night, when I flipped to a full-page feature story about Queen Priscilla. The article detailed Priscilla's coronation. It quoted some of Priscilla's classmates, and talked about her plans for studying design in college. There were grainy photos of Priscilla with her royal court, and then one with her date to the coronation. I almost dropped the scrapbook on the floor when I read the caption under the photo: *Queen Priscilla and her date, Steven Sham.*

Sham? Steven Sham?

I took a closer a look. Priscilla's date had a younger, clean-shaven face, and wore much less black, but he was unmistakably none other than Dark Fusion's slain leader—Sham.

Priscilla had dated Sham? I couldn't believe it. Why hadn't she said anything? She had acted like she didn't know him. That was an obvious lie.

Could she have killed him? But why? Maybe she

was so intent in maintaining her pristine appearance that she didn't want her past tainting her reputation? What would the princesses whom she was trying to mold into dignified young ladies think if they learned she had once dated an anarchist?

I tried to make sense of the photo. Were Priscilla's tears more than a response to spring allergies? Had she been heartbroken about Sham's death or had she been the culprit? I wasn't sure, but I knew that she was going to be the first person I found in the morning.

Chapter Twenty

Unfortunately, I didn't have a chance the next morning to speak with Priscilla. There was too much to do to get our float out of the float barn and rolling along Portland's streets. I momentarily forgot about Sham's murder and my suspicions that Priscilla could be connected, as I made my way through crowds of parade-goers pushing across the Hawthorne Bridge on their way to the parade route. I felt like a fish swimming upstream.

The weather gods had spared Portland from a soggy parade. Sun rained down on the Rose City. The atmosphere was electric. People chatted merrily as they toted blankets, picnic baskets, and pulled children in red wagons across the bridge. Police officers mixed in with the throngs of families, passing out shiny gold stickers cut in the shape of police badges and keeping a watchful eye on the festivities.

When I arrived at the float barn, the vibe was equally upbeat. Marching bands, cheerleaders, drill teams, clowns on unicycles, and stilt-walkers were packed in the parking lot, awaiting their marching orders. Juggling balls flew through the air. The sound of trombones warming up hit my ears. There was a heavy police presence here as well. Officers lined the waterfront pathway and had been positioned at every warehouse door.

Elin was waiting for me at the Blomma float. She wore one of our custom T-shirts, a black V-neck with our Blomma logo in the center. The logo, hand-sketched by Elin, was simple yet elegant. *Blomma* was written in a pale mint-green modern scroll, like a whimsical ivy vine. We had agreed to wear matching shirts for the parade. Mine was the same, only in cream instead of black.

"Darling, the float is a vision!" Elin greeted me with a firm hug and then kissed each cheek. "You've done a wonderful job. Simply wonderful."

"I wasn't sure it was going to come together until the last minute. Let's just hope the trees hold."

She looked up at our forestscape. "They'll hold. Not to worry."

We didn't have time to worry. Nicki shouted out commands on the bullhorn, running between float stalls to make sure everyone was ready to proceed to the route. We had the honor of hosting Oregon's most senior senator and congressional representative. Ted made grand introductions, bowing to both of them and gifting them with golden rose sabers. The politicians were humble and praised our float design.

Elin squeezed my hand as we climbed to our spot on the back of the float. Nerves welled in my stomach. It felt like a hundred bees were buzzing through my entire body. I was excited about finally having a chance to show off our hard work, but equally nervous about Dark Fusion's earlier threats of violence and disruption. Did having a senator and congressional representative make us a bigger target?

Relax, Britta, there are police everywhere. I clutched a handle carefully hidden under grapevines as the engine revved up and we slowly drove out of the float barn.

Sure enough, our trees didn't budge as we bumped over the gravel parking lot and turned onto Burnside, which led to the drawbridge that would take us over the Willamette. I felt my jaw drop as I took in the magnitude of spectators. People had crushed onto the sidewalks on either side of the open bridge. As far as my eye could see there were cheering mobs of happy Portlanders and visiting tourists.

Children screamed with delight as we tossed rose-shaped candies from the back of the float. People cheered and snapped photos of the Blomma float. Elin beamed with pride when we passed the grandstand, where Eric stood waving two miniature American flags. He was flanked on each side by Nora and Jon. In honor of the occasion, Nora had ditched her black leather for skintight red leather pants and a matching jacket. A band of red leather with sparkly rhinestones, tucked in her platinum hair, completed the look. Jon had opted for a more classic style—tailored black slacks and a burgundy button-down shirt.

Nora waved and hollered at us as we inched by. In hindsight I probably shouldn't have spent so much time worrying about the structure and whether our new design would hold. The parade was slow mov-

ing. We had to stop multiple times to allow the high
school marching band in front of us to finish an upbeat piece—"Louie Louie" on constant rotation—
and for the pooper-scoopers to sweep the streets. It
was a thrill to the see the blur of color in the crowd,
the happy mobs of people, and the expressions of
awe at our float.

"We love your violets!" a group of older women
wearing matching rose hats shouted. "You get our
vote for very best float!"

Elin beamed with pride. "I think they like it,
Britta."

"They love it," I replied, tossing a handful of candy
to three little girls dancing to the beat of "Louie
Louie."

The truth was, I loved every second of the parade, the jugglers on unicycles, the mounted horse
patrol with swags of roses draped from their sad-
dles, the sounds of tubas, the ethereal scent of flowers in the air. It was impossible not to get caught up
in the energy of our city coming together in celebration of all things floral. I felt like a kid again as I
grinned and waved with both hands. I didn't even
care that my arms were probably going to feel like
wet noodles tomorrow.

Priscilla stood at the helm of the queen's float,
three spots in front of us. Every once in a while, I
would catch a glimpse of her regal wave over the
marching band and the horses. I knew that we were
behind them from the trail of single-stemmed red
roses that the princesses were tossing to bystanders.
Beautiful, dainty, red, white, and pink petals littered
the streets like confetti.

Even if I had wanted to talk to Elin about what had happened last night, it would have been impossible over the sound of the bands and the clapping crowds. I pushed all thoughts of Sham's murder to the back of my head and smiled broader as we chugged down the streets.

The sun warmed my shoulders. My arms grew heavier and heavier, but I couldn't stop waving.

"This is a once in a lifetime, Britta! Soak in every moment," Elin said, tossing a piece of candy to a little girl in pigtails.

"I am!" I turned to face the other direction and my eyes landed on Pete Fletcher. He and Tomo were positioned at one of the barricades, making sure that traffic didn't interrupt the parade route. He caught my eye and winked. I felt the familiar tingle of a warm blush creep up my cheeks. Tomo didn't notice me. His jaw was tight. He methodically scanned one side of the block and then the other.

I knew they were keeping a careful eye out for any Dark Fusion action. Knowing that the police were out in force relieved some of my anxiety. Thus far there had been no sign of the militant group. I hadn't seen a single black mask or the sound of any protests. Maybe Sham's death had put an end to their attempt to disrupt the parade, or maybe the sheer number of officers patrolling the streets had kept them in check. Had all my worry and fear been for nothing? It seemed strange that the anarchists had opted to disappear, but thank goodness for small miracles.

When we finally made it back to the float barn at the end of the parade route, I heaved a sigh of relief. We had done it. We had successfully completed our first float, and the parade had been without any drama. Thank goodness.

Ted leapt onto a stack of pallets. "Attention, attention, everyone, please gather round. We are going to crown some winners in just a moment." He held a bullhorn with one hand and directed Nicki, who was arranging gold trophies in the shape of a bouquet of roses on a folding table next to him, with the other. "If I can have the float designers gather here in front of me," Ted continued, motioning for Elin and me to come forward.

We made our way to the front. A flutter of nerves danced in my stomach. It didn't matter if Blomma won an award. I was content with the fact that we had a float in the parade, but winning any award would be great for the shop. I wanted it for Elin.

"Ladies and gentlemen, first and foremost, let me congratulate you on a successful Rose Festival." Ted applauded us. "As you know, this was a challenging and trying festival, but because of you, Portland bloomed like a beautiful rose this morning. Without your hard work and tireless effort there wouldn't have been a parade." He paused and clutched his heart for dramatic effect. "This is why we do what we do, for the love of our Rose City. I made it my personal mission to see that Dark Fusion didn't rain on our parade."

What did that mean? I watched Nicki shoot Ted a look of disgust and roll her eyes. A handful of people cheered.

Ted encouraged them. "That's right. Feel free to celebrate that! No anarchist group is going to rain on us. Now, I can't take credit for Mother Nature, but I will tell you I put in a special request for a rain-free Saturday and she heard my prayers. What a morning! What a parade!"

Everyone clapped and cheered. Something about Ted's smug smile made my stomach flutter again. Had he just admitted that he had killed Sham to ensure his precious parade would go on as planned?

"On to the good stuff." Ted nodded to Nicki. She handed him the first golden trophy. "We've tallied the judge's votes as well as the ballots from the people's choice, and I must say that this is one of the tightest competitions we've seen in recent years. The overall winner received two—that's right, *two*—more votes than second place. What that tells me is that we had some stellar floats and designs this year."

Elin crossed her fingers.

"Our first awards go to craftsmanship, depiction of whimsy, and life in Oregon." Ted waited while Nicki handed him two more trophies. "This year's craftsmanship award goes to the team from the credit union with their elaborate and frankly slightly terrifying dragon!"

We hugged our fellow designers before they went to retrieve their award. I wasn't surprised that our neighboring float had won. Their dragon with its twelve-foot body and six-foot flames had definitely been a structural feat. Ted went on to name two more designers. I clapped enthusiastically along with the crowd.

Nicki removed the award for most outstanding. Ted posed for pictures with the winners. I could feel the anticipation building. He cleared his throat. "And now, the moment you've all been waiting for.

The awards for most outstanding and people's choice. We have a unique situation this year. This has only happened three times since I've been the grand marshal of the Grand Floral Parade. The winner for most outstanding and people's choice is one in the same."

I could tell that he was enjoying dragging out the process of revealing the winners.

"This year the winner of the people's choice and most outstanding is . . ."

The float barn went silent. I realized that my palms were sweaty. *You're being silly, Britta.* I brushed my hands on my skirt.

"Blomma!" Ted boomed.

Elin squealed. She threw her arms around me. "Did he say Blomma? Am I hearing that right?"

"He said Blomma." I pointed to Ted, who was waving for Elin to join him on the makeshift stage. "We won. Get up there." I nudged her toward the pallets. She looked genuinely shocked and humbled as Ted handed her not one but two golden trophies. No one deserved this level of recognition more than my aunt. Happy tears welled in my eyes as I watched her pose with Ted, and then immediately get swept up in celebratory hugs by the room of highly skilled designers. Winning both awards was the ultimate form of praise. Our peers and the public had bestowed the parade's highest honor on Blomma. I couldn't believe it.

Ted finished his presentation with a final bow. "Let me once again impart my thanks for making this a fantastic year. I know I'll see some of you at the dignitaries' dinner later this evening, and I hope you'll consider helping with the teardown process tonight. It's always quite a hoot. Some of you may have heard that this is my final parade. I'm hanging up my gardening shears and handing over my cape. It's been a great pleasure serving you and the Rose City."

A murmur went through the crowd.

"Please, please, no applause. I do this for you." Ted gave his cape a flourish. "Now let's break out the champagne."

The float barn was raucous. It felt like the locker room after a Super Bowl victory. Volunteers and designers who had worked countless hours preparing for the parade cracked open bottles of champagne and sparkling cider. People congratulated us and the other winners. I felt like I was floating in a rose-scented dream. Elin and I posed for pictures in front of the floats, which would be dismantled within the next few days. We toasted with glasses of bubbly.

Eric arrived with an overflowing bouquet of Deep Secret roses for Elin. I knew the dark-chocolatey rose was their special flower. "Rumor has it that I'm in the presence of winners." He offered her the bouquet. "I hope you'll let a non-flower guy like me hang around."

Elin cradled the roses. "Can you believe that we won? I'm in shock. I didn't see it coming."

Eric rolled his eyes. "Can I believe that you won? Of course." He gave Elin a look as if to say *Could there be any other outcome?* and then pulled a sweet bouquet of Stargazer lilies from behind his back. "For you, Britta."

"Thank you. That was thoughtful."

He winked. "It's a bribe. Now that you two have

been crowned the rose queens of Portland, I've got to find a way to stay relevant."

"I don't think that will be a problem." I nodded to my aunt, who planted a kiss on his cheek. I left them as everyone gathered around to be introduced to her paramour.

My thoughts returned to Priscilla. Overnight I had formed a new theory. What if Priscilla knew about the article? She must have remembered Gloria from years past. If she didn't want anyone to learn that Sham was her ex-boyfriend, had she killed him and then attempted to kill Gloria in order to keep it quiet? Sure, in some ways it sounded far-fetched that a well-respected businesswoman would go to such extremes, but then again, I had seen how intense Priscilla was about reputation.

I tucked Eric's gift of lilies in a bucket of water in the pigpen. He had chosen glorious stems that had obviously been arranged by a master floral designer. Lilies are one of the most fragrant flowers and can add height and drama to a bouquet. However, they produce a sticky yellow pollen on their anthers that can get everywhere. There's nothing worse than setting a lovely centerpiece on a dining room table, only to have everything coated in pollen dust. Whoever had created this bouquet had gently removed and discarded the anthers while keeping the delicate pink-and-white petals intact. Eric scored bonus points for purchasing artisan flowers rather than grabbing a stale, lifeless arrangement at the grocery store.

Next I went in search of Priscilla. I found her talking with a local reporter. She looked the part of a queen in her sparkling white ball gown that was darted in at her narrow waist and layered with fine tulle. Red rose-shaped rhinestones had been glued onto the tulle, making the dress shimmer with every movement. She wore yet another tiara and a silky red queen's sash. "This is the crème-de-la-crème of princesses," she said, holding a glass of champagne. "I was thrilled to be a part of this year's parade, and help instruct them on their very bright futures."

The reporter took notes. Priscilla sipped her drink with her pinky in the air.

When they finished the interview, I took the chance to confront her.

"Priscilla, do you have a minute?" I asked.

She snapped her head in my direction. "Sorry. I'm simply swamped with press interviews."

"It's about Sham."

A momentary flash of concern made the tiny creases around her eyes twitch. "What about him?"

I stepped closer. "I know about your history. You two used to date, didn't you?"

Priscilla's face went as white as the layers of tulle on her dress. She glanced around us. "Not here. Let's go outside." She handed her champagne glass to one of the princesses and made a beeline for the exit.

I practically had to sprint to catch up to her.

She stopped near the edge of the pathway. "How did you figure that out?" She fiddled with her sash, not meeting my eyes.

"I found an old article from the newspaper. It wasn't that hard."

Priscilla frowned. "Why were you looking at old papers?"

I didn't want to put Gloria in harm's way, so I lied. "For our display at Blomma. We were going to do a Rose Festival bouquet from each decade for our front window. I was looking at past years for inspiration."

She seemed to buy my story.

"You didn't want anyone to know, did you?" I paused for a moment. How smart was it to confront Priscilla? *If you're going to do it, this is the place, Britta.* There were people milling all around us. What could she do? Toss me off the side of the ledge, down into the Willamette? *Maybe.*

I pretended to pick a leaf from an oak tree and moved away from the edge of the path. "If people learned that you and Sham used to date, it would ruin your reputation, and you couldn't let that happen, could you?"

Priscilla started at me. "What?"

A clown wearing giant boat shoes and a floppy hat sped past us on a unicycle. High school cheerleaders danced in the parking lot and tossed their pom-poms around. Dignitaries and the princesses posed for pictures with fans, as more and more of the parade participants returned to the float barn.

"You killed him, didn't you?" I had found my stride and wasn't about to stop now.

"What?" She looked dumbfounded. "No. What are you talking about?"

"Sham, you killed him. I've heard how uptight you are about personal reputation with the princesses. Dating an anarchist certainly would damage your perfect reputation. If people found out that your high school boyfriend was an anarchist, that wouldn't look good for you or for Juvenescent, would it?"

To my surprise, huge tears welled in her eyes. She started to sob. I wasn't sure what to do.

After a few minutes, she gathered herself, and reached into her bosom and pulled out a tissue. "You have it all wrong. I loved Sham."

Now it was my turn to look dumbfounded.

"Not anymore, of course. I'm happily married," she continued. "I'm quite content with my SoCal lifestyle, and you're right, I have been trying to impart the importance of protecting your image and reputation with the princesses, but not because I was worried about my past. Because they're growing up in a digital era, and I've seen how quickly you can ruin your future by sending an inappropriate text. These girls are dealing with a brave new world of technology that comes with wonderful rewards and long-term consequences. I've been trying to explain to them how important it is to craft the right kind of appearance online. As in not texting naked pictures or posting drunk pictures on their social media."

She sounded sincere.

"In fact, Sham and I met for a drink the night before he was killed and were reminiscing about some of the crazy adventures we had had together and how lucky we were that social media didn't exist back then. That's what I've been telling the girls. We all make stupid mistakes and do stupid things in our youth. That's part of growing up, but I've been reminding them that their digital footprint lives forever. If they document their mistakes it could impact their ability to get into college or secure jobs in the future."

She had a valid point.

Her eyes misted. "Sham and I had amazing years together back in the day. We were just kids when we dated. Seeing him again brought back many memories from my youth. Happy memories. My husband knows about Sham. I have nothing to hide. I promise you that he was a link to my past. I would never have killed him, and yes, I care about Juvenescent and my reputation as a businesswoman, but the fact that my high school boyfriend lived an alternate lifestyle certainly wouldn't impact sales of our skin care line."

That was yet another valid point.

"When Sham and I met the other night, he shared that he had some serious regrets about the direction that Dark Fusion has taken. When he started the group years ago, it was a way to give voice to under-represented populations in the city. Sham didn't like big money or corporations, but he wasn't violent."

"Really. What else did he say?"

"Not much. He said he had a plan to make big changes. He was going to meet with Gloria and Nicki. He said something about the truth coming out."

"What does that mean?"

Priscilla shrugged. "I wish I knew. He was killed the next morning." She started to tear up again. She glanced at the expensive watch on her wrist. "I need to go. I'm due to take the princesses to brunch."

She returned to the float barn, fluffy layers of her dress trailing behind her. I stood near the pathway in stunned silence. I had been so sure that Priscilla was the killer, but she sounded genuinely upset about Sham's death. Why was Sham meeting with

Gloria and Nicki? And what did he mean that the truth would come out? I massaged my temples. There was a chance that Priscilla was lying to protect herself, but I was fairly confident she was being honest. Now more than ever, I had to talk to Gloria. She seemed to be the key to the case. I just hoped that she was recovering and able to have visitors.

Chapter Twenty-one

As soon as I could find a clear path through the celebratory crowds, I hoofed it to Blomma and wrapped a cluster of daisies in butcher paper, tied them with twine, and tucked them under my arm. Then I went straight to the sky tram. Now that the smoke had cleared, the aerial view of the blast-zone damage took my breath away. I placed my hand on my stomach as I thought about the displaced families, sorting through the charred remains of what had once been a quaint collection of cottages. Poor Gloria.

This time the receptionist at the nurses' station allowed me to see Gloria. I tapped quietly on her door.

A weak voice answered, "Come in."

"Gloria, how are you?" I entered the room to find her tucked under the covers in the hospital bed. Her skin was ashen. She looked frail and small. "These are for you." I set the daisies on her nightstand and sat in a plush chair next to the bed.

"They're lovely." She managed to give me a faint smile.

"Tell me what happened. Were you injured?"

Her eyes were dull. "No. I had made a pot of tea and curled up with a mystery when I began smelling gas. I thought I had left the stove on, but when I went to check, it was off. The smell of gas knocked me off my feet. I don't know what happened, but the next thing I remember I woke up here."

I could tell from the way she kept wincing that it was hard to speak.

"Are you in pain? Is there anything I can get you?"

She shook her head. "No. It's hard to find my breath. The police said that the gas line attached to my cottage had been rerouted into my kitchen. If one of the neighbors hadn't called 911, I wouldn't be here."

I reached for her hand. It was clammy and cool to the touch. "I'm so glad they got you out."

Her curly white hair was tousled, her hospital gown wrinkled. I wondered how much sleep, if any, she had gotten since being admitted. "Who would do such a thing, Britta? I've never had an enemy. I'm a little old lady who loves flowers."

"I don't know, but I know that the police are working every angle. There has to be a connection with Dark Fusion." I paused while Gloria shifted position in the bed. "Thank you for loaning me your scrapbooks. I might have found something in them. Did you know that Priscilla and Sham dated in high school?"

Gloria's glossy eyes widened. "Queen Priscilla?"

"Yeah. Can you believe it? I found a newspaper article. He was her date to the coronation."

"I had no idea they were high school sweethearts, but now that you mention it, there was something slightly familiar about Sham, but I never put two and two together." Gloria tried to reach for a water cup.

"Here, let me get that." I handed her the cup, and tilted the straw so it would be easier for her to drink. "I asked Priscilla about it after the parade this morning, and she told me that she had a special place in her heart for him."

"Oh, the parade." Gloria clutched her chest. "Please tell me about it. This is the first parade I've missed in thirty years."

I wanted to ask her about the meeting she and Nicki had had with Sham, but I couldn't deny her request. She listened with rapture, asking for every detail about the processional, weather, and crowds.

"It sounds wonderful," she said with a wheeze that sent her into a coughing fit. She hacked so hard it made my chest hurt.

"Should I call the nurse?"

She waved me off. "Give me a minute." Her voice quaked. "The doctor said this would happen for a while. They're sending me to a respiratory therapist later."

I felt terrible for her. "I should let you rest."

She reached for my arm. "No. There's something you should know."

I waited for her to clear her throat.

"It's about Sham. He wasn't what everyone thought he was. Now that I think about it, it makes sense that he and Priscilla knew each other years ago. He came to Nicki and me and asked for our help in a secret mission."

A secret mission? I scooted my chair closer.

Gloria coughed again. "Sham didn't like the direction that Dark Fusion had taken. When he started the group twenty years ago, his intention was to protest archaic government policies and give voice to the people, but over the last few years the group has taken a dark shift. Sham didn't want to hit small businesses or cancel family parades. That wasn't his mission."

Her words were exactly in line with what Priscilla had told me.

I waited while Gloria inhaled deeply through her nose three times, trying to maintain control of her breath. "Sham went to Ted first, but Ted refused to listen. That man can be so stubborn. Both Nicki and I tried to reason with him, but he's had it in for Sham and has blinders on." She pointed to her empty cup. "Can you give me some more water?"

"Of course." I grabbed the cup and walked over to the sink to refill it.

Gloria sipped the water. "Since Ted wouldn't listen, Sham came up with his own plan. He wrote up a contract with a promise that Dark Fusion would not block the parade. He and Nicki and I have been working on a secret float. It was meant as a peace offering. He gave the contract to Nicki and asked her to share it with Ted, because he knew that Ted would rip it up without looking at it if he tried to give it to him."

"A secret float?"

"Yes. On the morning of the parade, Sham and

the members he could rally to join his side were going to join in the procession on a float of dark flowers. It's quite stunning. If you reach into my purse, I'll show you photos."

"Is that what's hidden on the other side of the float barn?" I asked.

Gloria nodded. "Yes, Nicki told Sham that he could use that area since no one other than the carnival staff had access to it. Sham was very dedicated and a good designer." She motioned to her purse.

I found her phone. Gloria scrolled through her photos until she found the ones she was looking for. "Here."

I couldn't believe my eyes. The Dark Fusion float was incredible. It reminded me of something from the pages of *The Great Gatsby*. Decadent black dahlias and deep crimson roses shrouded the float in a gorgeous somber depth. Intermixed amongst the dark flowers were white orchids, cabbage blossoms, silver eucalyptus, and white anemones. The float was elegant and unlike anything I'd ever seen.

Of course, the dahlias! That's why Nicki had been hiding them. I couldn't believe they had been right in front of me and I hadn't pieced it together.

"Stunning, isn't it?" Gloria gave me a knowing smile.

"It's amazing. I can't believe Sham did this."

"Yeah. He funded the float with his own money. He did it all without the help of a major corporate sponsor or volunteers. Well, he and Nicki. They've been working until five or six o'clock every morning. They would get started after midnight. I helped some, but I can't pull all-nighters any longer. Nicki was a workhorse. She refused to give up. She worked her fingers to the bone every night. I doubt that she's slept in weeks."

No wonder Nicki had been so on edge and short-tempered. She had been functioning on no sleep. I flashed back to a vision of her covered in flower materials. That's why she had been sneaking into the warehouse. She wasn't building a bomb, she had been building a peace offering in the form of a float. I felt terrible for doubting her.

"The float wasn't part of the parade this morning." I handed Gloria her phone. What a shame that Portland didn't get to experience such an artistic twist on the theme of darkness. I wondered why Nicki hadn't included it.

Gloria struggled to catch her breath, holding a finger in the air.

"Let me call the nurse."

Gloria's face turned a scary shade of blue. She wheezed. "One minute."

I kept my hand close to the emergency call button.

Finally, Gloria cleared her throat. "I asked Zigs about that after Sham died. I told him that the secret float was almost ready and asked if any of his guys wanted to come finish it. He said he had an even better idea planned. An idea to honor Sham. He wanted to meet in private to talk about it. He was supposed to stop by my apartment last night, but then the gas leak happened."

My heart skipped a beat. "Zigs was going to meet you at your apartment?"

Gloria nodded.

Fear pulsed through my veins. I stood up. "Gloria, I need to go find the police. Are you going to be okay?"

She drank more water. "Yes. I'm fine. Thank you for stopping by, Britta. Your visit and flowers brightened an otherwise sad morning."

I squeezed her hand and left. I didn't want to scare her, but I was pretty sure I knew who had killed Sham and tried to kill her.

Chapter Twenty-two

Once outside Gloria's hospital room, I called Pete and Tomo. Neither answered. I left them messages, explaining my theory and telling them to meet me at the float barn ASAP. A sense of panic pulsed through my body.

I sprinted to the tram. It had to be Zigs. Why hadn't I figured it out earlier?

Of course. Everything made sense. Sham wasn't violent. Zigs was. I thought back to their interactions. I had wrongly assumed that they were working together to bring mayhem and destruction to Portland's idyllic parade, but it was the opposite. Sham had been trying to change the tone. To quell the violence. To shift Dark Fusion's mission. He probably would have succeeded if he had appeared on the stunning dark float this morning. I felt even worse, knowing that he had been suffering in silence, unable to right his past wrongs. No one had believed him—Ted. Me.

I sighed and clenched the cold metallic handrail as I rode the sky tram back to the waterfront. Staring out over the burnt block, I wanted to kick myself for how much I had missed. I thought back through every interaction I had witnessed with Sham and Zigs. I had wrongly assumed that they were cohorts. But I'd been mistaken. Sham had been trying to rein Zigs in, while Zigs had been staging an internal coup.

If Gloria hadn't mentioned anything about the secret float, she never would have been put in harm's way. Zigs must have realized that she knew too much. If he could keep her quiet, Sham was already dead. There was just one more person in the way—Nicki.

To think that she had been one of my suspects, and all along she had been working with Sham on a wonderful display of solidarity and blooms. She was in danger. I had to get to the float barn fast.

The Dark Fusion float was a thorn in Zigs's side. Both Nicki and Gloria knew the truth behind it. Zigs couldn't let that come to light. He had the strength to kill Sham, and now he had a motive.

If only Ted would have listened. Maybe Sham wouldn't have been killed. He certainly wouldn't have had to construct his float in secret. If only I had pressed Nicki harder. I shouldn't have run away that day when she caught me in the warehouse. I could have helped.

When I arrived at the float barn, the parking lot was deserted. A strange, cold vibe fell over the empty space. The volunteers, princesses, Royal Rosarians, and designers had left for brunch and afternoon high tea. Later tonight the decorators and a new group of volunteers would arrive to begin the process of dismantling the floats. We would process and arrange flowers harvested from each float. From there we would create bright bouquets that would be delivered to local hospitals and senior care centers.

For the moment an eerie calm fell over the parking lot. Elin had often talked about trusting her instincts when it came to floral design and life in general. My instincts were telling me to run. Something was wrong.

Yet, I continued on.

Britta, leave, my internal voice commanded, but my feet moved toward the front door as if being guided by a puppeteer.

Where was Nicki? Had she left with the others? I doubted it. She had been so committed to running a tight ship that, if I had to bet, I would guess that she was probably already organizing plans for disassembling the floats.

My inner voice screamed not to go inside. What if Zigs was here?

There was no time to spare. He had killed once, and almost succeed twice. I couldn't wait for Tomo or Pete.

I pushed open the front door. "Nicki? Are you here?"

My voice echoed back to me.

I glanced around the float barn. It looked like the morning after Mardi Gras. Debris in the form of flowers, candy, and confetti covered the cement floor. Volunteers had left scarves and raincoats.

Floats had been returned to their stalls, but many of them already had pieces missing. Probably souvenirs taken by volunteers.

"Nicki!" I called again. "It's Britta. I wanted to make sure that you're okay."

Nothing but dead silence greeted me.

I continued on, past the Blomma float. Our grapevine trees still stood sturdy and tall. I needed to do the same.

You can do this, Britta. I hoped that my positive self-talk would quench the tremors in my fingers.

I made it to the door to the attached warehouse. If Zigs had cornered Nicki, this was the most likely spot. I gathered as much courage as I could muster, and opened the door.

The second I saw what was happening inside I wished I hadn't. Unfortunately, my gut feeling had been dead-on. I recognized Zigs's wiry frame and mohawk. He held Nicki at knifepoint. He was tying her hands onto the Dark Fusion float. A gas can and lighter sat at his feet.

"Hey! What are you doing?" I hoped that I had the element of surprise on my side.

Zigs didn't flinch. "About to blow up this piece of crap float."

Nicki caught my eye and shook her head. Her eyes were wild with fear. "Zigs, you don't need to do this. You have nothing to prove."

"Nothing to prove. Ha!" His tone was laced with bitterness. It sent a wave of nausea through me. "Sham wanted to play nice. Kept telling us that violence wasn't going to get us anywhere. Yeah, right. What did his little kindergarten milk-and-cookies meetings get us? Nothing."

I had to get us out of here, but how? Should I make a break for it and risk him coming after me? Or should I confront him? I glanced around for anything I could use as a weapon.

Zigs's voice grew more intense. "Wanted to meet with the mayor. Wanted to make a pretty little float." He yanked off a handful of black roses and threw them at Nicki.

She tried to duck.

"That's right. How does that feel? You wanna play nice? You wanna sit down and have a cup of tea? Well, screw you and your rose parade. What a joke. A freaking joke!"

I stepped closer, careful to keep an eye on Zigs. He was in a focused rage, and Nicki was taking the brunt of his barrage.

"You and your pretty flowers and your roses, you want to dance down the streets." His voice had changed into a sarcastic singsong tone. It gave me the creeps. The man was clearly unstable.

With Nicki bound to the float, he reached down for the gas can. "Sham was out of touch. This is a new century, and the government is coming down."

He opened the gas can and doused the base of the float. The smell of fumes was too familiar. How could I distract him? Where were Pete and Tomo? If I didn't think of something, or if they didn't show up soon, Zigs was going to light the float on fire.

I moved toward a wooden crate labeled DUCK HUNT. I knew that carnival game didn't use real guns, but maybe I could fool Zigs. Thus far he had barely acknowledged my presence. Maybe he had forgotten about me in his blind rage.

He poured gasoline on the showpiece black and

red flowers. White orchids drooped under the weight of the toxic liquid. "Sham was a dreamer. No one was going to take him seriously. If you want respect, you command respect. And you know how you do that?"

Nicki shook her head.

Zigs made a fist with his free hand. "With this."

I inched toward the crate as Zigs went around to coat the other side of the float with gasoline. The smell made my eyes burn.

"Bet you thought your little parade was awesome this morning. Well guess what? It wasn't. You think you dodged a bullet? You didn't. We let you think that, but we have something bigger—much, much bigger—planned. It's going to send a message. A loud—LOUD—message." Zigs laughed.

What was he talking about? I didn't like the sound of it. I had to get into the crate. I ran my hand along the wood until I found the opening. I fumbled inside. My hand landed on a rubber duckie and something rough.

Zigs was rounding the front of the float. In a minute he would be directly across from me. I had to hurry. I tossed rubber ducks to the side and finally felt the barrel of a kid's plastic shotgun. I pulled it from the crate and held it out in front of me. "Stop, or I'll shoot."

"Go for it." Zigs tossed the empty gas can on the floor and stormed toward me. "Go ahead. Shoot." He held both arms up in the air.

I planted my feet and firmed my position. "I'm serious. I'll shoot."

He threw his head back and laughed. "With a toy gun. Nice try."

Was it that obvious? I mouthed "Sorry" to Nicki. She motioned to Zigs. What was she trying to tell me? In a flash he pulled his knife from his back pocket and lunged at me. Then he grabbed my wrist so tight I thought it might snap in half.

"Ouch." I tried to dig my heels into the floor but couldn't get any traction.

"Stop fightin' it." He dragged me through the gas. "What? Aw, did you think you were going to get out of here? How nice. Right! As if I would let that happen. You two little rose princesses can go up in flames together. That will add fire to tomorrow's headline."

He was strong. The tip of the knife pierced my neck as he pushed me onto the float. "That's right. Get up there with your little friend. You can be boom buddies. Yeah, you heard me right—boom, as in *kapow*!"

With surprising agility, he tied my hands behind my back and jumped off the float.

"He's out of his mind," Nicki whispered.

"How long were you here before I arrived?" I spoke in a hushed tone.

"Not long."

I'd lost track of time. How long had it been since I called Pete and Tomo? They must have gotten my messages by now. Surely one of them—or hopefully an entire police squadron—were on their way.

Zigs tugged a phone from his black cargo pants. "Smile pretty for the camera. You're going to be in the Dark Fusion hall of fame. Or should I say, hall of *flame*?" He laughed again and snapped a couple pictures.

I thought I might throw up. A woozy feeling assaulted my body.

"Any last words, before I light you up?" Zigs flicked a lighter. "Make it quick if you do, because we've got bigger things about to blow, if you catch my drift."

These might be my last breaths. I should have been sending out love to Elin, but instead I was terrified by his veiled words. What had he done? If I was going to die anyway, there wasn't any risk in asking.

"I don't catch your drift. You're starting a fire somewhere?"

"Ha! A fire. Yeah, right. Dark Fusion is putting our mark on this city—on this messed-up country—with the biggest blast ever recorded. Too bad you won't be around to see it. This place is going to blow, and then the real fun is going to begin." With that he flicked the lighter again and tossed it on the float.

Chapter Twenty-three

The next few minutes (or was it hours?) passed in a flame-infused blur. Heat seared as fire erupted around us. Nicki screamed, "We're going to die!"

I didn't disagree with her, but panicking wasn't going to help.

"Help!" Her voice pierced through my ear. "HELP!"

Zigs lit the other side of the float. Then he sprinted toward the door and flipped off the lights. "Burn in hell, girls. Burn in hell."

The flames grew around us. I couldn't tell if he was gone.

It was getting hot. Really hot.

Sweat poured from my forehead and dripped down my back.

Think, Britta.

I tugged at the ropes Zigs had used to tie me to the float. Rough twine cut into my wrists.

If only I had a pair of my garden shears, I could

make quick work of the rope. Instead I wriggled and yanked my wrists as hard as I could.

"What are you doing?" Nicki wailed.

"Trying to loosen the rope."

She snapped out of her frantic screams and began yanking her arms with so much force that the entire float lurched forward and back in rhythm with her body.

"It's not working," she cried.

I gave up. "I know."

The flames crackled, shooting embers into the air. They were creeping close to the float. A few more inches and we would be engulfed in fire. I had a feeling the float would go up in flames quickly. It was made of highly combustible organic material.

My skin burned from the heat.

"I can't breathe," Nicki coughed.

"Try not to panic."

"Panic! We're about to be torched. Of course I'm panicking. You should be panicking!"

Arguing with her was futile. I tried a new tactic. "Can you reach my hands?" I leaned as far forward as I could, bringing my face within in few feet of the flames.

"What?"

"My hands. Can you reach them?"

She calmed slightly. Then tried to wiggle her body next to mine. "It's too tight. I don't think I can get them."

"Fine. Switch." I leaned back.

"It's so hot," she yelled as she bent her body forward.

"I know." I inched forward as much as my bonds would allow me. It was a good thing I had inherited my mother's Swedish bone structure. I'd never been more thankful for my long, thin fingers.

Nicki's knots started to loosen. I fumbled in the darkness, desperate to free one of us.

"I think it's working. Try and pull your hand out," I commanded.

Nicki broke out into a coughing fit. The smoke was thickening all around us. We didn't have much time. If the flames didn't get us first the smoke would.

"I can't get it," Nicki choked out between coughs.

"Here, let me try again." It felt like someone was stabbing my fingers as I stretched them to their limit trying to loosen the ropes.

Nicki yanked her wrist. "It's still stuck. I think I'm going to pass out."

"No! Stay with me. We're going to get out of this. They're almost free." I wasn't sure where my confidence was coming from. Was this what people who reported "out of body experiences" felt like? I could hear the authoritative tone to my voice, but it sounded like it was coming from miles away.

"Okay." Nicki tried to clear her throat, which sent her into another coughing fit. The acrid air made me cough as well.

The flames were so close now they were lapping at the base of the float. We had to get out of here—now.

I didn't care if I dislocated a finger, I bent my index finger in a way that I didn't know it could bend, and tugged on the knot.

It came free. *Thank God!*

"I got it!"

Nicki gave her arm a ferocious tug and nearly

toppled into the fire. If her other arm hadn't been tied to the float, she surely would have landed in the fire.

"Okay, now what? What do I do?" Her eyes were wild. I could see the orange, yellow, and red glow in them. "What do I do, Britta? What do I do?"

"Relax. Use your free hand to untie your other arm."

She twisted around. "I can't. I can't reach it. I'm still stuck!"

"It's okay. You're fine. Try my hand." A blast of heat assaulted me as I moved toward the fire again. The flames were creeping close to our feet. I could feel the heat penetrating through the base of the float. Were my shoes about to melt?

Nicki's hand shook as she started to untie me. "Why can't I do this?"

"You can. Just focus." I could hear the urgency in my voice. We were out of time.

Her nail dug into my wrist.

I wanted to yelp in pain, but instead bit my lip. She was close. I could feel a hint of slack in the rope. After a few seconds, I wiggled my wrist free. Then I reached over and untied her other hand and waited while she freed me.

"Now what? The fire is all around us."

It was true. Flames over two-feet high burst in every direction. It was as if we were on a deserted island, only instead of being surrounded by cool blue waters, we were being consumed by hot, deadly flames.

Oh, what I wouldn't give for an ice-cold glass of water right now, I thought, licking my lips.

It was too late.

"We could jump." I didn't like the thought even as the words fell from my mouth, but what other choice did we have?

"Jump? Where?" Nicki waved in front of us. "The flames are four feet high. We can't make it."

"We don't have any other options." I tried to wave smoke from my face.

Nicki sputtered. "But . . . we'll catch on fire."

"Probably." My lungs ached. "It's our only chance. We jump together. The second we land, we roll. Isn't that what they taught us in school? Stop, drop, and roll?"

"But . . ." Nicki began to cough again.

"We have to do this." I grabbed her arm. There was no time to think. We had to act. This was our only shot. The fire was consuming everything in its path. "With me on three. Ready?"

She nodded but couldn't speak.

"One, two . . ." I was about to say three when the door burst open.

Someone was dousing the flames with water, or was it a fire extinguisher? There was too much smoke to tell.

"Portland Fire and Rescue!" a voice called. "Is anyone in here?"

Nicki went limp in my arms.

"Here! Here! We're on the float!" I yelled, trying to keep Nicki upright.

A voice called out a command and suddenly the large bay door opened. A huge spray of water showered down on me. Plumes of white smoke and steam made it impossible to see. I was damp. No, I was soaked. Water, or was it sweat, dripped onto my feet. In a flash a set of strong arms lifted Nicki off the float. Then another returned for me.

"Medic. We need a medic," a muffled voice called, just as everything went dark.

Chapter Twenty-four

The next thing I remembered was waking up in a hospital room. Aunt Elin was seated across from me. I blinked twice to make sense of where I was. My eyes felt as if they had been washed with sandpaper. I started to sit up and immediately fell back onto the bed.

"Britta, take it easy." Elin scooted her chair closer and wrapped her hand over mine.

Why did it feel like my lungs had also been scrubbed with a pumice stone? "Elin—" I couldn't catch enough air to speak.

"Take a minute. Just breathe. You took in a lot of smoke. The doctors said that you'll be just fine, but you're going to have to take it really slow and easy."

My breath sounded raspy and wheezy. "What happened?" I managed to squeak out.

"You were in a fire. Do you remember?"

I closed my eyes. It all came flashing back. Zigs, the gas can, the flames. I shuddered. "Yeah."

My chest felt like it was being weighted down with a basket of heavy gourds. Everything in the room looked like it was in soft focus. Was my vision blurry, or was I dreaming?

Elin squeezed my arm. "You gave me quite a scare. Eric rushed me here the minute I got the call. I can't imagine what would have happened if the firefighters hadn't arrived when they did. They said you were very lucky. Even a few more minutes of smoke inhalation could have been deadly."

My thoughts flashed to Nicki. "What about Nicki? Is she okay?"

"Yes. She's in worse shape than you, but they think that she'll make it through."

That was a relief.

I sat up a bit. Pain seared through my chest. My head throbbed.

"Britta, are you okay?" Elin looked concerned.

"I'm okay." I coughed. "Everything just feels tight."

"The doctor said that's normal. You breathed in soot. He said that you might have a headache and feel nauseous for a little while."

Check to both, I thought, positioning myself in the adjustable bed. "What about Zigs? Did they get him?"

Elin gave me a blank stare. "Zigs?"

"Oh no! Where's my phone? I have to call Pete right now."

"The doctor wants you to rest and said you should be talking as little as possible."

"Elin, I have to talk to Pete. You don't understand, the entire city might be in danger."

She looked at me as if I were speaking in a foreign language. "*Lilla gumman,* Britta, my dearest, what are you talking about?" She twisted the silky pale-green scarf that was tied around her neck and matched our Blomma logo on her T-shirt.

"Please. My phone."

She frowned, but she stood and walked to the opposite side of the bed. A strange wave of déjà vu washed over me. I had recently been in the same hospital room checking on Gloria. Now I was the patient.

Elin handed me the phone. "Be quick. You don't want to overdo it."

I nodded and called Pete. He didn't answer. I coughed out a weak message explaining that Zigs had set the fire and that he had hinted that he had something much bigger planned. When I shut off the phone, Elin's eyes were wide with worry.

"Is it true?" She tucked her hair behind her ears, revealing a sweet pair of hummingbird earrings.

"Yes. I know that Dark Fusion is planning to blow something up. The only thing is *what?*"

Elin thought for a moment. "The dinner for the visiting dignitaries. It's in less than two hours." She looked at her watch. "Britta, I'm supposed to deliver flowers to the Riverplace Inn. Our friends. They could be in danger?"

"Yes." Why didn't I think about it sooner? The dignitaries' dinner was Rose Festival's most elegant event. Visiting leaders and ambassadors from around the world would be in attendance at tonight's gala. If Dark Fusion had planted a bomb at the Riverplace Inn, not only would Portland be in danger, but so would distinguished heads of state. Zigs's words chanted in my head with new meaning. Suddenly I understood what kind of a statement he intended to make.

"I should go warn them." Elin hesitated.

"Go, yes. Go warn everyone in Riverplace Village. I'll call Pete again and Tomo."

"Are you sure you'll be okay?" Elin stood.

"I'm fine." It was true. I had new resolve and a mission. Zigs wasn't going to get away with harming anyone else or damaging my beloved Riverplace Village.

She kissed my forehead. "Call me with any news."

"You too."

With that she was out the door. I called Tomo. He didn't answer either. I left him a detailed message with my theory on Zigs's plans, then I hung up, called Pete, and left a similar message for him.

There was no way I was going to stay in the hospital while my friends were in danger. I had breathed in too much smoke. It wasn't like I had lost a limb.

I had to get out of there. I climbed out of bed, sending a piercing pain through my chest. I ignored it, found my shoes, and my jacket. After putting them on, I grabbed my purse and tiptoed to the door.

I peered into the hospital corridor. There were a couple of nurses and doctors at the far end of the hallway, but otherwise the coast was clear. I felt like a prison escapee as I ducked past the nurses' station and headed for the elevators. It wasn't as if I was being held captive, but a rush of adrenaline pulsed through me as I waited for the elevator to arrive.

Once I was at the main entrance, I simply strolled out the front doors. My mission was singular: I had to save Riverplace Village.

Chapter Twenty-five

Why weren't Pete or Tomo returning my calls? I hurried outside and immediately realized that the doctors were right. I wasn't in good shape. Just the act of walking a few feet left me gasping for breath. There was no way I could walk to the village.

I flipped on my phone and hired a car service. Within minutes the driver was at the curb.

"You're going to Riverplace Village, right, miss?"

"Yes." I tried to clear my throat.

"I'll get you as close as I can, but the place is crawling with cops. I heard a rumor that someone called in a bomb threat. I'm sure it's nothing, but they've shut everything down. Waterfront Village, the rides, the carnival—everything. You sure you want to head that way?"

"Yes. I need to get to the village," I said to the driver. Is that why Tomo and Pete hadn't answered? The police were already on the scene. They knew about the threat. A sense of relief flooded my body.

The driver wasn't exaggerating. It looked as if every police, fire, and emergency vehicle in the city was on the scene.

"This is as close as I can get," the driver said, pulling into a parking space on the street five blocks away from the entrance to the village.

"Thanks. This is great." I jumped out of the car and started sprinting toward Blomma. The magnitude of first responders on every street corner was mind-blowing. Temporary barricades blocked access in a five-block radius in every direction. My chested thudded with each step. My throat constricted, making it impossible to fill my lungs with air. I didn't care. I ran through the pain. If I collapsed, so be it. I had to warn everyone.

I arrived at the first barricade, gasping for air. "I need to get in there," I said to the officer stationed at the blockade.

"Miss, no one is getting in there. Not even the pope."

"The pope?"

He shrugged. "It's an expression my grandmother uses. My point is that no one is getting anywhere near the village."

"I own Blomma, one of the shops in the village."

"I'm really sorry about that, miss, but like I said, no one gets in. I have strict orders from the chief. Not even those limos are getting in." He pointed to the left, where a dozen limos were parked in a row.

The dignitaries, I thought. A woman in a deep-sapphire ball gown, and her husband in a black tuxedo, had exited their limo and were watching the commotion.

"So does that mean the gala is off?" I asked the officer.

He stared at me. I'm sure I must have looked like a drenched rat, between the fire and my brief hospital stay. "I don't know about any gala. All I know is that my job is to keep civilians clear from this area."

"Is there a bomb?"

"I'm not at liberty to answer that, miss."

I could tell I wasn't going to get anywhere with the officer, so I left. I walked toward the row of waiting limos. At that moment, members of Dark Fusion appeared almost out of thin air. They were on every corner, carrying giant banners and banging their drums. "Ready, set, boom! Ready, set, boom! Ready, set, boom!" they chanted over and over again as they marched to the police barricades.

A sick feeling rose in my throat. Where was Elin? She had left before me. Was she at Blomma? Or worse, the hotel? What about Tomo and Pete? *Please don't let harm come to my family and friends*, I prayed internally.

Dark Fusion and the police began to clash as the anarchists marched past each of the roadblocks. Their chants grew louder and louder.

I scanned the crowd for any sign of Zigs, but I couldn't spot him. Dark Fusion's members had grown in number and intensity. They appeared immune to the police as they pushed forward toward the village.

If a bomb was about to blow, why would they be heading toward it?

I stood in the center of the empty street feeling dumbfounded. What should I do?

"Ready, set, boom! Ready, set, boom!" One of Dark Fusion's members jumped on the hood of a police car. "Portland, get ready! There's a big boom about to happen. Out of the ashes will emerge a new world order. Your new leader is about to be born."

Huge cheers erupted from the evil-looking members, dressed in black.

A chill ran down my spine. Were they talking about Zigs? He was nothing more than a killer. He had killed one person, attempted to kill three more of us, and now was about to blow up a square city block. He was going to become Portland's new leader? No way. People would revolt. Portlanders would never let Zigs get away with bringing violence and mayhem to our beautiful Rose City.

The drums shuddered. More and more dignitaries emerged from their limos. It was a strange juxtaposition. Men and women clad in their finest ball gowns and tuxedos, blocks away from Dark Fusion's black mafia.

I wanted more than anything to be in the village with Elin. What about Nora and Jon and all of the other business owners? If only I had called Pete sooner.

I blamed myself. Dark Fusion was about to destroy everything I knew and loved and there was nothing I could do about it.

I sank onto the ground and watched the action unfold around me. The police held their ground, and Dark Fusion didn't gain ground closer to the village. For a minute I wondered why, and then it hit me. They weren't trying to get into the village, they were waiting. Waiting for the event. What was their plan? The minute the explosion happened they would take over the police with force? No wonder they had members camped at each corner.

A squad car with bomb-sniffing dogs arrived on the scene, followed by the ATF, who wheeled in robots used to defuse explosive devices.

That had to be a good sign, right?

I forgot about the pain in my lungs and the fact that it took a concerted effort to breathe. What was taking so long? The night grew cold as the sun sank behind Portland's skyscrapers. The crowd had grown so big that I didn't even realize I was surrounded by people now.

After what felt like an eternity, gunshots sounded. The crowd screamed and ducked. Where were the shots coming from?

I watched the faces of Dark Fusion. They looked confused. Something had gone wrong. This wasn't their plan. Then the police turned on the protestors. They used similar surprise tactics, taking Dark Fusion from all sides. The crowd scattered as pepper spray and batons started flying. I ducked behind a nearby food cart.

The sound of violence rocked Portland's streets. Only this morning similar crowds had cheered for our beautiful floral floats; now members of Dark Fusion were being cuffed and hauled away in police cars.

I felt a deep sadness. We could and should be better than this.

No explosion occurred. No buildings fell. The ground didn't shake. Shrapnel didn't fly through the air. Dark Fusion's mission had failed, and yet at the same time I couldn't help but feel like a small part of them had won as I watched the dignitaries return to their limousines to return to their hotels. The gala had been canceled, and our beautiful streets had been tainted with darkness. Litter was scattered across the sidewalks—ripped shreds of Dark Fusion's cardboard signs, smoke bombs, fire-crackers, and garbage. This morning's celebration of Portland's bounty had evaporated. Sham hadn't succeeded in changing the tone, and neither had I.

Chapter Twenty-six

"Britta!" I heard Elin's voice through the sound of sirens. The crowd had begun to disperse. It was obvious that the drama was over. "What are you doing here? You're supposed to be in the hospital." She ducked under the police tape and came to hug me.

I explained that I couldn't just sit there waiting for news. "What happened?"

"Pete and Tomo were here when I arrived. I raced from shop to shop, starting at Torch to alert Jon and then on to Demitasse to warn Nora about the bomb threat. I was on my way to tell the staff at Riverplace Inn when I bumped into Pete and Tomo. They were part of the effort to sweep the village. They did a great job. They got everyone out and had us all stay up the hill and out of harm's way."

"I was so worried about you. When I got here and saw the barricades . . ."

Elin linked her hand through mine. "I know. Me

too, but the police—Pete and Tomo—did a fantastic job. They deserve a medal of bravery. Or at the very least a flower crown."

I tried to smile. "What about Eric?"

"He's safe at his hotel. I called him and told him to stay put." Her hand was cold to the touch. "How are you? You really shouldn't be outside."

"I'm okay." Tears started to spill from my eyes.

"Oh, *lilla gumman.* Let's get you home." Elin wrapped me in a hug.

I tried to catch my breath between sobs but couldn't. Everything came flooding out—Sham's murder, Zigs trying to light Nicki and me on fire, and now tonight. "It's just that, after everything, I feel like Dark Fusion succeeded. They ruined tonight."

Elin led me through the crowd. "They didn't. Groups like Dark Fusion that try to spread hate and fear will never succeed, not in a town like Portland, not anywhere. And I can prove it. Come with me."

She guided me toward the waterfront, where a long line of people had steadily grown. The entrance to Riverplace Village was still cordoned off, but Portland's own stood shoulder to shoulder along the waterfront path. They were forming a long chain.

"What's happening?" I asked.

"Just wait." Elin smiled.

We made our way closer, where I spotted the Rose Festival Princesses handing cut flowers to everyone in line. I recognized them as the flowers salvaged from the parade.

"I don't understand," I repeated.

"Watch, you will." Elin and I joined the line. Priscilla came over to hand us each a cut ivory rose.

"This was a lovely idea, Priscilla. Thank you for making it happen so quickly," Elin said.

"Thank my royal court." Priscilla waved her arm toward the girls, who continued to reach into buckets and disperse flowers to the crowd. "I do believe that my duties here are complete. They have certainly learned and now are living the principles of what it means to be a Rose Festival Princess."

She paused and placed her hand over her heart. "This is a very proud moment for me. Ted and I were saying this might go down as the most memorable Rose Festival in history."

I followed her eyes and saw Ted Graham and other members of the Royal Rosarians dispersing flowers. At the far end of the pathway I could see police officers and firefighters funneling in.

Once everyone had a flower in hand, Ted Graham addressed the impromptu crowd on a megaphone. "Portlanders, I join you tonight in reclaiming our city. When your Royal Court heard the news that our Rose City was being overrun with darkness and violence, they came to me with an idea. Let's spread more light. Let's spread flowers. Tonight I ask you to raise your voices and raise your flowers in the air. Let's join together as neighbors and friends and pay homage to our city. Will you join me in singing Portland's song?"

People hollered and cheered as hundreds of bright and colorful flowers waved in the air. The sight was so beautiful that it brought happy tears to my eyes.

Ted led us in "Portlandia," the city's official song:

"Old town, downtown, fountains and
   lights,
The Willamette reflecting our city at night
From bridges, nightspots in
   neighborhoods, too.
Together, we grow in love and respect for
   you.

"Hours, days, weeks at a time,
Holiday weekends, time to unwind.
From winter's reign through summer's
   fall,
The lady of seasons belongs to us all.

"Portlandia
"Gazing upon the busy streets,
Reflecting the mountain's history
Through her eyes,
She fills me with pride."

There wasn't a dry eye when the song ended. Ted wiped his cheek and then held up a brilliant yellow gerbera daisy. "Now let's all raise a flower to the Rose City and toss it into the Willamette."

Again, everyone raised colorful blooms to the sky.

"To Portlandia," Ted boomed, and tossed his daisy into the Willamette.

"To Portlandia," everyone repeated. Hundreds of stems floated into the air. My breath caught in my chest, but not because of smoke inhalation. It was the loveliest sight I had ever seen.

Elin and I tossed our blooms into the river, which was alive with color. Streaming flowers, a reminder of Portland's beautiful bounty and unbreakable spirit.

"I told you," Elin said with a smile, tilting her head toward mine.

"Yes, you did."

We watched the parade of flowers bob along the surface of the river for a while, before we finally called it a night. Elin drove me home and tucked me in bed. She and Eric brought me soup and hot tea. After a sea of emotions and a roller coaster of a day, I felt contented. Everything was as it should be.

Chapter Twenty-seven

I missed out on the Rose Festival teardown. Elin forced me to rest, and to be honest the thought of returning to the float barn filled me with slight dread. Tomo and Pete stopped by the next day. I was propped on the couch in the living room. Eric had insisted on making a fire before he and Elin went to dismantle what was left of the Blomma float. I overheard him and Elin arguing.

"She doesn't need a fire. It's not that cold out. I'll get her a blanket."

"Elin, there's a chill to the air, and more importantly she's had a nasty scare. You know what they say about jumping back on the horse. It will be good for her to have a safe, cheery fire here in the comforts of home."

I couldn't hear Elin's response, but Eric's logic won because the next thing I knew, Elin was propping pillows behind my back and Eric was stacking logs in the brick fireplace.

"You're sure you don't want us to stay?" Elin handed me a plate of Swedish ginger cookies and a cup of steaming coffee.

"I'll be fine."

Eric poked at the fire. "Your cheeks have more color this morning. I would say your patient is coming along fine, Elin." He winked at me. "She'll be back on her feet and putting together beautiful bouquets in no time, isn't that right, Britta?"

I waved my fingers at him. "My fingers can't wait to start snipping."

I appreciated his support. I knew that my aunt was worried about me, but she didn't need to fuss.

"What do you say I make you two lovely ladies dinner tonight? My specialty, homemade fish and chips." Eric launched into a fake British accent. "So many years spent across the pond has made me a master at frying fish. Don't tell, but I'll share my secret ingredient with you two lovey ladies."

"What is it?" I asked, my interest piqued by Eric's bright eyes.

He pretended to check around us for listening ears and then whispered, "Beer. Not for the batter. For the chef."

Elin shook her head. "Oh dear, what am I going to do with him?"

The fire crackled and popped in a cheerful way. Maybe Eric was on to something. Unlike the fire at the float barn yesterday, his fire warmed the room and cast a wonderful glow.

"Fish and chips and ice-cold beer sounds great." I wrapped my hands around the coffee mug.

"Indeed. I'll make Britta's favorite dessert," Elin added. "A Swedish princess cake."

The cake was my favorite. Every year before my birthday Elin would ask what kind of a cake I wanted, and every year without fail I opted for her Swedish princess cake. Elin made it in traditional Swedish style with layers of sponge cake, pastry cream, and jam, covered with marzipan that was tinted green and adorned with a single pink marzipan rose. My mouth watered at the thought of it. I felt like I was twelve again as she fussed, tucking in my feet and reminding me that they would both have their cell phones if I needed anything.

Eric finally had to drag her out after I promised to send her a text update every couple of hours. On their way out the door he stopped and said, "Britta, I've been trying to convince your aunt to come spend a few weeks in London with me this summer. I'll show her the Buckingham Palace Garden, and as luck would have it I've heard that Elin has been invited to teach a workshop at the world-renowned London Floral Show. However, that would mean you'd be home alone." He gave me a goofy wink. "However would you survive?"

I matched his expression. "How would I? Hmm. Let's see. I suppose I could busy myself with keeping an eye on Blomma, watching the house and plants, and enjoying Portland in summer's full bloom."

Elin threw her hands up in protest. "I'm no match for the two of you. Don't think you can pull one over on me. I know that you're going to work in tandem to force me on a plane."

Eric caught my eye. "Yep. That sounds about right. Agreed, Britta?"

"Agreed." I laughed as they bantered back and

forth and headed for the car. It was a shame that
they had lost so much time, and yet it appeared they
were making up for it. I just hoped that Eric wouldn't
break her heart again. I knew that she could handle
anything thrown her way, but I wasn't sure that I
could take watching her suffer another loss. From
the outside it seemed that their blooming relationship was solid, and yet I knew that many decisions
lay in front of them: whether they could make a
long-distance romance work, or if one of them or
both of them would consider uprooting their life
for the promise of love.

You can worry about that later, Britta. I sipped my
tea and tried to focus on the fact that for the moment everything was as it should be.

Not long after they left, a knock sounded on the
door. It was Pete and Tomo. They let themselves in.
Pete looked as handsome as ever in a charcoal golf
shirt and black slacks. "How's the patient?" he said,
handing me a bundle of pale pink apple blossoms
loosely tied with raffia. An envelope with my name
written in beautiful calligraphy was tucked into the
ambrosial bouquet that smelled as if it had been
hand plucked from an orchard. "Read the card
later."

"Okay." I examined his face, but it was completely passive.

Tomo offered me a to-go container from the
Happy Spoon. The scent of ramen and savory broth
made me almost forget about Zigs and my brush
with death. "Good to see you upright, Britta."

"Thanks, guys." I set their gifts on the coffee
table and encouraged them to take a seat.

Tomo stood in front of the fire, shuffling his feet

and looking like he wasn't sure what to do. Pete sat in the chair next to me.

"We thought you would want to know that Zigs has been arrested. We finally got the film from the security cameras from the float barn. We have him on film going into the float barn the night that Sham was killed. Sham must have been working late on the float and Zigs took him by surprise. We have him in custody." Pete's tone was businesslike.

"How did you catch him?" I asked.

Tomo fiddled with a wax candle on the mantel. "It wasn't easy. We were on our way to the float barn. Got your messages, and then the call came through that there was a fire. A jogger running by smelled smoke and stopped to call it in."

"A good thing," Pete interrupted. "It sounded like the fire crew got there just in time."

I nodded.

"At the same time, someone called in an anonymous bomb threat for the Riverplace Inn," Tomo continued. "We were some of the first responders on the scene. As you know, there's been so much noise from Dark Fusion, but not a lot of action. This one felt different. It's hard to put into words, but ATF got called in right away."

"But I saw a van with dogs and a robot arrive long after everything had been closed off to the public," I said.

"Reinforcements," Pete offered. "That unit came from Salem. Standard procedure in situations like that, especially given the threat level."

"Right," Tomo agreed. "Our guys had already identified the device and were close to having it disarmed by the time they arrived."

"It wasn't a very complicated device." Pete stared at the plate of cookies Elin had left.

"Help yourselves," I offered.

They both took cookies.

"Yeah, pretty rudimentary." Tomo munched a cookie. "And our equipment is so sophisticated and mobile that we were able to have the robot remove and dispose of the bomb in less than an hour. What took so long was that we had to sweep the rest of the area to ensure there weren't any other explosive devices."

I thought about their line of work, and what it must be like to put themselves in danger on a daily basis. It made me more grateful that I got to spend my days surrounded by lush, gorgeous blooms.

He looked at Pete. "We were fairly confident, given the tip, that there weren't other bombs, but you can't be too careful."

Pete nodded.

"Who called in the tip?"

Tomo shrugged. "We don't know, but we're pretty sure that it was a member of Dark Fusion. They had too many details, such as specifics on where to find the device."

"Really?" I sipped my coffee, which had gone cold.

"We'll be investigating further over the next few days. We made dozens of arrests last night," Pete added. "Right now our theory is that Dark Fusion has two distinct factions. One that tended to be in line with Sham's vision and the other with Zigs's. We think that someone from Sham's camp called in the threat, but like I said, it's too early to know for sure."

"What about Gloria and Nicki? Any news on either of them?"

Tomo took another cookie. "They are both still recovering, but it's looking good. They should be fine. Among the three of you, we have solid testimony to put Zigs in jail forever. That's one silver lining in this mess."

"Any news on your family's shop? Have you been able to make a connection?"

He removed one of the iron tools for the fire and pushed a log that had fallen off the stack. "No. Nothing yet. But I'm working on it. I made a promise to my mom and dad that I would find the perpetrator, and I'm not giving up. Every explosive has its own signature, like a fingerprint. I'm crossing my fingers that the forensics lab will be able to make a connection." He looked at Pete again.

"Evidence never lies." Pete gave him a nod of solidarity. "We'll find something sooner or later."

"Let's hope it's sooner." Tomo fiddled with his earlobe. He never wore an earring while on duty.

Pete frowned. "It's too bad because we have plenty of circumstantial evidence, but nothing hard that we can tie back to Dark Fusion."

"That's why we should do a sting," Tomo said in almost a pleading tone.

"I'm going to have to go above my pay grade to get clearance on that."

Tomo wasn't deterred. "Then do it. Why are we sitting around here?" He stopped and punched his fist into his palm. "Sorry, look. I'm trying to be rational, but it totally sucks to sit here and do nothing, when we have the best lead that we've had in years. We can't just watch them go free after everything they've done—to the parade, to the Happy Spoon, to Portland."

Pete shot him a look.

"I'm not saying it's your fault, Detective. I didn't mean it like that. I get it. I get it. We have to follow proper protocol, but aren't there times when we have to bend the rules? My dad taught me that. That you have to know what the rules are and when it's okay to break them."

I got the sense Pete wanted to say something, but he let Tomo continue.

"I just mean that we need to follow up while the trail is hot, you know?" Tomo gave Pete a pleading look. "If we wait too long, they could bolt. The trail of evidence could go cold, or they could do this to someone else. You're with me on this, aren't you, Britta? You get it?"

"For sure." I gave him what I hoped was a comforting smile.

"I'm going to do everything in my power to bring them to justice," Pete said to Tomo, then he turned to me and changed the subject. "How are you feeling, Britta? You look a bit run-down."

Hadn't Eric just said I had more color than yesterday? Did that mean that I'd looked like a ghost yesterday?

"Okay. It's a relief to know that you caught Zigs, that's for sure." I twisted the blanket with my hands.

"Yep. He's not going anywhere. You're in no danger. Like Tomo mentioned, we've secured the barn, the place is clear, and Zigs will be going to prison for a long time."

A call came through on Tomo's walkie-talkie. "I better take this outside. Feel better, Britta. That soup is my mom's specialty, guaranteed to put hair on your chest."

"What if I don't want hair on my chest?"

Tomo laughed. "Fair point."

He went outside. Pete stood. "We need to get going, but I wanted to check on you. You gave me a scare yesterday." His tone changed. I got the sense that he had been trying to keep things professional in front of Tomo.

"I gave myself a scare." I fiddled with the blanket.

"Let's make a deal that you don't ever do that again." His eyes were filled with emotion. "Can we do that? Is that a fair deal? You stay far, far away from crazed killers and anarchists, okay?"

"Deal."

He glanced out the window and then scooted closer. I could smell his earthy cologne. For a minute I thought he might kiss me, but instead he picked up my hand and caressed it. "And, once you're better, I owe you a dinner. A real dinner. Or two. No interruptions. No murder cases. Just the most beautiful florist in Portland and this scruffy detective from LA."

"Sounds good."

"I'm serious. I want to take you to dinner and learn more about you, Britta Johnston." He kept his hand on mine. "The last two times I've tried to take you to dinner we've been interrupted, so what do you say, should we try for three? You know how the old saying goes, the third time is the charm."

"I'd love to."

There was silence. I could hear the crackle of the flames in the fire, and the scent of the ramen waiting on the coffee table. Pete leaned closer. So close I could feel the scruff on his cheeks and make out every indent in the scar that lined his face. Was I ready for this? Was it too soon?

My heart rate sped up.

Pete reached for the back of my head and massaged my hair. I closed my eyes.

Alas, the moment vanished. Tomo rapped on the window. "We have a call."

Pete let out a long sigh. He released my hair and kissed me on the cheek. "Dinner. Soon. Feel better." Then with a half wave, he went outside to join Tomo.

Our timing was always off. Is this how Elin had felt all these years with Eric? So close to finding love and then a string of unexpected detours meant that moments slipped out of her hands?

That was okay. I could wait for Pete. We didn't need to push things.

I watched them drive away and then opened the card. It was written in black calligraphy.

Dear Britta,
I found this poem from an old book of flowers and thought of you. Hope you feel better soon. XO, Pete.

> *There is a language, little known,*
> *Lovers claim it as their own.*
> *Its symbols smile upon the land,*
> *Wrought by nature's wondrous hand;*

And in their silent beauty speak,
Of life and joy, to those who seek
For Love Divine and sunny hours
In the language of the flowers.
   —*The Language of Flowers,*
Margaret Pickston, London, 1875

It wasn't hard to interpret the meaning of the poem. I clutched the card to my chest and let out a contented sigh. I had an upcoming dinner date with a man who intrigued me and brought me flowers and poetry. Everyone I knew and loved was safe. That was all that mattered. That, and returning to Blomma. I couldn't wait to get back to the shop and immerse myself in wonderful wild flowers. After all, a world without flowers is no world at all.

***Please turn the page for some gardening
and cooking tips!***

Welcome to Riverplace Village. Portland, Oregon, is bustling with Rose Festival activities, and Britta is eager to share some of her favorite Blomma tips and tricks with you as she immerses herself in a flower wonderland.

Blomma's Flower Tips:

Sensational Succulents—Succulents are a wonderful and hard-to-kill option for indoor displays and container gardens. Start with a shallow dish. Get creative. You can use everything from a traditional terra-cotta pot to a hollowed-out piece of wood, or a clear glass terrarium. Next fill three quarters of your container with potting soil. Then spread a thin layer of pea-sized gravel on the top. Blend the soil and gravel with your hands and add water. Mix thoroughly and begin arranging your plants. Position the largest plant on one side of the container. Cluster remaining plants based on size and shape. Finish by sprinkling more pea-gravel to cover any of the potting soil mix. Allow soil to dry out completely before watering again. Watering should be minimal. Elin and Britta use the guideline of watering succulents once a month in the fall and winter and once a week in the spring and summer.

Float Away—Britta got to try her hand at float decorating. Now you can take her techniques and use them to impress your guests at your next garden party or add a fun temporary splash of color to your backyard or front porch. Here's how. You don't need any moving parts or something on the scale of Blomma's float. Simply upcycle an old piece of wood, pallet, door, or window frame. Sketch out a whimsical design with a pencil. It doesn't have to be perfect. In fact, free-form is best. Next, cut flowers from your garden or hit up your local farmers market for an assortment of stems. Use whatever you have on hand—dried berries, twigs, leaves, and herbs. Challenge yourself to use only organic materials. With a paintbrush apply Elmer's glue to sections of your design. Then press flowers and organic material on by hand. Repeat the process until your design is filled in. Display on a deck, against a fence, or use as a backdrop for a party. Depending on outdoor temperatures and the type of flowers you use, your "float" should last a week or more.

Blomma's Featured Wine and Flower Pairing—In honor of Rose Festival, Britta has hand-picked a lovely selection of Pacific Northwest rosés. Don't be fooled by their dreamy pink color. Nothing about these wines is cloyingly sweet. Oregon and Washington rosés are vibrant, dry wines with notes of nectarine, peach, strawberry, and herbs. These crisp, luscious wines make for a perfect alfresco glass. Britta recommends that you serve your rosé chilled and with a gorgeous vase of fresh-cut, single-stemmed, pale pink Aphrodite roses. The fragrant, delicate rose scent will enhance your wine-sipping experience.

A Taste of Blomma

Aunt Elin's Spiced Coffee

Ingredients:
1 pound of dark espresso roast (whole bean)
1 tablespoon red peppercorns
1 tablespoon green peppercorns
1 teaspoon cinnamon
1 teaspoon nutmeg
1 teaspoon whole cloves

Directions:
   Add all ingredients together in a large bowl and mix together with a wooden spoon. Use a coffee grinder to grind the beans to your preferred consistency. Depending on the size of your grinder, you'll likely need to grind the beans in small batches. Store in an airtight container. Elin prefers strong coffee and uses two heaping tablespoons of her spicy blend per six-ounce cup of water. If you like a lighter cup of coffee, try one tablespoon instead. Serve with cream or a dollop of whipping cream with vanilla.

Swedish Butter Cookies

Ingredients:
1 cup butter
1 cup granulated sugar
2 tablespoons maple syrup
2 cups all-purpose flour
1 teaspoon baking soda
½ teaspoon salt
Turbinado sugar or powdered sugar

Directions:
Preheat oven to 300 degrees. Cream butter and sugar together. Slowly incorporate syrup. Once the mixture is fluffy and yellow, add in dry ingredients. Divide into eight portions and roll each portion into a two-inch by eight-inch log. Sprinkle with turbinado sugar. (This is Britta's take on her childhood favorite. If you prefer the traditional method, omit this step and dust with powdered sugar once you remove cookies from the oven.)

Bake at 300 degrees for twenty to twenty-five minutes or until golden brown. Cut (after cooled) into two-inch strips and serve with coffee.

Connect with Us

Visit us online at
KensingtonBooks.com
to read more from your favorite authors, see books
by series, view reading group guides, and more.

Books by Bestselling Author
Fern Michaels